# An Inconvenient Convent

## An Abbot Peter Mystery

Other books in the Abbot Peter series

*A Vicar Crucified* (DLT)
*A Psychiatrist Screams* (DLT)
*A Director's Cut* (DLT)
*A Very Public School Murder* (Marylebone House)
*The Indecent Death of a Madam* (Marylebone House)
*Another Bloody Retreat* (White Crow Books)
*A Hearse at Midnight* (White Crow Books)
*An Inconvenient Convent* (White Crow Books)

# An Inconvenient Convent

## An Abbot Peter Mystery

*Simon Parke*

www.whitecrowbooks.com

A CIP catalogue record for this book is available from the British Library. For information, contact White Crow Books by e-mail: info@whitecrowbooks.com.

Cover image: The Bonfire © 2021 by Harry Parke
Cover Design by Astrid@Astridpaints.com
Interior design by Velin@Perseus-Design.com

Paperback: ISBN: 978-1-78677-214-5
eBook: ISBN: 978-1-78677-215-2

FICTION / Crime / Christian / Suspense

www.whitecrowbooks.com

Dedicated to
Nick and Fiona Newman

*Kind and generous friends*
*for longer than is either legal or decent*

My deep thanks to Harry Parke, for the wonderful cover picture; to Karl French for his skilled and kind editing; to Shellie Parke, for her encouragement and voracious eye for error – though I fear some will still be found; to Jon Beecher, friend and publisher; and to every reader of this series; for you are the reason.

# Prologue

She'll die here in the chapel.

The abbess allows the truth to creep into her being, though it creeps fast that death has arrived, her own death, 'It comes to all, it really does, the hound of heaven, it chases us down' – she hears herself, some old sermon preached, and now she is the one caught, sooner than expected; much sooner. All of a sudden, she feels its breath, trapped underground in a cell where once she prayed, where once she knew God and now feels dread.

She has tried the door, pushing in fury, banging with her fists; and she has called out with wretched screams which disappointed her. Hildegard was not one to scream and looked down on those who did. 'Why scream? One must just get on with it.'

But she screamed tonight, hurting her throat, she didn't care, she'd scream again, for the door is jammed, it will not shift though how it was done, she isn't sure, she cannot imagine. *How is the door closed?* The prayer chapel door has no lock, it never has, that would hardly be right. No one is excluded from this holy place and no one trapped inside, free entry and exit, a sort of heaven – until tonight, the night of the bonfire, when all will be happy in the garden above and no one will give thought to prayer.

And now the first hint of the danger to come. The stone warms. She feels it. Slow at first, is how it will be; but warmth will become heat and heat will become – well, ask the martyrs what heat becomes, those incinerated at the stake, let their screams describe what heat becomes ... though tonight she will discover for herself. A life seeking knowledge, such a busy mind, but this is not the knowledge she wished for, a dark knowledge that no one should know, the boiling of blood, the burning of flesh, the bursting of eyes, the incineration of thoughts. Does the soul survive?

'*See*, Hildegard – see until you can no longer see!' She speaks with herself. 'Think before you can no longer think!'

And this will be murder. Hildegard knows it is murder, and not unfortunate chance. This is no accident. Such twisted souls surround her – had she not named them tonight, in writing, not half an hour ago? When really, she has tried to do what's best, who couldn't say that? Has she not saved this convent? Look what it was! It was *nothing!* And then look at it now! She could have listened more, this is true, she has never listened; but really, an abbess must lead, and not be forever debating the path ahead in mind-wearying circles. The leader does not debate the path – the leader *reveals* the path.

But her path is now changed. The path she imagined, a long and winding road, achievement along the way, a kind old age, is brutally barred. The path of her life is crushed and compressed down to minutes, as the wretched heat bites and her feet burn and she is crying and sweating and hurting and crawling onto the stone altar, and grabbing at the cross, holding it dear, she will pray again, 'Dear God, take this cup away from me! *Away* from me! My God, my God, why have you abandoned me?'

She will pray and she will scream, the two shall be one, scalded and charred, Hildegard's last voice on earth; and no one will hear, except perhaps the martyrs, who have ears to ear, and the knowledge to understand.

And tonight, beneath the Convent of the Holy Fire, their bleak knowledge becomes Hildegard's ...

# The Abbot reads the letter

Written by the abbess shortly before her end.
'She was not a happy author.'
'Are they ever?'
'So here we go. Unusual style.'
'She's a nun.'
*'How goodness struggles to appear in the world!'*
'Is this her or you?'
'It's her. *'How goodness struggles to appear in the world! How it struggles to find a home! As welcome, it seems, as the plague!'*

The abbot doesn't like so many exclamation marks, quite unnecessary, but reads on.

*'Like a bear in a trap, brought low by spiteful and unhappy souls – this is how good stumbles and falls; how its clothes are torn and its joints pierced along the way.*

*When all it wishes is to do right – to do right and to heal! How can objection be so loud, harsh and rude?'*

Tamsin interrupts: 'Is there more?'
'You know there's more.'
'There's only so much self-righteous guff I can bear. Can you summarise? Salient points only?'

'No, Tamsin, I can't.' He takes a deep breath and shakes his head. 'Because it deserves to be heard, in *full*, it's her last will and testament.'

'So there can't be a sequel.'

'Unlikely.'

'Small mercies.'

'Just hear her out. She deserves that, I think.'

'No one deserves anything.'

'And who knows, you might grow to like her?' He continues to read.

*'And so it is, here at Community of the Holy Fire, where pale-faced evil abounds – though it would not so name itself. Oh no!*

*Each creature names themselves a righteous saint, each a pillar of rectitude only discreetly advancing their cause, with small doses of smiling poison.*

*Casual alliance infects the sea air, polite and charming daggers, over drinks after prayers, un-named, unseen, unspoken and underground ... busy, like bramble roots in the abbey soil.*

*And each would quieten God! Oh yes! But I cannot. I tried and it made me ill.*

*In affliction I lay thirty days while my body burned, as with fever. And throughout those days, I beheld a procession of innumerable angels who fought alongside Michael against the dragon and won the victory.*

*And then one called out to me, and declared, 'Eagle! Eagle! Why do you sleep? Arise! For it is dawn – eat, drink and write what you must write!'*

*Instantly my body and my senses came back into the world. And, seeing my recovery, my daughters, who were weeping around me, lifted me from the ground and placed me on my bed; and thus, I began to get my strength back.*

*Yet now this place fears the truth. They insisted I write, to save me from affliction; yet now insist I tear it up, to save themselves from change, as if God's voice can be turned off.*

*Here in the Community of the Holy Fire, they fear the fire! Truly! They are frightened by the divine flame; they are burned in their souls by the blaze!*

*Let us understand. Evil is the power to crucify good for now. It cannot do so forever. Good shall prevail! But evil crucifies it for now. This I see; and I see it here.*

*All of you! I see you. Volmar the Worm, Louisa the Snake, Patience the Jackal, Daisy the Darkness and our Lord Bishop of Ego! Spare us your vile visitations!*

*God help the keeper of the flame in a place such as this.*

*And tonight, as we celebrate the autumn equinox and the lighting of the winter fire, the keeper of the flame is me, the most humble sinner Hildegard.*

*Lord, have mercy; Mother of God, have mercy. Lord, have—*

The abbot stops reading. There's nothing more to read. The words run out; sometimes they do. And Tamsin's face is curled with ridicule.

'Well, the Lord and his mother failed with the mercy,' she says and the abbot will not rise to it. What is there to rise to? Tamsin is right. Mercy had not troubled Hildegard last night; it had never come close, unless mercy and savagery are the same.

'And written on the night of her murder. Was Hildegard interrupted?'

'Interrupted, possibly; paranoid, certainly,' says the Detective Inspector. She's standing in a convent and feeling uncomfortable. Who wouldn't be? All this kindness and devotion, it is not what she knows; too much of the holy-hush for her liking. And it somehow makes her angry; all the humility and subservience on display; the stooped shoulders and averted eyes and the message is clear: 'No tall poppies here!' Which is difficult for as tall a poppy as Tamsin. And in reaction, she goes the opposite way; somehow compelled to be hard-boiled, callous and some way from humble. '"Just because you're paranoid, it doesn't mean they're not out to get you."'

'But they *did* get her, Tamsin.' He is surprised to have to say this. They most certainly got her.

'They did, yes.'

*'My God, my God, why have you abandoned me!' Hildegard's climbing on the altar, clinging to the cross.*

'So, not completely paranoid. What she wrote was prophetic. She dies by ... ' He decides against further description, for what can you say? 'She dies a few hours later, ensnared by "smiling poison". And it *is* how evil works, Tamsin.'

'We'll be *careful* with that word, Abbot.'

Rules need to be established at the start; she knows this. Especially when working with the abbot.

'Which word?'

'You know the word.'

'Evil?' Tamsin Shah winces like an actor hearing 'Macbeth', as if terrible luck is now unleashed and the gods must be appeased.

'I know this is a convent, Abbot; but it's also the 21st century ... for some of us.'

'Of course.' The deferential pause; the abbot does pause sometimes. And the pauses can go on a while, easing into silence; but it doesn't mean anything is over. 'So, no mention of *evil* then.' He accentuates the word and enjoys it. He won't be cowed. 'Here we are, the 21st century, hoorah and hooray, the century of enlightenment, Tamsin – such sweetness and light in our world, how could I forget? Turning our gaunt faces away from war, genocide, poverty, climate abuse, people-trafficking and repulsive injustice – who could possibly speak of evil in such idyllic days as these? Such sunny uplands we inhabit.'

'Can we get on?' For Tamsin, it's like giving a child his go on the swing. Give the abbot a go on his spiritual nonsense – and then we can all get on. But not today; today, we can't all get on – the child wants another go on the swing.

'Evil is accurate in its construction, don't you think?'

'I don't know what you're talking about.' She knows this is going somewhere but has no idea where.

'It is "live" backwards.'

'Are you brushing off an old school assembly?'

' ... I'm simply looking out the window, and seeing what I see ... '

' ... We now stand to sing *Morning Has Broken* – and could Year Five stay behind afterwards.'

'But do you not think some people make it very difficult for others to live?'

'How would I know?'

'Or to put it another way, do you not watch the news?'

'I have Netflix.'

'Oh, I'm sorry. Is it sore?'

'It's an entertainment channel ... oh, very funny.'

'Always sounds like a tropical disease. But to get back to the assembly ... '

' ... assembly's finished ... '

' ... for those who *do* rip life from others for their own advancement; for those who abuse their power with lies, and oppress others through their actions – "evil" is the only word, surely?'

Tamsin takes a deep breath. 'You can *think* it, if you must. It just cannot appear in a police report. We cannot have *that word* in any report. *Ever.* End of.' Her delivery is matter-of-fact; this discussion will now cease. 'No mention of ... '

'Evil?'

'Precisely. Stop saying it. It's not happening. OK?'

The abbot is a lean man in his sixties, who, despite his monk's habit, or maybe because of it, is quite beyond the reach of authority; and he couldn't give a merry fuck about police reports. Age is not good for many things; the decline of the body is harsh; the decline of the mind more savage still. But it is good for this. He proceeds with life as a man who has nothing to lose, which is always dangerous.

'And evil is a sickly soul, Tamsin; not as strong as it thinks. And this is case-relevant.'

'How?'

'To gain strength, it needs other diminished souls to collaborate in some manner. It needs others to collude. One evil soul can't do it by itself. Evil must become a community of inbreds to find influence. So – and now we arrive at the killing of Hildegard – is there collaboration here? Is that what Hildegard suggests? It's a thought.'

'It's a long-shot.'

'Indeed. But long-shots brought victory at Agincourt, so I am encouraged. Thank you.' Tamsin nearly smiles; the abbot is aware she would never knowingly encourage anyone. To call Tamsin encouraging is to deal a mortal blow to her persona. 'And perhaps first on our list are the famous five: Worm, Snake, Jackal, Darkness and Ego. Spoiled for choice, really. What delights await us.'

~

And Shah is happy that he's here in the convent. 'I thought you'd feel at home,' she says. 'Look at you, Abbot – like a pig in clover!'

'Have you ever seen a pig in clover?' She stalls. 'You've never seen a pig, have you?'

'So? You're still loving it. All the bells and smoke; the habits and crosses gliding round the corridors. Does it take you back to your monastery in Egypt?'

'Not particularly.' Though, in truth, it did a bit: but in a good way. Here is a place that exists for itself; and this is positive. It is not trying to sell you anything; not trying to tell you anything; not asking you to join or agree. It is simply trying to *be* something in the world – and yes, that did take him back to the desert.

Tamsin stands up and walks around in dismay. 'I mean, for me, there is absolutely nothing here that is normal. *Nothing.* It's like a walk on Mars.'

'I suppose the gravity is reassuring.'

'It might as well be a set from *Doctor Who*, frankly. But for you? For you, Abbot, it's a comfy pair of slippers. It's more like your own front room than your own front room.'

'If the alien has quite finished.' She's gathering up her things and the alien *hasn't* quite finished.

'And since you're so at home, I'll need your attention on the case.'

'My attention?'

'Your *particular* attention, you're sort-of in charge, do you understand?'

'I'm not sure that I do.' He is surprised. She has never asked this before; far from it.

'So, clear your empty diary, Abbot, as I may have, well – other commitments.'

'Really? Like what?' This woman never had 'other commitments'; commitments that were not concerned with her work. She was married to the job, even if the marriage was unhappy; even if her partner – the police – was to be abused at every opportunity. DI Tamsin Shah was a career woman, breaking her back on the treadmill of success at all costs, including her sanity, which was low on her list of priorities. She'd be hard pushed to say what a holiday felt like. A holiday was merely unfilled space in which anxiety could come out to play. As she'd once told the Abbot, 'I dread holidays. Terrifying vacuums of nothingness.'

But something had apparently changed. Now she had 'other commitments'. So what other commitments could they be? Apart, possibly, from a trip to that expensive hairdresser in Hove and yes – her hair was a stunning black glory, to accompany her stunning Arabian face. It was hard to find other words to describe Tamsin and this was a problem at work. Sadly 'stunning' is a disaster in police stations. Male police officers can't cope with beauty; the men become boys, fantasists, misogynists, lackeys or creeps. Evil, you might say; against life. But for now, the abbot is merely wondering about her extra-curricular commitments and so his question, 'Really? Like what?'

'Like none of your business, Abbot, which I think is our usual arrangement.'

They step out of Hildegard's large study – the perk of an abbess with an oak desk to die for - and begin down the ancient and enclosing convent corridor. It is indented with alcoves housing little statues of saints; though someone here, one of the living saints, had recently mislaid their halo – in a terrifying assault.

'None of my business?' He smiles. 'Yet you mention it to me, uninvited, so I'm getting mixed messages. You mention something to me that you don't wish to speak of. It's like jumping into the sea to keep dry.' Tamsin shrugs. 'You've met someone, I suppose.' How does he know?

'I haven't 'met someone'. And what is that even supposed to mean, anyway?'

'It means you've met someone.'

'I've met a lot of people; and a fair few since arriving here – most of them in very odd clothes. It's like a penguin colony.'

The convent bell tolls for evening prayer and suddenly the penguins appear like ghosts from the old stone walls; they join them silently in the corridor, making for the chapel.

'Not joining us for prayers, Abbot?' asks a voice from his past, sadly made present, the formidably bright and brisk Louisa. She recently appeared in Hildegard's letter as The Snake and she's no nun but a celebrity MP for 'somewhere up north' as she often says; and the financial saviour of the Community. No one can raise money like she can. So many contacts in her diary; and all of them have nannies.

'On this occasion, unfortunately no, Louisa. Duty calls.'

'Surely the worship of God is our first duty, Abbot?' Louisa doesn't give up … ever. She requires your agreement, requires you to be persuaded of her way. Yet always looks cheerful and wants to be your friend, even if she hates you. You may one day be useful; though probably you'll be crushed. She offers a smile of reproof at this failing soul, refusing evening prayer.

'My worship will be to catch a killer, Louisa. It's not you, is it?'

'Oh, I'm much too busy for murder, Abbot. I wish I had the *time* – my target list is long! But I always find time for prayer.'

'And for justice, I hope. Time for justice. I'm sure our Lord is as eager for that as *we* all are.'

'You're not becoming political, are you? That really would be the end.'

'Justice for Hildegard, Louisa. "Let justice roll!" as the prophet declared. Such an uncomfortable line for your government.'

'But maybe it's justice that she's dead, Abbot? Has that ever occurred to you?' She does like to shock. She has to do it every week in her newspaper column; confected outrage and colourful words about something or someone – and no quarter given. 'I mean, who knows? But maybe this *is* justice rolling, Abbot. One does wonder sometimes if the murderer doesn't actually have a point? Not here, of course. It's a complete and utter tragedy, poor woman. But doesn't it ever cross your mind? I'm sure it does. After all, no one's overly harsh on Von Stauffenberg who tried to kill Hitler. A hero, if anything. But it would have been murder. So, are murderers in fact heroes sometimes? Removing people who are unpopular ... which, to be honest, the murdered usually are.'

'I'm sure you're making sense to yourself, Louisa.'

'What a very rude man!' She is playful, as she can be on the satirical panel shows she appears in. 'The Tory who can laugh at herself,' as one newspaper framed her.

'And in the meantime, I'll rudely seek justice for Hildegard.'

They walk on towards the chapel caught in the hallowed rush to prayer.

'So, we're not getting the professionals, Abbot?' She really doesn't give up; like a battering ram with a mind of its own – but assault with a smile.

'You most certainly are. My colleague here, DI Tamsin Shah, is the S.I.O. obviously; she will be leading the investigation.' Tamsin arrives in Louisa's sight lines and the two women assess each other unfavourably. 'I shall merely assist where I can with due humility.'

Louisa nods in a concerned and supportive manner. 'Photo copying, that sort of thing?'

And now Tamsin intervenes, because this place is getting on her nerves with its long corridors and alcoved saints; and this woman is a cow. She has seen her on the news, and can take no more of her snide remarks. Tamsin can abuse the abbot with impunity; but others cannot. That's the moral order and Louisa has transgressed. 'Well, thank you for your offer, madam – and it's much appreciated. DI Tamsin Shah.' She shows her card. 'Are you a nun here?'

'Er, no.' Louisa is taken aback. She assumes her celebrity goes before her.

'And if we need photocopying or simple filing, we'll certainly be knocking on your door. But we do have administrative back-up; probably better minds than yours, to be honest; while the genius of the abbot lies in other directions, which would be wasted in the chapel right now.'

Sometimes Peter struggled with Tamsin, and with good reason; so many reasons, in fact, it was hard to know where to start. But sometimes he loved her, and today, in the convent corridor, in the bloody teeth of condescension, it was the latter.

They would be a team, the hounds of heaven, on poor Hildegard's behalf. And the question which begged for an answer: Who hated her that much, to do ... *to do what they did?*

# What a wonderful fire!

And the convent certainly knew how to arrange them. It was a grand night in the life of the Community of the Holy Fire, on England's south coast – 'a stone's throw from the sea,' as the abbess would say; and there were plenty of stones to choose from on Stormhaven beach, maintained in an un-maintained sort of a way, in order to deter visitors to the town. It was town by the sea, rather than a seaside town.

'No one in Stormhaven wishes for visitors,' as Geoff in the hardware shop explains to any who'll listen, which is a fair few. The town is not flush with entertainment. 'Apart from Mr Whippy on the seafront, obviously. *He* wants visitors. But then he's a visitor himself, is he not? Someone said he lives in *Crawley.*'

Case closed.

But each year the Community of the Holy Fire breaks the Stormhaven rules of inhospitality and welcomes visitors for the Grand Fire of the autumn equinox. It is quite an event, when wine is poured, warm clothes worn, baked potatoes eaten, a huge bonfire ignited and from the blazing fury – wild orange flame against the dying light – a torch is lit that will burn throughout the winter in the convent garden. It will be a symbol of light in the darkness; and a sign of hope in the barren winter months.

'Be our light, O God, through these winter months and so lighten our way unto eternity!' declares Stephen, the eager Bishop of Lewes. He loves an audience. And Michael the gardener is telling everyone to stand back, "cos it can get fruity' as he lights the match. And how quick is the response! Such immediate conflagration! Louisa Knowle-Makepeace, celebrity MP and a woman of barnstorming energy, had earlier given a wonderful speech. She had called the convent 'a light to the nations!' It was aspirational, clearly, and unencumbered by supporting facts. Indeed, it was Louisa who referred to it as 'an inconvenient convent' to friends. 'Absolutely ghastly place, full of atrocious humbug – but believe me, we might make something of it yet!'

She could sometimes sound like Margaret Thatcher; and it may not have been unintentional. But tonight, the fire roars with crazy delight at such a bold commission. A light to the nations indeed! Louisa knew how to stir a crowd.

'Is this the best fire ever?' asks Sister Roisin, for it does seem particularly energetic this year, caught in the westerly wind from the Azores, via Newhaven. 'Perhaps that's why they moved it, to catch the wind better.' The fire has indeed been moved from its usual site. And it's like the flames are in a hurry, rushing and whooshing through the wood, quite insatiable, cackling and cracking, with Michael, 'at a safe distance, ladies, always be safe,' feeding it with fuel tossed into the blaze as the smoke begins to swirl and the temperature rises. And when the large Christmas tree is thrown on, saved for this moment, the flame explodes and everyone gasps.

'I was asked to give it a hand,' says Michael, in the voice of the half-deaf, different vowel sounds; and people sometimes thought him German, which didn't go down well. 'Are you deaf or something?' he'd reply. 'You couldn't be more English than me!'

And he's 'giving it a hand' for the abbess. She had 'asked for something special, she even wrote me a note,' he said. 'I got a hand-written note and you don't get many of those these days, like none. It's all bloody emails. "Give it a good hand," she wrote. "We want a fire and an evening to remember!'" So, a generous dose of petrol, poured earlier on the wood, was presently helping things along nicely. Along with the Christmas tree.

'She loves a good fire, Hildegard,' says Sister Roisin who is wondering where she has got to. Hildegard is a visible person and she can't see her anywhere. 'She says God is in fire as both light and heat: the light of revelation and the heat of dismantlement. She says we live daily in the presence of this brilliant burning!'

Sister Roisin admires Hildegard hugely and came here because of her letter writing, as the abbot discovered that night. 'Hildegard writes to anyone with power – prime ministers, archbishops, leaders of industry.'

'What about?'

'Morality, usually. She wants high standards in politics, the church, in industry.'

'Well, she won't be short of material.'

'And the environment obviously. They all hear from her about the environment. She doesn't mince words when it comes to green issues.'

'So, she keeps the rich and famous in order.'

'Tries to. Which is how Louisa heard about us, I think. I mean, Louisa is quite brilliant as well.'

'She is indeed! And clearly loves a good fire.' The celebrity politician is dancing by the flames with the gardener, Michael. 'She's not shy either.'

But Abbess Hildegard is not enjoying the fire tonight; and didn't write the note to Michael. Trapped underground, there's no dancing for her; only the scream and her clawing at the door; and the shouting out, shouting 'til she's hoarse, for the fire will incinerate her, she knows this; she knows where she is and how it works. She knows what's coming, locked in the Prayer Chapel, made entirely of soapstone, and as anyone from the convent is aware, it is the very last place to be on a night such as this; with the fire where it is. Who ordered it to be moved?

She's in the right place – for, as she tells her nuns, it is always good to pray, this is holy ground. But it's the wrong time, really very wrong; for this holy ground will soon become an oven.

*'My God, my God, why have you abandoned me!' She's climbing on the altar, clinging to the cross, the ground too hot, brief relief, but the altar is warming, the heat passing through – 'Bishop!'*

## It was hardly a choice.

⁓

It was obvious Tamsin had to bring the abbot onto the case. It was a convent, for God's sake, where large police shoes, in the investigation ballet, could look particularly clumsy. Even Chief Inspector Wonder, never the abbot's biggest fan, suggested his inclusion on this occasion.

'No-brainer, Shah, surely? As sure as night follows day.' He must have a book of cliches. 'I mean, what's not to like? And I'm not saying you can't handle a murder in a convent – it's probably two nuns and a spade, it usually is. But the abbot might help with some of the jiggery-pokery.'

She had no idea what he meant, none at all; and nor was she interested. The relationship between herself and Wonder had been fragile for a while - ever since the famous Christmas party; as in, the *in*famous Christmas party. It was a party still sniggered over at the nick, passed on down generations of recruits; the one described in police stairwells with spite and relish. And he was embarrassed by his behaviour that night, who wouldn't be? He should not have touched DI Shah in that manner. I mean, it was just an alcoholic squeeze, no harm meant, but no – it should never have happened. And all bloody embarrassing.

The DI, who walked out on the party immediately, said she wasn't surprised – 'for what surprises anyone about men these days?' Though away from public view, she was surprised, what with Wonder being the Chief Inspector and not that sort of a man at all ... until he was; until his drunk hands began wandering in messy and pathetic ways.

'Men should not drink alcohol,' was the moral of the story for Tamsin but she didn't report it.

'You should have reported it,' was her friend's view, and fair enough, perhaps she should; but she wanted promotion more than a reputation for causing trouble. That never worked and so she tried to move on and shrug it off; though like a stain on the window, it remained in view. He was her boss; but in a manner, she was now his. She'd kept an 'arm's length' between them ever since; and Wonder felt the distance, because he liked her, or rather, admired her. You didn't really 'like' DI Shah; that wasn't the transaction. But you did want her on your side, and you wanted her on any case that needed solving. She was graceless, stressed but relentless.

And looking on the bright side – 'because it's not all doom and gloom, chummy!' – all was not lost in the Chief Inspector's professional life. Leaving the Christmas party aside, because you have to move on, the 'Trusted Citizen' scheme was going splendidly in the Sussex Constabulary. And the 'Trusted Citizen' scheme was his own creation, Wonder's brainchild, which only last year had actually won a national award for 'Imaginative Policing'. He had collected the trophy in person at the Doncaster conference; and had done so with great pride. The exact number of schemes on the short list was never made public. He'd heard it wasn't high. 'But a win's a win, sonny,' as he'd told one PC. 'A win's a bloody win. I'll take it all day long!' Then adding, in a moment of largesse, 'We should *all* be proud. It's not just about me; it's an award for us all, the whole Sussex constabulary! So why can't they all be a little more excited?'

The scheme allowed a trusted member of the public to assist in a police investigation, 'if deemed helpful'. And the abbot, working with DI Shah, had been deemed helpful on a number of occasions previously; in fact, he'd been rather more than helpful, if you wanted the abbot's opinion, which he was happy to give. He could also be deemed irritating, obviously – because Tamsin liked to lead and, despite his protestations and denials, so did the abbot. And two chiefs is always an issue.

'You're in charge, Tamsin.'

' ... and now as though you mean it.'

But somehow it worked, despite the woman also being his niece, an accidental discovery which was a bit of a bombshell at her age and another story – another story she'd so far had time to tell no one, because why would you? Golden rule: tell no one anything because knowledge is power; and she wouldn't be giving that away. Neither had she ever referred to him as 'uncle', because it didn't seem right or comfortable. No one suddenly becomes an 'uncle', appearing out of thin air; her mother's lovers had tried that and failed.

'Where is the man?' asked her eight-year-old self.

'I wish you wouldn't call him "the man", Tamsin.'

'Is the man staying tonight, mother?'

'He does have a name. His name is Ramon. You can call Ramon "uncle" if you like.'

'But is the man staying?'

As it turned out, Uncle Ramon wasn't staying, mother was shouting at him, and uncle was moving on, as uncles did. So, any prospective relation, with a view to a title and a place in her heart, had to earn their stripes; and Tamsin made stripes very hard to earn. And anyway, that wasn't for now, family sagas could wait; because there was an incinerated body at a convent in Stormhaven, and help would be good; help she could abuse and ridicule, certainly, because that was her way; but equally, help she could trust, and she did trust the abbot; the trust was deep between these two – as deep as the deep blue sea she lived near in Hove ... but avoided. She was not a sea-swimmer. 'No one sensibly chooses cold in their life,' she'd say.

And maybe the trust would need to be deep, because suddenly – and against all good sense – Tamsin might actually have a 'love-life'. Most people seemed to have a love-life of sorts. Whether creaking, joyous or an absolute bloody disaster, they had a story to tell. But Tamsin had never had a love life; or not one with any love in it, or life; and she hated the phrase 'love-life' with a passion. What on earth was a 'love-life' anyway? But maybe something had changed, and her partner on this case would need to understand that sometimes, she'd need to leave. Evenings might need to be free.

And then the phone had rung and it was the abbot, returning her call about the convent job, saying he'd do it. 'I'll do it,' he said. 'I'll help with the killing at the convent.'

'Good,' she said, sounding casual but pleased and surprised in equal measure. He usually put up more of a fight when asked to participate. He would embark on some sad ego-propping operation, which wallowed in the hunt. The abbot was so rarely in demand, so rarely of use to anyone, that he just had to make the most of it when he was. So, while she *was* pleased, almost hysterically so, she would not sound pleased. *Give him a sense of his own value and he'll start making demands and become grandiose.* So, her 'good' was restrained, held so far back in the throat, it was almost bad.

'And you will need me,' he adds.

'It's possible you can help, yes.' Her throat contracts again with these words of faint praise; they are forced out. She has never praised anyone, not knowingly, and she's not starting now.

'The murderer will be the one with the lovely smile who works tirelessly on behalf of the less fortunate. Shall we meet there? Oh, and I'll need Bancroft. Is that possible?'

The abbot had worked with PC Bancroft on a previous case and found him an honest work colleague who knew his way around police procedure, IT and forensics; and remarkably, wasn't on a personal mission of self-aggrandisement – so, all in all, an unusual policeman. 'I remember he wanted to join CID when we last worked together.'

'And he's still being considered,' says Tamsin.

'*Still?* That was over a year ago.'

'There's considerable competition for places in CID; they only take the best.'

'It doesn't show.'

'But I'm sure we can get hold of him. I've nothing against the man.'

'High praise.'

'We'll give him a title, something like Senior Investigative Liaison Officer.'

'SILO?'

'He likes a title.' And this was true, Bancroft did like a title. A title calmed him, reassured him of his value. He was probably the milk monitor at school; so eager for a role. There was always a sense of the outsider about Bancroft. He never quite felt at home with his fellow officers here in Sussex, and it wasn't just that he came from Dorchester. Clearly this didn't *help*, and equally clear was the fact he was regarded by his colleagues as an 18th century yokel. Brighton thought highly of itself. Brighton imagined it was London-by-the-Sea and the Brighton police, the Mets-by-the-Sea. Like the Mets, they liked to think they did things differently, more violently, more corruptly; like an insecure teenager copying his dodgy elder brother. So, Bancroft did not feel at home at work. But then Bancroft didn't always feel at home at home either – and his wife *came* from Dorchester and her father had been the town's mayor! Maybe one day he wouldn't feel like an outsider, a stranger on this earth, but until then ...

~

So, Tamsin has both Bancroft and the Abbot on board; and in record time. Employing him, as has been noted, was usually a game of cat and mouse, though who was which, wasn't always clear. They'd probably both see themselves as the cat. The rules of the game were simple: would he say 'yes' or wouldn't he? Negotiations were sometimes extended, swinging this way and that, with him whining about how difficult she made it for him, how insecure she was, *blah blah blah*. But, in the end, the offer of some money in the bank, even a pitiful amount, usually swung it for the abbot. The abbot had needs, with his keen interest in stationary and expensive bubble bath. And really, there are only so many ways a former abbot of a desert monastery can make a living, so, when the Old Bill come calling and offer fool's gold ...

'It's Abbess Hildegard,' she said, 'Do you know her?'

'Hildegard? I know *of* her. Met her once. A force of nature, by all accounts. Leads from the front.'

'Not so much now.'

'What's happened?'

'She's charcoal.'

'She's ... ? OK.' Even the unshockable abbot seems shocked, which pleases her. 'And how did this occur? Not an accident with the barbeque.'

'Unlikely. It was in the prayer chapel, and I know things have changed in the church, but ... '

'So many questions.'

'Something about the soap stone.'

'The soapstone?'

'It's what the chapel's made of. But whatever she prayed – and I imagine she was praying quite hard towards the end – God must have been out.'

*'My God, my God, why have you abandoned me!'* She's *climbing on the altar, clinging to the cross, the ground too hot, brief relief, but the altar is warming, the heat passing through, sudden scalding –* 'Bishop! *– someone! – Jesus, help me!'* She's *clinging to the cross, clinging for dear life, her hands burning,* 'Into your hands I commit my –'

'Are you there now?' asks the abbot.

∼

It was a fifteen-minute walk along the beach to the convent, set in noble isolation on the Stormhaven side of Tide Mills, all salty air and sea spray, with views across to Newhaven harbour. The landscape was rough and stony with the occasional touch of wildflower, the tough variety. 'It *so* reminds me of Dungeness,' people would say. 'But without the artists.'

And then there was the remarkable delusion of the convent itself. Embarrassingly, being a newcomer himself to these parts, it had also fooled the abbot. The Community of the Holy Fire was not as it appeared. Not at all.

# The jackal has a small office.

~

It is not as large as Hildegard's, but then Hildegard was abbess and the Jackal – née Patience, to a car mechanic and a teacher in Peckham thirty-eight years ago – was sub-abbess; and lucky to have an office at all.

'The sub-abbess is traditionally one of the girls,' Hildegard had said, mindful that whatever else occurred, Patience would not be sharing her office space. 'Yours is a more pastoral vocation, a sister among the sisters. Do you really need an office?'

'I think so. I need a place where—'

'Surely you should be removing walls of separation between you, rather than erecting them?'

But Patience was true to her name, adding Persistence and Bloody-mindedness, because she'd always had to fight for her worth; and a cleaning cupboard had been duly converted into an office.

'Well, if you must,' said Hildegard, in reluctant acceptance. Patience had also had an office when she worked in the city of London. It was an office larger than Hildegard's and with a striking view of the Thames. It was everyone's dream office. Clients loved meeting her there. 'It's like a film set,' they'd say. But while being head of marketing for some very large companies had blessed her bank account – her financial cup running over – it had left her soul cold. And now her office was a former broom cupboard in Stormhaven-by-the-sea.

'I am sub-abbess Patience,' she says, reaching out a hand to them both.

'Sounds more like a naval appointment,' says Tamsin.

'Near to the sea; but nothing to do with boats; though I used to love watching them from my office on the Thames.'

She will get that in early. The police woman's looking smug.

'You weren't always a nun?' says Peter, and Patience tells of her former life in the city 'with more money than I knew what to do with.'

'How much?' asks Tamsin because, while it is hardly part of the enquiry, it is the obvious question. And Patience isn't afraid to say.

'Eighty, ninety thousand a year, plus bonuses; which is all very nice but I wasn't happy.'

Tamsin is disorientated, in stone-cold amazement. This woman had earned more than her, (she wouldn't mention that) enjoyed an office on God's own river - and then walked away from it, kissing goodbye to success and enrichment, because 'she wasn't happy'. Who in the City is happy? And did such people as Patience really exist? Well, clearly they did, here in the asylum also known as the Community of the Holy Fire.

Tamsin has to ask. 'Did you miss anything, when you, er, changed direction?' This was the second choice ending. The first choice had been 'when you lost your mind.'

'My jeans,' says Patience with a smile. 'I didn't mind about anything else. It was easy to let go of most things. But getting into this habit and leaving behind my jeans, that was hard. It took a while.'

'But now the jeans are gone.'

'They are, yes. Gone forever.'

'The abbot here didn't struggle in the same way,' says Tamsin, woman-to-woman. 'Plenty of jeans available in Stormhaven; yet still in his old work clothes.'

'Your *old* work clothes?'

'I was an abbot of a monastery in Egypt.'

'Oh, I see. But no longer?

'It's a difficult commute.'

'I mean no longer a member of a community?' asks Patience, without guile. She is confused.

'Er, no – not presently. I mean, I was for twenty-five years, near Sinai – and not St Catherine's, which is the famous one, with the nice library, but the other end of the valley, St James-the-Less, not so well-known!' He has lost his train of thought in his defensive ramble. 'But not since I returned to England, no.'

'Yet the habit is still your identity in some manner?' Again, without guile which leaves the abbot on the ropes.

'Well, in a manner, I suppose, it still is my identity. I was an abbot for a long time; though in another way, I have left it all behind very happily.'

'So happily you still wear the clothes?'

'Like an old pair of socks, I suppose. Familiar.' This is getting worse.

'Well, hardly a pair of old socks, Abbot. No one sees your socks but everyone sees your habit.' It is genuine interest from Sister Patience; but mixed with distaste. A man still wearing a habit when he is no longer a member of a religious community? For her, it's odd. And for Peter, it's becoming strangely embarrassing, when he has never been embarrassed about this before – even when the police were finding it all very funny with their jokes about stocks, gallows and witch-dipping. So why is he bothered now?

'I'm clearly due an existential crisis,' says Peter.

''I think it's arrived,' says Tamsin, 'in a gold limousine.'

'Though hardly the crisis that faced Hildegard as the chapel warmed.' Peter needs to reclaim some ground, so opts for on some questions. 'Unimaginable. Did you two get on well?'

'I believe we had a professional relationship.'

'Despite her beating you to the position of abbess?' This information was courtesy of Sister Agatha.

'That really made no difference.'

'She got two thirds of the vote, I hear.'

'There may be twenty-three nuns here, but only one person knows the exact voting figures.'

'One times twenty-three, I think. News travels in a community. But was that difficult to live with?'

'Why would that be difficult?'

'Well, I suppose I'm a traditionalist in these matters; that is, one who doesn't believe there has ever been a clean and fair election. And, in my experience, it can leave a residue of bitterness.'

'I think half the present cabinet stood to lead the party last time there was a leadership election. They failed – but their voice was heard. So maybe they succeeded. And at least they valued themselves enough to stand. All to their credit.'

'I don't think anyone in the cabinet could be accused of under-valuing themselves.'

'And now they get on with it.' Frustration contained lifts her voice up an octave. 'Just as I get on with it. There's no failure if you are on the right path.' No failure? Tamsin is again mystified. Is this the sort of nonsense she's going to have to put up with in the convent? The failure was clear and obvious.

'I suppose it's a rejection, though, which can, as the abbot says, be difficult. And, believe me, he knows all about rejection.'

'I see it more as an affirmation, actually.'

'Really? And how does that work?'

'Not a rejection of me but an affirmation of Hildegard. And there's a lot to affirm. Or rather, there was.'

'So, like the cabinet, you're just "getting on with it", as you say?' Patience nods. They'd spent long enough with this matter in her eyes. But Tamsin can't put the bone down. 'No resentment at all.' It is layered with disbelief.

'It's not a question of resentment, Detective Inspector.'

'Well, I think it is.'

'And, to be honest, this is sounding more about you than about me.' Respect from the abbot. This was *all* about Tamsin.

'You just feel you could have done a better job than her?'

'A *different* job, Detective Inspector. I would have done a different job.'

'But a better different job?' Patience smiles.

'I'm simply acknowledging a reality. It is not the same as resentment.'

'Thin line.'

'But a line nonetheless.'

'And no racial prejudice in the vote? You don't feel your colour was a factor?' Someone had to ask and it was Peter.

Patience takes a deep breath and shifts her position. 'I don't know.' Her defences are down a little. Years of pain appear in her eyes; too many memories – casual racism in the supermarket and everywhere beyond. Why should she even have to consider this? 'One hopes not.' There is more grace than conviction in her answer. 'You must remember that Hildegard has – I'm sorry, *had* – been here since childhood. She attended the convent school.'

'There's a school here?'

'There *was* a school here, not the finest educational establishment, and wisely closed down some years ago – it's not a given that the holy can teach.'

'Or even be holy,' adds the abbot absent-mindedly.

'They weren't always kind, no. But in its day, it was a place for daughters of the rich and religious to be left by their parents. Hildegard was dropped off by her father and mother at the age of eight and barely saw them again. She often spent her holidays here in the convent.'

'An unusual childhood.'

'They were an intensely religious family and saw her as an offering to God.'

'You mean she was a child-sacrifice of some sort?' Tamsin is incredulous.

'A "thank offering", they called it – for their ten children. They felt they should give one back to God. Hildegard was like a tithe, whereby you give a tenth of everything to God.'

'And she saw it in the same way?' Peter steps in, while Tamsin recovers from shock and disgust.

'Hildegard always said she was glad to be free of them. I once asked her how she felt being left here. "Best day of my life," she said.'

'She had to say that,' says Peter. 'It was the worst day of her life. A sad little lie she had to tell herself in the face of parental neglect; a rationalisation in the cause of survival, to keep her rage at bay. Banished knowledge.'

'Don't mind the abbot,' says Tamsin. 'He really won't leave childhood alone.'

The abbot's hands plead to the sky and Tamsin offers a 'see-what-I-mean?' look to Patience.

'It's childhood that won't leave *us* alone. And while it may not be significant in this case; no one is made happy by neglect. The shame is profound because the child blames themselves. They were not worth the care. So, they must make a different story of it, a better story. I very much doubt it was the best day of that little girl's life. Rather, a moment of traumatic abandonment by the sea.'

Patience responds briskly: 'Well, whatever the ins-and-outs, Abbot – I don't really have time for that sort of thing – she was part of the fabric here. Hildegard was the convent girl who inevitably became a nun and then inevitably became abbess. I was an outsider – a complete outsider, ethnically, geographically, culturally.'

'And what happens now?'

'How do you mean?'

'In terms of the succession. How will the next abbess be chosen – and crowned?'

'Hardly *crowned*.'

'You know what I mean.'

And she did know what Tamsin meant, but must pretend a certain indifference towards advancement. This is not the City where greed is good and ambition a virtue and Patience is good at pretending; she has pretended much to survive. 'Well, I'm not sure we've quite reached that time yet.'

'And when you do?'

'When we do? I suppose there will be a fresh election.'

'You suppose?'

'Well, there will have to be. I mean, it's obvious. But really, no one's thinking about that.'

'Maybe someone is,' says the abbot. 'Maybe someone has thought very hard about it.'

Tamsin ignores him. 'So, it's not an appointment, Sister Patience – the bishop doesn't step in and appoint someone?'

'The *bishop*?' It's as if Tamsin has blasphemed. 'The bishop has *no* power in the matter at all!' Patience realises the unnecessary force of her response; or how it might be perceived, at least. 'I'm sorry, but he'd probably like the power; he'd probably like it very much.'

'You don't like the bishop.'

'It's not a question of whether or not I like him.' *No, it is.* 'It's a simple fact. He doesn't have it; he has no power at all here. The new abbess will be chosen by the good sisters of the Community. That is how it is in our Order.' Tamsin wonders if the bad sisters will feel excluded.

'And you will stand?'

'Me?'

'Well, you are the sub-abbess; with a record for desiring advancement.'

'I don't know how you can say that. And really, it's much too early to say ... way too early. I have given the matter no thought at all.'

*So, she can lie when she has to.*

'Did you like Hildegard?' asks Tamsin.

'Did I like her?'

'That was the question. You don't like the bishop but did you like Hildegard?'

'She was a remarkable woman.'

'Not quite an answer.'

'I believe we got along well.' Her shoulders tighten a little. 'Though no one could replace Richardis as far as Hildegard was concerned.'

'Richardis? Who's Richardis?' A new name appears in the mix.

'A former nun here, much loved by Hildegard. No longer with us.'

'She died?'

'Her death would have been easier for the abbess to handle. It was her living that was problematic.'

'Meaning?'

'Richardis decided to leave the Community and Hildegard was – how can we say it? – "rather upset". But even that doesn't quite capture her mood. Richardis was her favourite, her protégée.'

'That sounds awkward.'

'It's not awkward, it's just plain wrong. It's *wrong*. One should not have favourites; it is made clear in our Benedictine rules.'

'I suppose every boss has favourites; those they like more than others.'

'But not every boss makes it quite so obvious.' The resentment of Patience lives on.

'But Richardis went?'

'She did, yes, two years ago.' Tamsin loses interest in Richardis, the errant nun. Women falling out is hardly headline news; and it was a while back and probably not relevant. Something more pressing demands their attention now.

'Hildegard called you the Jackal.'

'I'm sorry?'

'It's what she called you. "Patience the Jackal", she wrote in her final testimony. Why did she say that?'

The body of the sub-abbess locks up, her shoulders become rigid. The scowl across her face comes and then goes. She is now in explanatory mode, in teaching mode – explaining the situation, but uninvolved herself. 'Hildegard had strong opinions, everyone knows that. She had her good books and her bad books. You didn't always know which book you'd be in. And it could change: good books one day, bad books the next. Perhaps it wasn't my lucky day, who knows? She was a remarkable woman, though, you had to be impressed.'

'Well, someone wasn't.'

# A small parlour had been set aside

for the investigation.

And beneath a portrait of the Virgin Mary looking depressed, a beguiling fire burned in the ancient hearth where fires had burned for hundreds of years, surely? It was rightfully called 'The Snug' and Tamsin is for once seduced by the deep sense of history around her; the strong presence of time past holding the present, communicating with the present. *I'm getting old*, she thinks, drawn in by the ancient wooden doors, the arched and aged stone window frames, the panelled wood ceilings and the flagstone corridors, worn away by centuries of feet – the feet of the devoted on their way to prayers.

'I feel like I'm in the 16th century,' says Tamsin.

'Be quiet, woman,' says Peter and Tamsin is shocked. 'It's the 16th century, remember? I can say what I like.'

'I don't want the immersive experience, thank you. The architecture will be just fine.'

'Well, he'll be pleased you've been fooled.'

'Who will be?'

'The architect.'

'How do you mean, fooled? How have they fooled me?' Tamsin is not keen on being fooled – by an architect or anyone else.

'It was built in 1927.'

'This place – built in 1927? But how could it ... ?'

'Convincing, isn't it? Deceived me as well; reeled in hook, line and sinker, like a prize trout. But it was built in 1927 by a rich landowner who wished to create an ancient retreat house.'

Tamsin is shocked. 'You mean this is all *fake?* It can't be.'

'No, none of it is *fake*, Tamsin. Not in its parts. Everything is real. It's just the place which is an illusion. Everything here is as old as it looks, everything quite genuine – the arches, the doors, the flagstones – but everything here started life somewhere *else.*'

'How do you mean?'

'In 1923, this was just a scruffy patch of beach. But by 1927, there was a 15th century convent, with some 16th century additions.'

Tamsin is not generally interested in architecture; the amenities in the hotel matter more than its shape or provenance. But she is intrigued by this story. 'How? I mean, how was it done?'

'The architect, who had built nothing before this and built nothing after, went on a journey.'

'Not a spiritual journey, I hope. I hear they can go on a little and I really don't have time.'

'He went round England, Scotland and Wales, scouring the countries for ancient settings – old farmhouses, old homes, antique fairs, old institutions. Sometimes entire buildings – including a 14th century pub – were moved and rebuilt here. It was an early attempt at recycling, in a way – using the already used. So, everything here is old, but the convent itself is an illusion.'

'Will you be long?' asks a middle-aged woman, standing in the doorway, and staring. She's in an overall and leggings; furniture polish and a cloth in her hand. 'I'll need to clean.'

'This is a private space,' says Tamsin, unimpressed.

'Private? I don't bloody think so.'

'Police.' She holds up her card to end the conversation. They don't need visitors, especially a cleaner.

'But good to see you anyway,' says Peter. 'And you are?' Will he get an answer? It's touch and go.

'Daisy,' she says and it seems too delicate a name for the trooper before them. 'Solid' is the word that comes to mind ... and 'intense'. She can certainly stare. 'My name is Daisy Munch.' And then adds, as she has presumably done many times before, 'like the painter.'

'Which painter?' asks Tamsin. She needs more clues.

'Edvard Munch.' A pause to see if that means anything. It doesn't. 'He painted *The Scream*.'

*An unusual cleaner,* thinks the abbot who sees how her words cut all small talk off at the pass. And now she mentions it, there is something of the scream about her; eyes which tell of the twisted caverns of lost childhood. Is this why Hildegard called her the Darkness?

'Quite a painting,' says the abbot, picking up where Tamsin cannot. She is still wishing this woman gone. But Peter knows the story. 'Munch was out walking with friends, when he "sensed an infinite scream passing through nature." I've always remembered that. And it's topical as well – as we try and save the planet.'

'Hildegard was a snob. But she heard the scream.'

'Why do you say that?'

She pauses. 'It doesn't matter.'

'It might matter.'

'She was keen on saving the planet, that's all. Some say she liked the planet more than she liked people.'

'Do *you* say that?'

'Her and her secret plans.'

'Which secret plans?' asks Tamsin.

"Who can say? The plans were secret.'

'Secret from whom? Secret from you?'

She nods. Too long a pause. 'Secret from everyone.'

The abbot doesn't wish to lose her. 'And are you related to the painter?'

'Who knows? I am Danish, so it's not impossible. Danish blood anyway and related in feeling. The scream connects us all; that's what I reckon. Some say it's love that connects us; but I say it's the scream, end of.'

'Maybe both?' Daisy shrugs. 'And you are – not a nun?' That sounded so crass. But then Daisy creates an atmosphere in which anything might offend; in which words are best chosen with care, which means the worst words are chosen. Fear is a terrible writer.

'It depends what you mean.'

'Isn't it like pregnancy? You either are a nun or you're not?'

'Hildegard could tell you why I'm not a nun. Were she here.'

'Or you could.'

'I am the servant of the Lord.' She nods at her cloth and polish. 'May it be unto me according to his word. Cleaning is my calling, now and forever, amen.'

It is hard to say whether these words are spoken in acceptance or rage; in peace or fury, though the grimace suggests the latter. And after she leaves, Tamsin turns to the abbot.

'What was that about?' But before he can answer, Daisy is back in the room.

'If I were you,' she says, 'which I'm not, thank God – and which I hate people saying to me, sanctimonious bitches. But, if I were you, I'd ask about the Green Chapel.'

'Ask who?'

'Hildegard's worst kept secret – the Green Chapel. You haven't heard?'

# 'Sorry to disturb you, ma'am,'

~

h e says. Bancroft is at the door of the snug, looking excited. And he's not sorry to disturb them, he's absolutely delighted. But since when did anyone speak the truth?

'What is it, Bancroft?' Her mind is with the Green Chapel, the well-known secret, left to them by Daisy. She doesn't need Bancroft at the moment.

'It's just that I found this, pushed under the door of Hildegard's study.' He's holding some writing paper.

'When?'

'Not today. I mean, it wasn't put there today. It was missed by SOCO, caught in the door stop, it was!' He holds up the discovery.

'Could it be litter, Bancroft? *Maybe?* In which case, the bin is probably your best bet.' She's still with the Green Chapel – a precious lead, currently being stalled by Bancroft, who smiles knowingly.

'There's no litter in that study, ma'am. Cleaner than a nun's conscience, that place!' Tamsin can normally kill enthusiasm dead, but Bancroft is a challenge. Gifted with a marvellous lack of awareness, he picks up on nothing. Or perhaps he's just smart – smarter than a bride groom at the altar rail; the fool who knows more than the queen.

'We'll see about that,' she says. 'One convent conscience is a swamp.'

'The note is type-written. And dated.'

'Dated?'

'Well, it says "After the fire" where you'd expect the date. Like it was put there last night, after the fire.'

'So, pushed under the door of Hildegard's office *after* Hildegard was killed,' says Peter. 'Odd.'

'What does it say?' Tamsin is more interested now. It's possible the Green Chapel can wait a moment. Against all odds, she may need to listen to Bancroft.

He reads. 'NO CHAPEL. ACCIDENTS OCCUR. LET US PRAY.'

'So, it's a warning, presumably to Hildegard ... '

'She's not actually named,' says Bancroft.

Peter: 'But it was her door, Bancroft; it was pushed under *her* door, so let's imagine – a warning to her about an accident, which feels like a threat ... when the accident has already happened.'

Tamsin, pondering: 'No chapel. No *Green* chapel?'

'What's the Green Chapel?' asks Bancroft.

'We don't know,' says Peter. 'We've only just heard of it ourselves; though I feel we may hear more.'

'It doesn't make sense,' says Tamsin. 'Let me see it.' She reaches out.

'Gloves!' says Bancroft cheerfully. He hands her a pair, and once they're on – a process slowed by irritation at her mistake in front of the milk monitor – he gives her the note.

She reads it again. The date: AFTER THE FIRE. And then, below: '"NO CHAPEL. ACCIDENTS OCCUR. LET US PRAY" So, she's being warned to behave – being warned about something to do with a chapel. Do they want a chapel? Do they not want a chapel?' Another thought. 'And she's being warned, when she's already dead.'

'So, who warns the dead?' asks the abbot.

Silence.

'Someone who thinks she's still alive?' says Bancroft. Is he allowed to be so brilliant?

'And therefore written by someone who isn't the murderer.' says Tamsin. 'Because the murderer knows she's dead. You'd have thought.'

'So, not the killer – but someone who's frightened, angry or both.' More silence. Everyone's mind is busy but no one quite ready to commit.

'Tomorrow, the interviews start in earnest,' says Tamsin.

'I do like an earnest interview,' says the abbot.

'And Bancroft, we want to know of everything inside Hildegard's laptop. Everything of *interest* – find it.' He nods. He can do that. 'First thing, yes?'

'First thing, ma'am. Let the dog see the rabbit, eh?'

'*What?*'

'I don't mean you're a dog, ma'am,' he adds hastily. 'I'm the dog. Just a saying my wife uses.'

'You can go, Bancroft.'

## 'He's a cartoonist,'

She says, as her car pulls up outside the abbot's home. It is set in a small row of cottages on the corner of Clarendon Road and the sea front. And he has lovely views, if you like the sea; for there is only sea. And no protection from the paint-wrecking salt, wrapped in the westerly winds. It is another expense for the abbot, as if the bubble bath wasn't enough ... and the stationery, particularly the notelets, featuring winter snow, disappearing paths or inglorious ruins, that sort of thing; though who receives them remains a mystery. He buys them – but does he send them?

The abbot is aware of Tamsin's unkind glance at his property.

'A re-paint every third year,' he says. 'Or it does begin to look a bit down-at-heel and tired of life.'

'Then we must be in year five. There should be a "home most like its owner" competition. I think you'd do well.'

They're still in the car; he hasn't got out. After the first day of an investigation, it's good to pause and imagine they're two normal human beings who chat about things. Obviously, that isn't how it works between them, but the abbot can dream.

'A cartoonist?' She nods. She has already shared too much and regrets it. 'So, how did you meet?' It's a risky question but

with the door half-open and exit lines clear, it seems worth it.
'Online, I suppose. I still don't know how that works.'
　'Don't try. You'd be way too niche.'
　'I'm not talking for myself.'
　'And anyway, what about your neighbour, Annabelle Rusty? Is she still mustard-keen?'
　'She was never mustard-keen.'
　'She *was* mustard keen.'
　'Our relationship has never involved any sauce at all.' Tamsin hikes her eyebrows. 'Perhaps a little mustard. But I thought this was about you.'
　'More fun if it's about you. And she did invite you round for supper. How did that go?'
　'It went as well as it could go between two people who share a garden fence but very little else.'
　'Maybe the fence is just the beginning. Fence today; holiday in Spain tomorrow.'
　'Or maybe it's just a clear boundary, which I won't be crossing. A neighbour can just be a neighbour. So is your new man a neighbour?'
　'Who said it was a man?'
　'He is a man.'
　'He *may* be a man, yes. But it's a rather big assumption.'
　'It's a deduction, not an assumption. They're different.'
　'Well, we didn't meet online. Why would you think we met online?'
　'It's all right, Tamsin, there's no need for shame.' It had only been to stir the water, and now it was spilling everywhere. 'I'm told it's OK now. No, *more* than OK ... now everyone works from home – including my doctor, I think. No sighting of him for a while. We're all online. So it's almost the only way to meet people in our brave new world.' A slight pause, realising there are exceptions. 'Unless you're involved in amateur dramatics obviously, where furtive backstage liaisons have ended more marriages than death itself.'
　'We did not meet online.'

And it was true, they hadn't met online. The story was a good deal odder. Jason – hardly Tamsin's name of choice – had been giving a talk at the Brighton Festival on political cartooning. It was called 'The Art of Ridicule'.

'Quite a catchy title,' said Fiona, a work colleague, who had a spare ticket and thought of Tamsin, because Fiona was kind like that, with a discrete eye for the lonely. 'I can't go alone, Tamsin – you'd be doing me a favour, honestly. And no one knows more about ridicule than you. You could swap notes with him afterwards.'

The kindness had to be disguised because Tamsin struggled with kindness; this was plain. And if the invitation was seen as a charitable act, there'd be no way back for Fiona; only some very dark and awkward woods.

'He works for *The Sunday Times, The Spectator, Private Eye* – well, everyone really. Just thought you might be interested.'

And surprisingly, Tamsin, drawn by the word 'ridicule', thought 'Why not?' So, fast forward in time to the Brighton Centre, and we find them sitting in the audience, waiting. Tamsin liked the look of the crowd – young and trendy – which meant she need not hide her face; indeed, she relaxed, as much as she ever relaxed. Just for a moment, she forgot the perceptions of the world, and almost missed his appearance on stage, which was the opposite of a grand entrance. He'd clearly learned nothing from the Queen of Sheba.

'It's him,' whispered Fiona.

'I know,' said Tamsin as she watched a man with a slightly stooped walk – mid-to-late thirties, dark hair, decent height, corduroy jacket and trainers. He was clearly astonished anyone had turned up to listen; though as Fiona had said, his cartoons were enjoyed by hundreds of thousands every day.

'That's quite some power – but he doesn't seem to have noticed.'

And Tamsin liked that. Either his ego was a devilishly clever disguise artist or something he left home without.

'Out of my comfort zone, I'm afraid,' he said, struggling with the mic. It was making odd noises as the sound system, along with the audience, settled down. 'I'd prefer to be holding a pencil, to be honest. Or a stick of charcoal ... a brush even. But is that OK, can you hear me at the back?' Vague affirmative grunts. 'I remember the last person I heard asking that. Fellow in the audience replied, 'I *can* hear you, but am happy to swap places with someone who can't.' Gentle laughter. 'A face for radio, obviously, so you must forgive that; and I'm very much hoping you didn't pay too much for the ticket. That would be simply tragic. Not for me so much, but certainly for you.' Was he being played by Hugh Grant? 'Refunds are available from the Chancellor of the Exchequer, as long as you're a billionaire. If you're not a billionaire, then what have you been doing with your life? And I'm afraid you'll have to pay double, you lazy bastards.'

Brighton likes that. 'But seriously – as if anyone was laughing – asking a cartoonist to speak is like asking a politician to tell the truth. It's just not what either of us *do*. We wouldn't know where to start. So, I apologise in advance for what follows. Mozart wrote a very good tune but was really crap at football. So tonight, it's like you're in the stadium, expecting musical heaven – but it's a football match and Mozart is in central midfield.'

He went on to talk about his craft, as though it was really something everyone could do, if only they didn't have a proper job. He discussed politicians' noses, eyebrows and bottoms with indecent interest and the help of a white board and pen, and then took questions from the floor, begging everyone not to ask where he got his ideas from, which was the cue for the first question, to much laughter: 'Where do you get your ideas from?'

'I sit at my desk and beg politicians to make an arse of themselves – and the response is heart-warming.'

He'd also heard the next question before: 'Are you jealous of Quentin Blake?'

His normal answer was something avoidant like, 'How can you be jealous of a national treasure?' But tonight – and he doesn't know why – something invites him to be a little more truthful. Who knows, may be truth matters?

'I used to be jealous of Quentin.' The hush in the house deepens. No one had expected anything honest. 'Or was it envy? I must find out the difference. But then I met him at some do and realised he's a very hard man to be jealous of; he has such heart, which is there in his drawings. He understands the terror and despair of life; but also understands its heart. I couldn't be jealous anymore.'

'Biggest influence?'

'Oh, everyone, really; we stand on the shoulders of giants. But maybe Honoré Daumier is a special reference for me, absolutely wonderful 19th century French artist. He could catch a face.'

'And a bottom?'

'I'm sure his bottoms were outstanding – everything else was.'

He ended up doing a cartoon of a member of the audience, randomly chosen; or in this case, randomly volunteered by Fiona.

'Is there anyone out there willing to be caricatured?'

And this is where Fiona leapt in. 'Tamsin – here!'

'Damson?' Jason hasn't quite heard.

'No, *Tam*-sin.' Though Fiona wouldn't forget 'Damson'. It would have a time and place. 'It's *Tam*-sin.'

'Sorry, Tamsin, sorry – my fruit-fixation is cruelly exposed. But could you bear to be drawn?' Jason peers into the darkness.

'Well, off you go, Damson!' says Fiona. 'It would be rude not to. Incredibly insensitive of you – and I know how much you care about other people's feelings.'

Ordinarily, Tamsin would never have gone up, however insensitive it might appear; she might even have left in a temper, at such manipulation by her friend. And making a mistake with her name was never wise. That was a very bad start for Jason. She didn't much value those who had given her the name; but she valued the gift itself – and people would need to get it right or find themselves in the chill winds of her disdain.

Only today, at the Brighton Festival, the chill winds didn't blow for some reason; and Tamsin is stepping out into the aisle, doing something with her hair; and instead of turning right towards the exit, she turns left towards the stage, because – well, she wanted to be near him. Can she believe that? It's ridiculous, and she's denying it even as she approaches the stage. Has she been drugged? He's not what you'd call attractive. But she just wants to be near this man she doesn't know. And when has she ever felt that?

## 'You completely misunderstand me!'

~

The bishop is talking with the sub-abbess; the Ego with the Jackal. 'I have no intention of taking over! Absolutely none! I just wish to stay close to events. So I can *support* you, Sister Patience.' And he's very close to events in this tiny office, with the sub-abbess trapped behind her desk.

Stephen, the Bishop of Lewes, is a media bishop – *Thought for the Day* on Radio 4 and any other studio he can get himself into. He doesn't have an agent, that wouldn't be good, but he can at least write emails, make phone calls; make himself available. Patience has heard him and he's pretty good. He has the gift of clarity. You can't always remember what he said, but you can remember how clearly he said it. And he is a dab hand at the confirmation sermon, apparently; very popular in the area.

'We can always rely on you for a good one, bishop. Don't know where you find all those clever words. Do you keep them in a "clever words" store cupboard?'

Speech somehow brings him alive; as does his purple shirt of office and the large silver cross hanging beatifically from his neck. Without these, he impresses slightly less, with a drifting waist, disappearing hair and dandruff, like gentle snow, on his shoulders.

'You have no authority to take over, even if you wished it.' Sub-abbess Patience remains calm, and the abbot remains listening in the corridor outside, the door left ajar. 'And it may be best, bishop, if you stay away from the community for a while. Until this is all sorted.' She looks up at him from her desk.

'*Stay away?*' He is flustered – when he merely came here to be a figure of calm and support for these dear and well-meaning ladies. He thought it might help to have a man about the place; particularly a man of status. But if she wanted to play hard ball ... 'I hardly think you have the power, sub-abbess, to keep me away, I'm not sure what Louisa would think.'

'Louisa?'

'And I mean ... !'

She cuts across him. 'We need each other at this time, bishop. And when I say "we", I refer to the community here. Not you, not Louisa – the community. We had a special meeting this morning to listen to our pain and discomfort at recent events. We *do* need each other – but I am not sure we need *you*.' And, because she can't help herself, 'And if you have issues with female authority, I suggest you see a therapist. They're not for me, never in a thousand years; but I'm told they can be helpful for some. Perhaps the church will pay for six sessions.'

Well, he had never expected this from Sister Patience; never in a month of Sundays. She was always such a placid girl, restrained – well, she's not a girl, she's a woman in her late thirties – it's just a manner of speech. But she was always compliant; and he he'd always been respectful of her culture, because Africans are different – as he'd learned recently attending a Black History Month school assembly. All rather worthy, but some good points made. And possibly he could re-cycle some of them to sound more ethnically-diverse, which might be wise in terms of his career. 'I wish only to be a reassuring presence.'

'Reassuring yourself, perhaps.'

'A focus of unity.'

'I'm not sure an outsider can offer that.'

'I'm so sorry to bother you,' says the abbot who feels he must save the bishop from further humiliation. He appears as a man drifting ever further from the shore of human connection – but too panicked to pick up the oars. And now the abbot wishes to help him home; and provide relief for the trapped sub-abbess. 'I was just wondering whether anyone could give me a tour of the chapel where Hildegard died. I'm told it has very particular powers. And bishop, I hear you are uniquely qualified to tell me about them. An expert-in-waiting, so to speak.'

The bishop is delighted to assist.

⁓

'It's made of soapstone,' says the Ego, slowly regaining a sense of authority. And the abbot is happy to hand it to him. They sit underground on the dark stone seats in the prayer chapel where Hildegard died. And they both feel sick. Forensics analyse but they don't clean and the stench remains. Burned flesh, like rotting pork, takes a while, however many windows you open. And there are no windows to open down here. You might as well be down a mine.

'We won't stay long,' says the abbot, with a handkerchief over his mouth. They do have their uses.

'Like Thomas à Becket martyred at the altar of Canterbury Cathedral,' says the bishop.

'Oh?'

'A place of prayer, Abbot, a place of devotion – but not a place you expect to die.'

He shakes his head censoriously, whether at God or the murderer or Henry 2nd.

'Well, quite,' says Peter. 'And I'm aware you're a bit of an expert in all this, bishop; an expert in the science of it.' And the bishop is glad he's aware. 'With a degree in geology from Southampton, I understand?' Stephen nods, as if to say, 'Oh, it's nothing really!' with which the abbot would have agreed.

'Clearly busy with your research, Abbot! The tainted baubles of academia!'

'But baubles nonetheless. We won't be sniffy about baubles.' That didn't sound quite right. Move on. 'So, you of all people can help me make sense of the snippets that I've learned.' The bishop nods again, sagely this time, happy with this consultancy role, happy to be teacher. 'So what I understand from forensics is that Hildegard was killed by the soapstone, a fire – and a door wedged shut? Is that possible?'

The bishop sighs. 'The heat would have been unbearable.'

'Why?'

'The seats are part of the wall and part of the floor which is part of the ceiling which is part of the slab of stone above us, in the garden where the fire burned.' He indicates above ground. 'Like a cave, this chapel is one piece of rock.'

'Really? So, just to step back a little, this underground chapel was built in soapstone to be a place of private prayer.'

'Yes.'

'Warmed, in the summer and autumn by a huge slab of the rock on the south-facing lawn, absorbing the sun's heat and passing it through the rock to the chapel.'

He nods like a professor with a promising student. 'Stones with the highest energy density are best for absorbing heat quickly,' says Stephen. 'Gypsum, soapstone, basalt, marble – they're the best.'

'Really?'

'Oh yes. Excellent thermal conductivity. They hold the heat, you see; they're insulators, they don't pass it on – unless you're inside the oven obviously.'

'So basically, whatever happens to the slab above, happens to the chapel below? Natural energy, I suppose.'

'Indeed. Hildegard was very hot on the green agenda – though that's probably an unfortunate phrase on this occasion.'

'And perhaps no one, in the planning, had quite reckoned with the absorbency of the rock – and how the warm chapel in winter could become the Penance Hole in the summer, something of a sweat box for the faithful.'

'I have heard this said. The law of unintended outcomes.' He likes this phrase.

'But on the night of the murder, Bishop, something much worse.'

'Murder?' The bishop chokes.

'Oh yes, Bishop, it was murder, unfortunately. Hildegard could hardly have locked the door herself.'

'No, I suppose ... '

'And because of the fire on the slab above us, it became more than a mere sweat box, more than a Penance hole – it became the Murder Hole.'

The bishop does not look well; his face is drained of blood.

'Not murder, Abbot. No, really.' His head shakes with scepticism. 'Probably a tragic mistake; *that*, I think, is the more likely explanation. We neither wish, nor need, to be melodramatic.' Peter wonders if he has been listening at all. Having been a bishop for a while, he may be out of practice.

'And the locked door?'

'A thousand possibilities.'

'Absolutely. Yet here's me unable to think of one. I'm clearly in the wrong job!'

'Who knows who might have walked past the door and locked it without thinking?'

'Why would they do that? Why would they wedge the door shut, a deliberate act, without thinking?'

'The clue is in my words, Abbot. *Without thinking.*' This isn't an answer, but he stands up, like the boss closing the meeting. 'You'll no doubt do your best, Abbot, and with the very best of intentions, venture down "rabbit holes various". But the sad truth is, we will probably never know what happened that night.'

'I'm sorry?'

'I'm just saying – and not pleased to be saying it – that we'll probably never know. And it won't bring her back, of course.'

'Oh, we will know, Bishop,' says the abbot, also standing up. 'It won't bring her back, as you say. That is beyond our reach. But light will shine in the darkness and reveal all. We'll know everything. *Everything.*'

He allows the silence which follows. And they leave the chapel in silence.

~

'I'm just a visitor, of course,' says the bishop. They approach the stairs. 'So, probably not the person you need to be speaking to.'

'Every little helps.'

'But anyone here would have known not to be in the chapel at this time.'

'Yet Hildegard was there. I wonder why.'

'I have no idea, absolutely none.'

'It does seem curious behaviour. I don't know – perhaps someone invited her.'

'I can't imagine that. Ridiculous.' They are climbing the stairs out of the cellar and the Ego is sweating. 'I mean, the Grand Fire is a great event for the community, one of the most important of the year, she wouldn't miss it, however keen on prayer she might be. A remarkable woman ... '

*'My God, my God, why have you abandoned me!' She's climbing on the altar, clinging to the cross, the ground too hot, brief relief, but the altar is warming, the heat passing through – 'Bishop!' – someone! – Jesus, help me!' She's clinging to the cross, clinging for dear life, her hands burning, 'Into your hands I commit my –* '

*And suddenly Hildegard is alight, flesh in flames, the thoughts die.*

'Her body was found on the altar,' adds Peter, 'wrapped around the cross, seeking refuge there; though the cross will have been a heat stick by the end, an extension of the oven.'

They have reached the Elizabethan hallway and the bishop is struggling with the image. He wishes to get back to the science, to things technical and quantified. 'Well, the transference of heat would have been considerable down there; very considerable. It would have resembled a wood burner. Of course, she should have walked out; she should have walked out.'

'She couldn't walk out, remember – the door was wedged shut.' Is he stupid? 'It wouldn't have opened. Someone wedged the door shut.'

'Well, it *shouldn't* have been shut. It absolutely shouldn't have been.' Stephen is tense; a man utterly bemused by events. Is this delayed shock? 'Why was the door locked?'

The abbot turns towards the bishop and places his hand on his shoulder. 'Is there something you're not telling me, bishop? Do you know why Hildegard was there in the chapel on the night of the Grand Fire?'

He's looking at a ghost; and then the ghost pulls away, says 'I cannot help you, Abbot,' and he hurries down the corridor.

## 'I've decided to live on site,'

declares the abbot.

'Oh?'

'I thought it for the best.'

' ... and forgot to ask me.'

'I didn't forget. It's just better, Tamsin. And I think you mentioned I was in charge.'

'A degree of responsibility was my suggestion. I'm not sure I ... '

'I can be around, I can meet people here, chat with them – you know, unplanned encounters which reveal character, weakness and desire.'

'Yours or theirs?'

'It's about the story on the ground. The police can struggle with that sometimes. They just see the story on the white board.'

'So you say; quite often, in fact. It's almost on a loop.'

'Spontaneous encounter has fewer walls than the formal interview; it has to be more revelatory.'

'Revelatory? Is that even a word?'

'It's why job interviews so often deliver the wrong choice. If you only know someone officially, then you hardly know them at all.'

'Finished?'

'Possibly.'

'Though of greater concern, Abbot, as I consider your "sleep-over" idea, is the nuns' sweet virtue.' The abbot raises a weary eyebrow. 'Which, as Senior Investigating Officer, I have some responsibility for. In short, can you be trusted?'

'The day you become this convent's moral guardian is the day the convent must close. And on a brighter note, the sub-abbess has kindly offered me lodging in the confessor's room.'

'So many images.'

'Then let them pass.'

'Is that where confessions are extracted by any means possible?'

'It's a bedroom, with neither thumbscrew nor rack; and above the kitchens, so well away from everyone.'

'And does the confessor know of his eviction – or are you top and tailing?' Tamsin is enjoying this. It must be the ridicule, which makes her think of Jason and their meeting in Lewes later. Oh God, how was that going to go? 'And while we're here, who or what on earth is a confessor? I remember the Inquisition used them; but most organisations now have HR departments.'

'His name is Volmar.'

'The Worm?'

'The Worm, yes. And he is – was – Hildegard's long-time confessor.'

'Meaning?'

'He heard her sins.'

'Meaning?'

'Times when she felt she'd fallen short of the mark.'

'Which mark?'

'God's, I imagine. She'd tell him about whatever it was, get it off her chest and in doing so, find some sort of peace, some sort of reconciliation.' Tamsin is struggling to engage. She cannot imagine being eased by telling anyone anything – particularly not a perceived error or failure. Why would you tell someone about it? 'In her early days, he was something of a mentor to her, apparently.'

'Who told you that?'

'Sister Roisin. We met by the compost. It's where you learn things. Volmar was a guide, an encourager, a boundary-keeper for Hildegard. Do *you* have a mentor?' For Tamsin, it was probably the abbot, if it was anyone; so, she simply screws up her face at the absurd question. 'As we know, it was a relationship from way back.'

'And then something went wrong.'

'It seems so. We don't yet know how the much-loved confessor became the Worm. But there are other nuns here who prefer a male confessor as well; so, he stays over sometimes; and they can book in to see him.'

'The dumping ground for convent sin? I can't imagine he's detained *that* long. I mean, just how much can there be to confess here?'

'There could be a great deal. It's all about our attitudes, isn't it?'

'It's presently about murder.'

'This death is about attitudes.'

'I think it was the fire that killed Hildegard.'

'A fire lit by attitudes, which kill in different ways.'

'Of the two, I'd probably take death by attitude. And one thing's for sure: the Worm must know all of Hildegard's secrets.'

'All the secrets she's revealed to him, yes. But it may be there are some that she hasn't. People do edit, even in the confessional; *particularly* in the confessional.'

'Well, there'll be no editing outside it.' A surge of anger inside her. 'We'll hear the truth, the whole truth and nothing but the truth.'

'The eternal optimist.'

'And with that in mind, having met the Darkness, I think it's time we formally met the rest of the Famous Five – Worm, Snake, Jackal and Ego.'

# The Jackal is sitting pretty

~

behind Hildegard's desk. She takes her position as if it was only a matter of time; to the manor born, as they say. Tamsin and the abbot sit before her, almost as supplicants. The sub-abbess knows the power of a desk from her city days, the corporate world, where most sackings are done by text, which is less fuss. But if you were to be sacked face-to-face – something of an honour and a definite feather in the cap – it was always from behind a desk. A desk ensured distance, it removed the 'human' from the meeting. 'It's nothing personal.'

And now Patience is on different adventures – from corporate to convent, from power to prayer; yet still mindful of the desk, the power of the desk ... old habits and all that.

'The importance of vocation is under-estimated in society today,' she declares confidently. Her audience is captive and she seizes the moment. 'Especially in our disintegrating culture of self-determination and choice.' She feels the need to educate Tamsin, who has a manner towards both her and the place which her mother would have called 'pinched'.

'Which are good things, from where I'm sitting,' says Tamsin politely and obviously. 'Self-determination and choice? To be encouraged, surely?'

'Good things?' The nun laughs. 'Can a puppet make any serious choices? *Really?*' She's looking hard at Tamsin. 'From what I see of the world, few know who or what is pulling their strings.'

'Perhaps you mix with the wrong people.'

'And perhaps you mix with the deluded, Detective Inspector!' Spoken in jest but with a sledgehammer in attendance. 'Talk of self-determination is nothing more than a pot of froth, based on the illusion of being in control. At least we in the Community of the Holy Fire don't imagine we're in control of anything.'

'Someone here does. Or someone here *was*.' Time for Tamsin to break out of this convent neck-hold. 'Two nights ago, someone in this establishment took control rather savagely. There's nothing holy about putting someone in an oven, locking the door, turning up the heat – oh, and laughing through the torment.'

'Laughing?'

'Well, there was considerable merriment, I'm told; much laughter round the fire that night.'

'And that is a crime?'

'Only when *one* of the laughing faces – or maybe more – knew exactly what the fire was doing as they made merry.'

There is silence in the room.

'It does lack comedy,' admits Peter.

Patience offers a dismissive snort, a glimpse of the teenager, a petulant moment. She will not back down. 'All attempts at control are futile.'

'But, in this case, deadly.' Tamsin speaks with a smile, with great and deliberate calm. Her work is done. She has left the Jackal rattled.

'Deadly but futile.'

'Why do you imagine it's futile?' Incredulous.

'All murder is futile. What is gained? Nothing is gained.'

'Unless it's the life insurance.'

'For which you have sold your soul.'

'A price you think worth it, perhaps.'

'It is futility incarnate.'

*A good description of the convent*, thinks Tamsin. 'But what if it isn't futile, Patience?'

'What do you mean?'

'What if it changes everything? What, for instance, *won't* happen now that Hildegard is dead?'

'How do you mean, "What *won't* happen"? She won't walk through that door now, I know that!'

'That would be a surprise, yes. You'd lose your desk for a start. But I suppose I'm wondering if the killer might be trying to stop something.'

'I don't understand.'

'Well, let's exclude the usual suspects, shall we? Money? This isn't about money. I don't think so. There's no life insurance; no hidden accounts in the Cayman Islands. Family? No, the killer is not the next of kin, I don't think that either. This isn't a next-of-kin murder. And neither is the murder related to sexual gratification. I'm not feeling that. Are you feeling that, Abbot?'

'Not unduly.'

'Not even the abbot's feeling it. So, it's an unusual murder, because those three – like Einstein – explain almost everything.' The abbot watches as the power is removed from the one behind the desk. It can be done, and Tamsin is a fine exponent of the art. 'So, I'm thinking the killer might be trying to *stop* something.' Patience nods in acceptance. 'Something Hildegard might have done, if she hadn't been incinerated. Still with me?' She nods again. 'So, Patience – what might the killer be trying to stop here in the convent?'

'Who can say?' Casual and dismissive. She doesn't like to be told – or investigated.

'Well, we hoped the Jackal might.' Silence. 'You must have known something of her thinking, her plans.'

Patience ponders a moment; though Patience doesn't really ponder – she thinks, which is different; and quick decisions arise. 'I suppose the Green Chapel might now be under threat.'

'The Green Chapel.' Tamsin can't help but look at the abbot. 'To which all roads seem to lead.'

## 'I do apologise,' says Tamsin.

'The abbot taking your bedroom is all rather sudden and renders you homeless, I imagine.' She looks at the abbot, the bed-stealer, who looks at Volmar.

'Oh, it's hardly *my* bedroom,' says the Worm, in self-deprecating tones. Bangladeshi roots but officer class English. 'Really not, Detective Inspector. I don't believe in ownership.'

'Maybe your toothbrush?'

'Maybe my toothbrush. But we are all pilgrims here on earth.'

'So, it's not your bedroom?'

'Well, in a manner it's mine; in a manner, I suppose.' He clearly *does* believe in ownership. 'But the abbot must lay his head somewhere, if he wishes to stay – if stay he must.'

'He must, yes.'

'I'd heard he lives quite close by, not much of a walk; a walk many would relish at the end of the day, I'd imagine, but if he must ... '

'He really must,' says Tamsin who can't abide passive-aggressive men; men who hide their fury behind pretended calm.

'I hope it will not be for long,' says Peter, smiling warmly at the Worm. 'And presumably you are only an occasional visitor here?'

'I come when called upon.' Which manages to sound pompous and then, as if to explain, 'I have known Hildegard for many years, *knew* her for many years. I taught history and maths at the school here, so I was here when she first arrived.'

'Oh?'

'Left by her mother and father, aged eight years old. I remember the scene very well. How can anyone do that? Drive off and leave them – so young!'

'It's called private education, I believe.'

'Quite.' Volmar has no wish to become political. 'And, in time, I was given special responsibility for her ... before moving to my present community in Alfriston. Not far. So yes, I knew her as a young girl; watched over her as best I could.'

'Her guardian angel?'

'Maybe.' He is moved by the thought; and saddened. 'And Hildegard wished for me to remain as her confessor as she grew into a woman; and to be available for other nuns, should they wish for it.'

'And some do?'

'Some women prefer a man as their confessor, yes; it was, of course, the tradition in all holy orders until recently.' Volmar is settling into amiability, perhaps even self-importance. His ageing eyes are wistful in remembrance of the little lost girl, who grew up to be abbess. Tears arise and his hands begin to shake. 'She never got over Sister Richardis, of course.'

'Tell us more.' *Let's hear his version with appropriate ignorance.*

'So sad.'

'She died?'

'No, she left – she left the community ... in a manner.' There's that phrase again.

'In a manner?'

Volmar retracts. 'No, she left.'

'Why did she leave?'

'They fell out, Hildegard and herself.'

Nuns at war? 'Why did they fall out?' asks Tamsin.

'You must know how it is in communities.'

'Not really. I've managed to avoid them so far.'

'Sometimes those closest to us, those who we imagined most dear – they hurt you, do they not? You make a mistake and suddenly you are cast adrift; and left all alone in desperate loneliness.'

'You speak of Richardis?'

'Of course!'

'I thought you were getting autobiographical for a moment.'

'Hardly.'

'Though as Hildegard's confessor, she must have confided in you?' He grants her this. 'She must have spoken of the hurt of this departure? In fact, you must know a great deal about the deceased.' Fresh vistas of revelation open up before Tamsin's eyes. Thank God for confessors.

'Clearly, I cannot speak of these things, Detective Inspector.'

'Oh?'

'You wish me to speak of the confessional; that is clear.'

'Good.'

'But I cannot speak of the confessional. *No.*' He is putting in a boundary, a line in the sand, erecting a strong and sturdy fence, though this doesn't work well with Tamsin, who recognises none of the above.

'Not even on behalf of the incinerated?' she asks and the abbot watches Volmar's twitching soul, all nerves and discomfort. 'Perhaps she would actually *like* her voice to be heard now? Don't you think she might? I think I would. After all, when she spoke in the confessional, about her miniscule sins, she didn't know what was to come. Perhaps having tasted the future, there are things she would now like heard?'

'I understand your sudden interest.'

'You "understand my sudden interest"?' Now she's angry. 'Like I'm some nosy-parker or voyeur? My sudden interest, as you call it, is in justice for the dead.'

Volmar smiles and nods. 'Quite, quite, and no need for upset – but really, one cannot dishonour the integrity of the confessional; it is sacrosanct, you must understand.'

Tamsin doesn't understand. 'I don't understand at all, I'm afraid. Not a word. All I'm hearing is pomposity and raging self-importance.'

'The integrity of the confessional is sac ... '

'Only the truth is sacrosanct, surely – don't you think?' Volmar seems suddenly absent. 'And when the confessional gets in the way of that ... '

'We just want to find the person who locked the prayer chapel door,' says the abbot, in kinder tones; but they calm nothing; they are like petrol on the fire.

'Oh my God!' And now Volmar is weeping, head in hands, his heels banging the floor, up and down, up and down. This is all too much; the man is a wreck.

'Louisa?' mouths Tamsin, already somewhere else, and the abbot nods.

The Worm is a mess. It is time to meet the Snake.

## But there's trouble on the way.

L oud voices from Hildegard's study interrupt their journey down the corridor. A man and a woman ... it's Bancroft and someone. He shouldn't be shouting in a convent. Why is he shouting? It doesn't fit well. But then maybe he isn't shouting; maybe it's just that everyone else is so bloody quiet.

'Where are you going with that?' says Bancroft.

'I'm just cleaning,' says Daisy.

'In the abbess' study - the day after her murder?'

'Life goes on.'

'Hers doesn't.' He's flustered. 'And why the laptop in your hands? *Why?* Is that Hildegard's laptop?'

'What if it is?' The Darkness thinks he's a fool. She fancies her chances here; just another stupid pig.

'So, you put it down straightaway.'

'I'm just giving it a clean, sergeant.' All police are sergeants.

'Do you often clean laptops?'

'Occasionally. All part of the service.' And she is feeling good; but does need to get out of here with the laptop; this delay is so irritating. Why had the plod come in now? She feels confident, though, she feels fine – until that detective inspector arrives in the study doorway. Holy shit! What *was* she doing with the laptop?

'So, where were you going with it?' asks Tamsin, stepping in.

'I wasn't going anywhere with it.'

'She was leaving as I arrived,' says Bancroft. 'The laptop was going somewhere.'

'OK, so I didn't want to stay in here. I find it really spooky, what with – recent events.'

'Yet your instincts to clean were stronger, Daisy. Commendable.' Daisy shrugs. She's burning inside. 'So, you braved the ghouls and the ghosts of the dead woman's study to offer a computer cleaning service for the deceased.'

'Respect for the dead.' Daisy really wishes she was somewhere else. Lying is like walking through a bog – increasingly tiring. 'And someone else might need it. They're not flush for computer's here.' *Awful.* Rule 1 in the Liar's Handbook: '*As much as you can, stick to the truth.*'

'Well, PC Bancroft needs it, OK? So, you can put it down now, Daisy, nice and carefully – and we'll leave any cleaning to him. He's good with a baby wipe. Do you understand?' Daisy nods. This woman is a complete cow, like Hildegard. 'Oh, and stay out of here from now on. Resist any urge to clean anything else in this room. You're trespassing on a crime scene. All right?'

'All right.'

'And we'll need to talk, Daisy. So, do work on your story or you'll be surprised at the trouble that falls on your head. It will make a cleaning job at the convent a warm but distant memory.'

'Good,' says Daisy, 'because this isn't what I am.'

'Oh, and while you're here, why did Hildegard call you the Darkness?'

'The Darkness?'

'Yes.'

Daisy shrugs and offers a "thinking" face. 'Perhaps because I shone a bright light in her eyes – and light leaves you blind?'

And with that, she leaves, as churned inside as the sea in a storm; rolling emotional waves, breaking on her shores, leaving her hardly able to walk.

'And leave to marinade in fear for a few hours,' says Tamsin, watching her leave. And with Bancroft duly instructed, they follow her down the corridor, past the saints in glory and ever closer to the Snake.

# 'Have you two met?'

~

Asks Tamsin. She's aware the abbot looks awkward, which is unusual. 'I feel you *have* met before, in a previous life – and it didn't go well.'

And Tamsin is uncannily right. The abbot and Louisa have met in a previous life, and no, it hadn't gone well; or not as far as the abbot was concerned.

'Nothing we can't handle,' he says. 'Water under the bridge.' His smile reaches beyond the pain and is acknowledged by Louisa, a former blond bombshell and still striking in her late forties, if strikingly hard – as if there's no one to look after her apart from herself. Her skin is toughened for the fight. Louisa doesn't blend into the background and nor, probably, would she wish to. Even when seated, she is an energy in the room.

'Not a problem for me,' says Louisa, looking at the abbot, 'It was nothing at all, it happens all the time.' Though they're not saying exactly *what* isn't a problem or *what* happens all the time. The silence remains sticky.

'It's called body language,' says Tamsin, feeling like a referee taking two wrestlers aside. 'But if the contestants don't wish to speak ... '

'I think we should just proceed with the interview,' says Louisa. 'We're all big boys and girls here. And the tape recorder will be a great deal more interested in my understanding of events around the death of the abbess, than in long-forgotten slices of irrelevant back story. So shall we crack on?'

It was not long-forgotten for the abbot; but then it's the victors who forget, not the losers. The victors have forgotten the next day, while the loser can mope around for years. 'Cracking on' is definitely for the winners.

'So how long have you lived here, Louisa?' says Tamsin, brightly. 'It's an unusual residence for a politician. Especially for one whose constituency is in the north.'

'The *best* residence for a politician, Detective Inspector – away from all the nonsense of Westminster. And my constituency organisation is a well-oiled machine. Ted runs it like clockwork. They hardly need me!'

'And so they hardly see you?'

And then the abbot joins in. 'Though, I suppose, you're *part* of it.'

'I'm sorry?'

'Oh, it's nothing really. Just something you said.'

'What did I say?'

'Well, I suppose you remind me of those drivers who speak of hitting a traffic jam, when they *are* the traffic jam.'

'What are you talking about?'

'Because *you* are the nonsense. You are a constituent part of the nonsense in Westminster. It's not separate to you.'

Tamsin applauds the abbot silently. She hasn't recovered from Louisa's control-snatch of the interview. *Shall we crack on?* That wasn't Louisa's call. And she must be made to pay.

'One does ones best to bring sanity to the corridors of power,' she says, humbly.

'Then you're best isn't working,' says Tamsin. 'And, in between, you hide away here.'

'A sweet refuge; an absolute Godsend. And I use the word advisedly. I really do believe it was sent by God.'

'And that *you're* sent by God?'

'I couldn't possibly comment!'

'But you have other homes, I imagine?' She'd been policing by Wikipedia in bed last night.

'Of course.' No embarrassment.

'Of course, indeed! How anyone can manage with just *one* home remains a mystery to us all.' Louisa smiles. It takes more than this to de-rail a force of nature. 'And one of the other homes is a large estate in Scotland?'

'Is this relevant?'

'Who knows at the beginning of an investigation? Everything is material. But not all material matters.'

She will explain. 'It's a family home, my mother and father still live there, bless them – in the east wing ... so they can have their independence. So crucial for the elderly, I feel.'

'And even more crucial for you, I'd imagine. You don't get on?'

Louisa smiles. 'It's the only way, isn't it? Love them to bits, of course; but humans are not meant to live together – not even close by. It simply doesn't work.' And Tamsin's thinking she has a point. So, what's she doing with Jason? Can it lead to anything but a nightmare? 'But I do enjoy summers in the glens. Always have done. I actually think *everyone* should summer in Scotland, it's a different air, a different pace; it would do us all good.'

'And does the Community of the Holy Fire do you good?'

'Immeasurable good.' Suddenly serious, suddenly sincere – like a bull-shitting politician trying to find an emotional connection with the listener. 'You know, I regard it as my family, in a way.'

'And you have a house in the grounds here.'

'A small cottage, yes. I could ask for nothing more.' That's true, thinks the abbot; otherwise she would have done. 'And believe me, I didn't wish for the cook and her family to be forced out. Poor Gemma. Not my idea at all; last thing on my mind. And I spoke up for her. Spoke up for her strongly.'

'Oh? Why did you need to do that?'

'She turned out to be a thief, poor thing. So sad. She stole some items from the chapel, including a silver chalice. But I so wanted her to be forgiven, like in *Les Misérables.* Such a lovely scene at the beginning, don't you think? When the bishop forgives the thieving Jean Valjean – and indeed, gives him more of his silver! Inspirational. And that's me, I'm afraid! I'm the bishop in that story. I wanted her forgiven and free – but sadly, Hildegard felt she had to go. And she's the abbess. Well, she *was* the abbess. And I understood. It's not my place. I just wished it otherwise.'

'So why did they give you the cottage? It's quite a gift.'

'So generous, yes. I mean, I suppose I have raised funds for the community, quite significant funds ... '

'How much?' Tamsin had never found the topic of money vulgar.

'Well, the work is ongoing, I hope for much more, obviously – but so far, something well over one and a half million pounds.'

'Quite significant, as you say.' Pause for a moment. 'That's quite a financial investment by you in the place.'

'It's just money.' Which is what the rich always say. 'The worth of this convent in the world, and the worth of this convent to *me* – these things cannot be measured on a spreadsheet.'

'And so, they gave you a cottage in the grounds to say thank you.'

'It's more a beach hut, really!' Compared to the Scottish pile, maybe. 'But it's all I need and it seemed a good marriage, mutually-beneficial – which I imagine marriages are supposed to be.' Another novel thought for Tamsin: a relationship in which two people are happy and help each other to live.

'Not married yourself, Louisa?'

'No one would have me!' You'd have no one, more like. Or are you perhaps gay when it's not quite allowed by the church – or by your party membership?

'And so, you must have known Hildegard well?'

'Remarkable woman.'

'As everyone says.'

'Maybe it's true.'

'And tell me, have you heard anything about the Green Chapel?'

'Not that I know of. The Green Chapel?' She performs a stage think. 'Is that something to do with here?'

'We believe so. I'm slightly surprised you've not heard of it. Everyone else seems to have done.'

'Oh, I am *very* junior here ... .and that's just as I like it, believe me!' No one in the room does believe her. The idea of Louisa being a junior anywhere is a big imaginative leap.

'But a junior who raises significant sums of money – so maybe one with a *little* influence.'

'Oh, I don't know – I occasionally drop a pebble in the pond of discussion, I suppose. Of course, it has been difficult with Hildegard's health.'

'What about her health?'

'Well, it's not a secret. Bed-ridden for weeks a while back. Not quite the leadership we're looking for, obviously.'

'I suppose no one can always be ... '

' ... she had visions, you see, which cause all sorts of trouble – and I did encourage her to see a doctor, get something to calm her. There's a pill for everything these days but – well, you couldn't tell Hildegard anything.'

Peter feels discomfort. 'You speak of her visions as though they were a disability.'

'Well, it's all about mental health these days, Abbot. We're bound to be concerned, which I don't think is a crime.'

'But were her visions not a gift from God?'

'Let's just say I think some were godlier than others. Our task was to spot the best ones – and quietly ignore the rest!'

'And was the Green Chapel one of her best ones?' Tamsin wants her back on track and away from dull lectures on mental health.

'The Green Chapel?'

'Yes. You have no memory of that?'

'Er, no, really not – and you're going to have to excuse me,' she says, suddenly feeling inside her jacket. She glances at her phone. 'Ah. I've got Robert on the line, housing minister, desperately unimportant – God spare me from being a junior minister! Responsibility without power – or "All shit and no gold," as they say! But a sweet, sweet man, owns the next-door estate in Scotland actually, and we're working on something, "Hello, Robert, no, of course, this is a good time, couldn't be better … "'

And she is up and out the door in moments. Tamsin and the abbot are left alone, in silence. It is the silence of shock and awe, as though a whirlwind has just passed through.

'Definite housing experts, her and Robert,' says Tamsin. 'They own six properties between them.' Wikipedia again.

'Six?' says the abbot. She nods. 'That's a good number. They still couldn't afford Hove, though.'

'And she didn't like mention of the Green Chapel, did she? Hasty exit.'

'I suppose she had to take the call.'

'You don't believe that.'

'I don't, no. It was a huge act of insecurity. Only the needy *have* to take a call.'

'And I'll swear that phone wasn't even ringing.'

'I assumed it was on silent. That's a thing now, isn't it?'

'What's a thing?'

There had been no smart phones in the desert when Peter was there, thank God. The young Bedouin boys led the way in their arrival, which kept them busy beneath the startling stars of the desert night; but that was after the abbot shook the sand from his feet and left. Instead, in the monastery office at St James-the-Less – where the filing cabinet was the height of technology – there had been a phone which they dialled; and which sometimes led to a connection. This wasn't always so and this could cause frustration and a profound sense of cosmic alienation; but on the flip side, made success and connection, when it occurred, a particular delight.

'We're connected? Really?!I can't believe it! I can actually hear you!'

It was the shock that made phone conversations so joyous. And that was how phones should be, with ringing bells, powerlines to plug in – and surprise. So yes, Smart phones were a disappointment to the abbot, whose advance into the territory of cordless communication, like an old man on ice, was cautious.

'Putting phones on silent,' he says. 'It didn't use to happen.'

'It didn't happen today either. It was silent, Abbot, because no one was ringing her. Louisa was on the run, running for cover, run rabbit run. We must speak with her again. But I'm encouraged by the panic. And now tell me – where did you meet?' The abbot looks confused. 'You and the Snake – how or where did you meet? Or to put it another way, where exactly was the car crash?

'Oh, it was nothing really.'

'The atmosphere was one hundred per cent awkward.'

'She turned me down for a job.'

'Surely not?!' Tamsin is laughing.

'On returning from the desert, I applied to be warden of a retreat centre. A rather prestigious one in the middle of nowhere, which would have been perfect; and she was on the interview panel.'

'She gets around.'

'She was the chair, unfortunately, with not only the casting vote, but – like some Russian despot – probably the *only* vote, parliament be damned. She didn't like me and made it quite plain.'

'Which bit of you didn't she like?'

I'm not sure.'

'Or was it the whole wretched package?'

Peter now remembers the difficult day. 'I shouldn't have disliked their chapel. That was a mistake.'

'How do you mean?'

'I said it reminded me of a dull Thursday in Littlehampton. And it turned out she liked the chapel very much indeed. Her grandfather had built it and two members of her family were buried there.'

Tamsin shakes her head. 'You haven't a clue, have you?'

'The truth is important.'

'Not at job interviews.'

'It was truly awful.'

'Again, not at the job interview. It was a *wonderful* chapel, an inspiration to generations of both those with a faith and those with none.'

'You would have got the job.'

'Of course, I would.'

'She was quite rude at the time. I was only a short time back in this country, feeling my way and not ready for it.'

Tamsin laughs. Other people's discomfort had this effect. Though, for a moment, she is distracted by her own discomfort, wondering what the evening would hold with a cartoonist she barely knew at all. It was unheard of and insane.

'Don't worry, Abbot, it's not over with Louisa. She may even regret not putting you out to grass in that care home.'

'Retreat House.'

'Whatever. But first we'll speak with the Ego, Stephen, Bishop of Lewes. And I have just the opening line.'

# 'Is there a Bishop of Ego in the church?'

~

'I'm sorry?'

The bishop is determined to enjoy this police interview; and he'd hardly be human if he didn't find the Detective Inspector attractive. No sin in that. Rather, thank God for the creation of such beauty. That's not lust – that's worship.

'I'm not religious myself, Bishop, so I'm still learning how it all works. How does it all work?'

'With difficulty, on occasion!' Humour and humility – absolutely the best way to start.

'And I'm told you're the Bishop of Lewes?'

'I am, yes ... though – and I realise this is not particularly for now – I prefer Bishop *for* Lewes. I'm not *above* them, you see, but right there among them, cheering them on, so to speak. I'm very much the facilitator of God's people, their *servant.*'

'It's a rare servant who sits on a throne in gold robes and a very large hat,' says Tamsin. She's flicking through her notebook, as though her mind is elsewhere.

'It's just symbolic.'

'As opposed to shambolic.' She is still looking at her notes.

'A low blow, Detective Inspector! But I've survived worse.'

'Really?' And now Tamsin looks up. 'Then I must try harder.'

The bishop thinks it's a joke and remains confident and chatty. He's keen to impress this beauty. Well, he's keen to impress any authority figure really. It is always important to impress. 'You'd have to ask the pews, of course.'

'The pews?'

'Sorry, in-house slang for churchgoers. But I hope that's their understanding of my leadership.' A deprecating smile is offered. 'I'm a great believer in collaborative leadership, in *servant* leadership.'

'As you mentioned: instead of a messiah-complex, a servant-complex.' The bishop smiles before he is kicked squarely in the balls. 'Yet Hildegard didn't see you as a servant.'

'Oh?'

'No, she called you the Bishop of Ego.'

'Really?'

*Let it sink in.* 'It was in a note the abbess wrote the night of her death; a last will and testament, as it turned out.' The facilitator for Lewes is unsettled. 'So, like fresh blood on the kitchen wall, it's quite – how shall we say? – relevant to our inquiry.' The bishop sits quietly, looking down at his feet. 'So, what do you think about that?' He looks up and shrugs like a caught-out schoolboy. 'I mean, you must have an opinion.'

'I'm shocked, of course.'

'Angry, I'd imagine.'

'Not angry. But disappointed, certainly. I mean, who wouldn't be?'

'So *why* did she say that of you? Why so rude?' Tamsin shakes her head in disapproval at such behaviour. Her acting has improved over the years. 'I mean, it's not very – well, Christian, is it?' She sounds almost like a crusader for niceness; as if Hildegard is due a reprimand for her lack of it. But the bishop now strokes his thigh in professional amusement, flicking away an imaginary crumb. He won't be intimidated; he really won't. He's seen off bigger beasts than this one; and though this isn't true, a man can always dream.

'A remarkable woman,' he says, shaking his head in admiration.

'We're getting that impression,' says Tamsin. 'The same words are on everyone's lips.'

'Well, she was. My wife's a huge fan.'

'Your wife?'

'Thinks the world of her.'

'But not you?'

'Oh, she likes me as well.'

'No, I mean *you* didn't think the world of her. Or why tell us what your wife thinks?'

'Oh no, they were my thoughts as well ... a remarkable woman.'

'Almost a mantra. So, now I'm wondering who wrote the script everyone seems to have in their hands?'

'Or perhaps it's simply true,' says the Ego, who really doesn't have time for all this. He's not enjoying this interview as much as he had hoped; they don't appear impressed and he's irritated, to put it mildly. 'Sometimes the truth is simple, Detective Inspector. It's not called "the plain and simple truth" for nothing.'

'But, in a way, that makes it worse, Stephen.'

'How so?' A polite smile cracks his face.

'Well, we all get abuse in our lives from the unremarkable. Don't you find this? Online tirades from anonymous keyboard cowards. It sort-of goes with the territory for anyone in a public role. I'm sure you experience that. Tell me it's not just me.'

'Oh no, it's par for the course, we need thick hides.'

'Yet here is a *remarkable* woman – your words, bishop, no script, not some reprobate but a remarkable woman, calling *you* the Bishop of Ego.' She makes a surprised face. 'I suppose I might, in your shoes, take note.'

Again, he laughs easily. 'Then consider note duly taken.' He now brushes his right shoulder, in his absence of concern; an act of disdain, dislodging some of the dandruff. 'I'm not everyone's cup of tea,' he says – a badge of honour, wear it with pride. 'Which, I imagine, our Lord might also have said?' He looks to the abbot for support.

'We'll be speaking to him as well,' says Tamsin – because what on earth was one meant to say to that? The man's a complete—

'And Hildegard's green ambitions?' asks the abbot, scrolling slowly through the emails just sent to him by the Bancroft. The milk monitor had been busy with Hildegard's laptop and this particular batch contains correspondence with the bishop. It is dew from heaven – and the timing is divine.

'Visionary,' says the bishop. 'She'll be remembered as a green visionary.'

'You seem to be falling over yourself in admiration.'

'No more than she deserves.'

'But visionaries do need killing, I suppose – or who knows what will happen?'

'The green agenda is one of the leading issues of our time; and one that we in the Sussex diocese are most mindful of.' This feels like a press statement. 'And I'm now wondering if you have any serious questions.'

Tamsin has been looking at the same emails appearing; and getting the gist of them rather quicker than the abbot. And actually, since the bishop asks, some serious questions do come to mind.

'So, I presume you must have been four-square behind the Green Chapel.'

'I'm sorry?'

'The Green Chapel.' Pause. 'Surely you must be aware of it?'

'I may have heard talk of something. I was never quite sure what it was all about, to be honest! Ideas came and went here at a furious pace. She was that sort of a woman, always advancing some cause or other. Never at peace. And, I mean, I'm at a distance, so snippets are all I get to hear!'

And now the abbot has found something. Miracles happen. 'Though you did write to her about it.'

'Write to her about what?'

'Yes, you wrote' – *hang on, he's lost it*, and stepping into the pause, Tamsin takes over.

'About the Green Chapel.'

'Did I?'

'Yes, you wrote to her suggesting she "give up on this Green Chapel nonsense".' Tamsin leaves a silence. Sometimes silence is best. Sometimes silence crucifies people better than nails. 'So do you wish to respond?'

'I write many emails. I really can't ... '

'I'm sure. You're a busy man, bishop ... a busy *busy* man. And the busy bishop cannot remember everything – he's too busy.' If scorn could kill. 'But the Green Chapel was obviously "a snippet", as you name it, with some *substance*. I mean, it was a snippet you were very forthright about.' The bishop looks blank. 'Shall we send you the correspondence? To nudge the memory. It's there on Hildegard's computer, so presumably on yours – were we to look.'

'I have no idea where this is all going.'

'And neither do we, bishop, it's something of a white-knuckle ride for us all. My knuckles are getting whiter by the second, as more and more emails appear. So, we'll not waste any more of your valuable time. We're aware how busy you are, and we'll continue this conversation tomorrow, when you'll probably need a new story about the Green Chapel – or certainly a revised one. No need to go "back to the drawing board" as such – but maybe some significant adaptations? Adaptations more closely related to the truth than those attempted today.'

They'd need to continue a number of conversations tomorrow with Bancroft's revelations multiplying by the minute. From a quick glance, Louisa had also got away a little lightly, no question about that.

Though Stephen is thinking mainly about Margaret and hoping she doesn't need to know. Things were not good with her at present. They hadn't been for a while and messy conversations with the police were the last thing they needed – absolutely the last thing.

They'd been so much better in the early days, obviously, when they *did* love each other, you'd have imagined so; or at least liked each other, enjoying trips out and so forth. It had actually all felt pretty special, and he was remembering how special it felt in the car this morning, as he drove over. Had Stephen ever been liked before? He didn't think so; and so being liked by Margaret was intoxicating, quite overwhelming. And perhaps Margaret had never been liked either. And so, everything he did was good; it was like walking on air; and it only started going downhill when they got engaged, really; that was when things changed, when he wasn't so good apparently, and consequently she wasn't so good. But by then it was too late, because family had been informed, wedding plans made and cancellation would just have been too embarrassing for everyone. He could imagine what his father would have said; and he feared that man's judgements above all things. So, as with the tide, Margaret withdrew and Stephen was left stranded. This was his take on the matter, but who knows? Perhaps she'd say he withdrew. Only now he's helping the police with their enquiries and it feels terrible. It feels like his father all over again.

'So, do please be here, bishop,' says Tamsin as he gets up from his chair. 'We wouldn't want to drag you from your home in an unseemly manner, with a clumsy and unnecessary show of force. I know how you men can stay calm in these situations. But wives can get quite hysterical. Women, eh?'

## A first date is a terrible thing.

~

Especially when you are thirty-eight and it is literally your first date.

Other relationships in Tamsin's life had not featured dates. They had included sex and arguments, brief connection and confused and raging distance; but never 'a date'; never a dressed-up arrival at a restaurant you don't know, to meet a man you don't know; and being pretty unsure if you wish for either. What was she thinking when he rang her and suggested a meal? And she said – she can still hear herself – 'Why not?'

There was a moment of pleasure; he'd chosen her from the crowd at the Brighton Centre. Though really, it was Fiona who had chosen her, not him. He was staring out into darkness. He hadn't chosen her at all. But perhaps that's her best look – invisible. And you had to wonder why he was still looking for someone in his thirties? Tamsin had to wonder anyway, and she wondered with increasing intensity as the evening beckoned. Because, if he wasn't 'a catch', then this was just embarrassing. And how can a single man in his late thirties be a catch? Imagine the baggage he must carry that makes him quite so untouchable. And what on earth would they talk about ... and how would she let him down at the end?

'Hello,' he says, unsure whether he can touch her shoulder to announce his arrival. She's absorbed by the menu in the restaurant window. She doesn't hear him; or maybe she does, but she doesn't turn. He refrains from touch. Sometimes in life, as well as cartooning, less is more. So, he stands to her side, not too close, and says 'Chosen anything?'

'Jason!' she says, looking up and nervous. 'Good to see you.'

'Good to see you too,' he says which is better than 'tell your face.' Jason is strong on the message of a face. He can draw it in a few lines; and he can see it in half a second. This beautiful woman is terrified. By way of greeting, he manages to half-touch her arm and she nearly touches his.

'So, you made it!' he says.

'Close thing. So many reasons not to come.'

'Why, thank you, ma'am!'

'I didn't mean.'

'I know.'

Pause. A bus goes by offering helpful distraction; and a gust of wind ... and then a mother with her child, late back from after-school club. They stand in the street light, the day having left.

'Been cartooning?'

'Pretty much. Policing?'

'Pretty much.' They start laughing. 'Shall we go in?'

'Only if the dialogue improves.'

~

There was movement by the bushes, rushed movement; which in the light of the crescent moon, felt furtive and hasty.

The abbot was walking the convent grounds. He always walked last thing at night, wherever he was. He walked to commune with the sky, the wind, the rain and the stars. In the desert, the clarity of the stars had been frightening – 'twinkle, twinkle' really didn't do it. They demanded awe, each and every one of them. They demanded he fall on his face in the dusty courtyard, and declare himself a sinner, an inadequate – for who could compete with such glory?

But then perhaps they looked at him in a similar way. Perhaps the stars were in awe of humans. He sometimes spoke of this, particularly when one of the monks was down on himself.

Tonight, however, he walked in England, on the coast, in convent grounds; with more cloud and less light, but still a day to be considered, a day now past. What is to be made of it? So many introductions and relationships begun, different coloured threads appearing in the tapestry, and the walking is good. The clear-minded sub-abbess, called Patience or the Jackal, depending on who you believed. She knew all her lines; but perhaps that was because they were true. And Tamsin was still in recovery at her decision to leave behind £90,000 per annum, a Thames-side office and her jeans. He remembered also her quiet amazement that he still wore his habit of calling, when his calling was gone. Were the clothes he wore now the clothes of a fraud?

Then the force that was Louisa, known also as the Snake; and if she was a saint, she'd be the greatest saint, quite magnificent in her glory; and if a sinner, likewise, a deep and dangerous nightmare. No half-measures with Louisa. She was a liar obviously; but it was probably all truth to her; in the way that both religion and politics made truth and lies almost impossible to discern; with every cover-up, a lie on behalf of the truth. But the price is high in the end. If you lie for the truth, then truth is lost. She'd need to face at least one of her lies tomorrow; though in her hands it would probably become a scented rose.

And then Volmar, whose room he had stolen, whose identity he had stolen – it felt like that, something quite personal. A man with a long history of affection for, and care of, Hildegard; but now down-graded by the remarkable woman to the status of Worm, which was quite a fall from grace. So, when did the fall begin? And what pushed him over the edge?

And then earlier in the day, he was forgetting, the Munch-loving Daisy. And he wondered if she had been forgotten all her life. She was the woman with *The Scream* in her eyes; the cleaner who mimicked the Virgin Mary, 'Let it be unto me according to thy will' – without any sense that she was happy about his will. And when she said 'Let it be,' it was a line of resignation rather than trust. She knew about the secretive Green Chapel and maybe, as the cleaner, she knew many other things. She'd need to be careful, because knowledge is sometimes dangerous; often only the clueless survive. And if she's a reluctant cleaner, which she is – then why? Why carry on? And why does Hildegard call her the Darkness?

And finally, the Bishop of Ego; the man with a small bishopric. He would perhaps like a larger one, a more significant, posting. Winchester. London. Liverpool, at least. Suffragan Bishop of Lewes, his official title, was only halfway up the greasy pole of advancement in the Church of England. This media darling, this man of bright and clever words, this frightened shell of a human being ... he wanted more. He was a man Peter wished to feel sorry for; but a man who made such feelings so hard. And he was lying about the Green Chapel which seemed almost like another character in this story; a ghost-figure moving through this convent as a rumour, a discomfort – but not yet in the open; not yet anything anyone could actually touch. Tomorrow, the Green Chapel needed to be brought out into the open.

And it was then he saw the movement – a figure in the moonlight running across the rough sea grass. His eyes followed her, it was a woman, he thought so – a young woman carrying a bag. And as he watched, she disappeared behind an old boat, its tattered sail waving in the westerly wind; rotting as boats do over time. He followed her slowly, no chase; and there, behind the boat, he saw a tent and inside the tent, a torch beam.

So, who ran in the convent grounds after dark? Who lived in a tent in the grounds of the Community of the Holy Fire – or at least on its edge? He walked towards it, state-of-the-art camping; it somehow looked expensive and unlike any tent he had ever slept in. It could perhaps sleep two, but there was only one figure inside; a clear but hunched silhouette.

'Excuse me,' he calls out. He stands away from the tent, not wishing to frighten. 'I'm a visitor here, working with the police

– I was wondering if you could help me? My name's Peter ... '
A hooded face appears in the tent doorway, pointing the beam straight in his face. 'My name's Peter ... Abbot Peter. And you are Richardis, I presume?'

~

'Incinerated?' Margaret drops the pie dish on the kitchen floor. The bowl fractures; fish, cheese sauce, pottery and pastry mingle and ooze on the terra cotta tiles. *Incinerated?* 'Was it deliberate, Stephen? I mean, how could ... ?'

A bishop's partner is familiar with tragic stories. The church attracts them. By setting up as an institution of concern, the church invites them in. If you claim to care, tragedies – and their victims – will come and find you in their pain; and expect helpful words and infinite compassion. Of course, in reality, one cannot be too concerned, not all the time; or one would be crushed by the sheer weight of the world's endless scream. But even so, *even so*, the incineration of an abbess – and one hugely admired by many, including Margaret – well, what to do with that?

'A remarkable woman,' says the bishop, with due solemnity.

'You're not in front of the cameras now, Stephen. I know you didn't like her.'

'My personal feelings are really not ... '

'You felt she was an attention-seeker.'

'It isn't the time ... '

And then a thought strikes her. 'So, is that the end of the Green Chapel?'

'You know as much as I do. And it's hardly the issue.'

'I never understood why you had such problems with it.'

'I didn't have problems with it.' *Sound casual.*

'I mean, I know it stole some of the thunder from your "Make Lewes Free from Plastic" campaign. But there wasn't that much thunder anyway. And if you'd only cooperated with the school children's plastics campaign – but then your name wouldn't have been on it, I suppose.'

'I'll be in my study.'

Sadly, Margaret is way too smart to be hysterical. Hysteria would have been easier to handle; he could have played the man, calmed her down; he could have said 'There, there, everything will be all right.' But a lawyer doesn't need calming; and Margaret, who had recently returned to professional practice as a barrister, pushed him away further by the day, or so it seemed.

And as he had diminished in her estimation, Hildegard had grown, which really wouldn't do. Every cloud, as they say ...

**It was a good morning's work.**

~

Though the chapel was an odd setting for a police inquiry. There were more crosses and hymn books than usual; and the temptation to kneel, pray or sing was strong. But instead, they had sat together in restrained excitement and reconstructed events around the bonfire on the night of the killing; and discovered quite a lot. They had, for instance, discovered who saw who, what and when. There were no arrests, which was disappointing. Many of the nuns had attended 'Murder Mystery' weekends in previous lives which sorted things out pretty fast. Real investigations needed to speed up a bit, perhaps. But chided and harassed by the glamour girl at the front, they'd all done as well as they could, with the dark, smoky and slightly inebriated memories available.

So, what did they know? They knew that everyone had been there, except Hildegard. No one was absent from the fire apart from the abbess. And, of course, no one knew that *she* wasn't there at the time; no one noticed and why would they? They all assumed her to be out of sight and talking with others. Why wouldn't she be there on this most important of nights? And the fire was large, the flames high, the smoke thick, the group scattered and the wine plentiful, like the wedding at Cana. The biblical precedent somehow made their hangovers more decent, more rooted in the faith; almost an act of worship.

Daisy, who ran the convent bar, also minded the bonfire bar that night; while Michael – big, wild Michael, the convent gardener – tended the fire, endlessly on the move, prodding the beast, feeding the beast and asking anyone too near if they'd like to dance, which no one did – apart from Louisa. He had brought his CD player and the best of ABBA. A few nuns remembered his solo rendition of "Dancing Queen." 'I think he'd been at the sauce,' as Sister Cecelia said. 'Along with Volmar. I'm not sure he was standing at the end. '

'He wasn't standing,' confirms Sister Maria. 'I found him in the roses.'

'Perhaps a proper end for Satan,' says Sister Roisin.

'Satan?'

'You haven't heard?' says Sister Rowena. Tamsin looks blank. 'Clearly not. And frankly, who knows the truth of these things. But some say – and I think I speak truthfully – Volmar hasn't been himself since the Satan episode.'

'The Satan episode? Can we follow that one up with you?'

'Of course.'

Not all of the sisterhood drank wine, particularly Sister Roisin, who was brought up by an alcoholic father; so more 'let down' than 'brought up'. He was forever saying sorry, and forever lapsing, until the sorry was worse than the crime.

'No one hears your "sorry", father.'

'I mean it.'

'They might hear you taking responsibility. But not your "sorry"'

Such a weak man; weak and violent.

And so, for her and her like on bonfire night, there was apple and elderflower cordial and some out-of-date tins of Sprite, given to the convent by the local newsagent.

While those who *did* drink of the vine, they needed watching. As Michael observed, loudly, 'These folk can't handle it, remember! Can't handle it! And when the wine is in, the wit is out, eh – my mother taught me that!'

And he wasn't wrong. Maybe it was the vast night sky, or the lingering harvest moon, all fat and creamy, heaven so close – but a certain freedom came over many of the otherwise sober-minded souls when offered 'one for the road'– even though there was no road; they were going nowhere apart from their cells. And the one soon became three.

'Let's make it a Trinity!' someone exclaimed as the bonfire burned, darkness deepened and winter crept into their souls.

But they'd all been there; this was the thing. Or at least they'd all been there some of the time, including Louisa and Bishop Stephen. Everyone remembered them drinking, chatting, laughing. 'That Stephen's a charmer. And it's all very embarrassing but I asked him to preach at my funeral.'

'People always ask me to preach at their funerals,' Stephen admitted.

And Louisa was also remembered, 'She can tell a surprisingly rude story! Nothing like she is on *Question Time!*' And everyone remembered her dancing with Michael and everyone remembered the rocket, of course – a huge and star-whooshing firework, exploding again and again against the luminous dark as the wine flowed and everyone gazed into the sky.

'What a night!'

⁓

Peter hangs around afterwards.

'All very tragic,' says a nun, arriving by his side, and clearly wishing to be known. 'Sister Rowena. And I know who you are, of course.' She has a round face, bright eyes, clear skin, five feet eight and approaching middle-age. Peter wonders about her hair, though he'll probably never know. 'Shaved,' she says, reading Peter's mind with quiet accuracy. 'But it isn't just tragic.'

'Oh?' *Is this about her hair?*

'It's evil.' *It isn't about her hair.* 'Tragedy is so often evil.'

'Indeed.'

'Hildegard was a one-off, Abbot. Not perfect by a million miles; maybe two million. But a great light burned in her. So bright, she struggled to contain it, I think. That's why she was ill so much. She didn't know what to do with it.' Peter is tuning out the noise around him. He's interested. 'I genuinely think she wondered if she was mad. She wouldn't say that, she divulged very little about herself to anyone. She was well hidden behind her shell. But I wouldn't be surprised. I've seen genius struggle before. She could certainly turn on herself, the self-loathing could be quite extreme – and, as I say, it made her ill sometimes.'

'Louisa mentioned.'

'I'm sure she did.'

'She's not a fan of visions.'

'I think her visions were rather fine. Full of light ... light which is now snuffed out ... by evil.' Was she testing him? 'Do you believe in evil, Abbot?'

'I'm happy with the word,' says Peter.

'A rather limp answer.'

Peter smiles. 'Not everyone on the case would use that term; it is banned from police reports. But I have no difficulty with it. Think of me as an ally.'

'And you are to be our white knight, I hear?' *Is this an interview?* 'Sent to save us.'

'I'm more a speckled knight.'

'How disappointing. Everyone prefers a white knight, I think. Effortlessly powerful and true.'

'Definitely speckled. But on your side, if that's any consolation.'

'Well, I don't know if it is. What if I'm the murderer?' She speaks playfully.

'Then the best thing for you, Sister Rowena, is that I bring you in and see you convicted.'

'And why is that best?'

'So, you can start again.'

'I might not want to start again.'

'Well, that's your issue, not mine.'

'So, not much of a friend.'

'I didn't say I was your friend. I said I was on your side.'

'So, you're on everyone's side?'

'Of course.'

'Then I'll tell everyone to watch out.'

Sister Rowena takes her leave with a bow, so easy in her movements. And Tamsin appears.

'That all looked very intense. Was she flirting?' The abbot shakes his head. 'Or were *you* flirting?'

'We were discussing evil.'

'You know the way to a nun's heart. And I hear you've found the mythical Richardis?'

'I have, yes.'

'So, she actually exists.'

'She actually does.'

'And what on earth is she doing back here?'

## The Snake had lent them her front room.

R ichardis had asked to meet here. She was unhappy about
returning to the convent building for the interview;
wary 'about stepping inside the four walls'. She said it
didn't feel right.

'I don't feel worthy,' she said, with the humility of an averted
gaze. She was a posh girl and elfin-like; the wind might blow
her away; though the abbot notes the steel in her eyes, which
makes an occasional appearance. You sensed that somewhere
behind the diffidence she knew exactly what she wanted.

'Why aren't you worthy?' asks Tamsin. 'It's just a building.'

'It's not just a building, Detective Inspector; it was never *just*
a building. It's a calling, a way of life – and one that I walked
out on.'

'Perhaps it was time to go.'

'Jesus told the story of the prodigal son.' The abbot nods.
'Well, *I* am the prodigal daughter. I walked out!' She gazes at
them intensely, as if she really wishes for them to understand;
as if something very deep has just been revealed. Tamsin looks
to the abbot for help.

'Though the story ends happily, as I recall,' says Peter.
Richardis looks like she missed this bit. 'The son left home

rather rudely, yes, with no thought for anyone's feelings but his own.'

'That's me.'

'And then had a rather bad time of it, in faraway lands.' Richardis nods. Were her London days like this? He somehow doubted she ate pig food in Knightsbridge. 'But finally, when abandoned by his friends and starving, he decided to return, to go back home and face the music of condemnation.'

'Again, that's me.'

'Yet there was no condemnation, Richardis. Instead, the prodigal found himself welcomed with great joy and warmth.' The abbot smiles at the thought. 'Could it not be the same for you here?'

'I don't think so.' She shakes her head at the thought.

'Not even with Hildegard gone?'

'Well, who knows?' she says airily.

'We hear you two fell out.' Richardis looks at the ground. 'Well, did you fall out?'

'It depends on what you mean by the term, Abbot.'

'I mean did you fall out?' Richardis shrugs. 'The shrug takes us nowhere, Richardis.'

'She wasn't best pleased with me, one might say that.'

'Why not?'

Doe-eyes. 'I suppose I wasn't being her obedient little girl.'

'I see.'

'Do you?'

'So, if the place troubles you so much,' – Tamsin intervenes – 'why live in a tent in the convent grounds? Why not rent a flat in the Lake District or the Norfolk Broads, somewhere far away from here?'

'It's a long story.'

'We have time.'

'Time for all things,' says Peter, reassuringly. 'Rush has no place here.'

'And some of it we know, of course – like the bit about you being Hildegard's favourite.' Richardis blushes a little. 'I mean, was that awkward? Being the boss' pet?'

Richardis will not rise to the bait. She will stay calm and in control. 'Hildegard saw something in me that I did not see in myself. So, I am grateful for that.' And now Princess Diana's earnest innocence as well. Richardis comes across as young, almost a child; though she must be well into her thirties.

'So, you left the convent out of undiluted gratitude to Hildegard? An unusual motive for departure.'

'Not quite.'

'Oh?'

'She had been very ill, of course.'

'Is that important?'

'She wouldn't eat. And I thought it might be me.'

'You?'

'My behaviour.'

'And was it you?'

'No.' She shakes her head. 'No, it wasn't me, I was imagining that. She was holding back God's word. This is what she said.'

'Holding back God's word?'

'Holding back a vision God had given her. She had visions, Hildegard. Many visions, she always had, ever since she was a child. But she wouldn't speak them.'

'Why not?'

'Because she was a woman, and felt unworthy. I mean, obviously women aren't unworthy. But it was how she felt; so she kept them inside. God's word was festering in her, she said afterwards, making her ill.' Tamsin is struggling. Isn't this asylum territory? 'Volmar was the only one who could reach her. He said she must speak of her visions. And when she did, she recovered. So, he was right, wasn't he?'

'And what were her visions?'

'We never knew. But something was going on, we knew that.'

'Yet still you decided to leave.' Richardis takes a deep breath. 'Well?'

'I felt she smothered me.' There, she'd said it. This was how she'd felt in the end. She hadn't felt it at first, not at all. In the early days, Hildegard took an interest in her. She had made her feel good about herself, which was a first for one so given to anxiety and self–doubt. But down the line, there was a price to pay – Hildegard's increasing involvement in her life, as if she somehow owned it now and directed it; and by the end, she had felt smothered by Hildegard.

'You felt smothered?' Richardis nods. 'How do you smother a nun?' It sounded like the set-up for a joke, but the question was serious. From where Tamsin was sitting, a convent would smother anyone, with its rules and conformity. So how could Hildegard take it further?

'Always wishing to see me, that sort of thing; asking me what I'd like her to pray for, always wishing to direct me, guide me.'

'Did she fancy you?'

'Who knows?' A careless laugh but not exactly a denial. 'I have no idea. She suggested that one day I would take her place.'

'You mean become abbess?'

'She spoke of that, yes.'

'Well, there's a promise.'

'And it wasn't hers to make,' says an angry Richardis. 'I mean, it's not hers to hand out. It's an election.' Richardis clearly didn't like the idea of an election. The word was spoken as if such a thing was a massive shame; as if democracy held back those who were truly born to rule.

'And did you like that idea – of taking her place, I mean? Becoming the big cheese.'

'Maybe. I don't know. I didn't really think about it.'

'But when you did?'

'How long would I have to wait?' There's sudden frustration in her. 'I mean, Hildegard wasn't old. Or not *old* old. She could live forever. Some people are like that. They just carry on. And then what of me?'

So, thinks the abbot, this girl/woman is a schemer. Behind the doe-eyed unworthiness sits red-clawed ambition. She'd already worked out the risk of waiting too long.

'But as it turned out,' says Tamsin, 'and here's the silver lining, I suppose – she didn't live forever. Someone roasted her, and left her clinging to a cross, like a pig on a spit, which was a bit of a thing. Someone deliberately wedged the door shut which sealed her inside an oven.' Richardis looks down at her feet again, perhaps in sorrow. 'And now she's dead. So, unlike the wedged chapel door that night, maybe the "Richardis for abbess" door is open again.'

'I really can't think about that.'

'It wasn't you who locked that door of the night of the fire?'

'Of course not!' A forceful and shocked denial.

'It's just that everyone else is accounted for.'

'How could I do that?'

'Any one of us can do anything. That's how.' Richardis shakes her head. 'Do you know Louisa well?'

'Louisa?' She is surprised by the question. 'I hardly know her at all.'

'It was kind of her to lend us her cottage for this interview,' says Peter amiably. 'Not many get in here, I'm told; quite a fortress. She likes her privacy. So, generous of her to consider your particular needs.'

'I suppose so. I find people are kind. And Louisa has a heart of gold.'

'Really?'

'People seem to form opinions about her; not always nice. But you have to be tough in her line of business. And there's nothing she won't do for people. In many ways – and I'm not the only one who thinks this – she's the beating heart of this place.'

'And not Hildegard?'

Richardis well remembered those final days of her time in the convent; the days when Hildegard had withdrawn from her, and then blanked her, as if she didn't exist. It was so painful. And on her final day, there were no kind words spoken in chapel; no leaving card organised, no mention made of it at all; and she left alone on that Thursday morning, after a silent breakfast – made to feel like a traitor, a lost soul spurning salvation.

She remembered the walk of shame, out of the gate, journeying to oblivion – also known as Stormhaven, along the sea path, with her ruck sack and case, a one-way ticket purchased; and from there by train to Brighton, where she had friends. Or hoped she had friends. When you don't have a bed, then you know who your friends are. Sofa-surfing is not as merry as it sounds.

And the final meeting with Hildegard, still not forgotten; it still woke her at night.

'Do you know what you do, Richardis?' Hildegard wore her glasses, which usually meant a telling-off.

'I know what I must do, Abbess.' Richardis hated confrontation; she always had; and she longed to be out of here now.

'One day, you could sit in my chair, Richardis. I have wished that for you, as you know, and still do. It is here, it awaits you, if you can only learn patience ... holy patience.' So, it was her fault. It was Richardis who was to blame for all this. It was her sin, her lack of 'holy patience' that was ruining everything. 'But know what you do, Richardis; know what you do now. Walk away from this place, turn your back on your calling, and the dream I offer will be gone, truly; there will be no way back for the prodigal.' That wasn't Jesus' version but it was the more common one. 'And the ingratitude on display, the ingratitude you *show*, will leave a very bad smell here, believe me; and one that will not be forgotten; not for a very long time. And though you leave the *community*, if that is your decision – and there is still time to turn back from your sin – you will never leave the sense of shame inside you ... ever. There is no train or plane, no trinket or treat, no person or pill that can take you away from shame.'

Such hammer blows; and so many of them. Richardis fears a panic attack but calms as she hears herself saying, 'I have to leave, Abbess.' How did she manage that?

'Why?'

'Sometimes one doesn't now the "why". One just knows the need to go.' She heard herself sounding weak, her voice breaking, but what was there to say? 'Did you never find that, Abbess? Have you never known the need to go?'

'No.' That was telling her. 'I could have gone many times. Perhaps I wished to, yes! But I have always stayed – stayed to do my duty.' Richardis plays with the cross round her neck; she does it when anxious, and it irritates Hildegard. The crucifix should not be used as an anxiety aid: this was not encouraged in the community. And then the question Hildegard has never asked; never believing it would come to this. 'And what do you go *to*, Richardis?' She stiffens further as she asks, like a woman asking about her husband's lover.

Richardis is careful. She cannot tell the whole truth; and cannot say how she feels. She has no wish for a fight. 'I don't know. I have friends who have intimated ... '

'"Friends who have intimated?"' Hildegard bursts in. She can't listen to any more of this. 'Is Richardis, dear Richardis, now the whore of dubious recruiters? What of your *calling*, girl? St Paul listened to no recruiters on the Damascus Road! He had seen the light, just as I thought you had.'

Richardis is confused; she doesn't know what to say anymore. Has the light faded? She knows only darkness. 'The adventure here is over,' she says. 'What can I do?'

'*Stay!* You can stay.'

'If there's a fire in the kitchen, you must leave.' She'd read that somewhere.

'But there's been no fire in the kitchen. What fire do you speak of?' Hildegard has taken this literally.

'Maybe you do not see it.'

Hildegard shakes her head. The kindly instructor has done her best but what can one do with wilful intransigence? 'And do you not *know*, can you not *understand*, that night after night you will wake at two in the morning and regret miserably this decision so hastily and insubstantially made? Do you not know that? Do you really believe you will ever sleep soundly again?'

'I do not sleep so soundly now.'

'You know I am right, Richardis.'

She had got up and left Hildegard's office and been sick in the corridor, beneath the statue of St Cecilia, who never gave up on her calling but carried on until the very end, until bloody and painful martyrdom. Hildegard was right: Richardis could not be easy on herself and her sleep would tell the tale.

~

'And what happened then?' asks Peter. He's interested in the journey of an ex-nun; and doesn't need psychoanalysis to know why.

'I worked in London for a couple of years.'

'I'm told you hoped to be an actor.'

'A lot of people hope to be actors.' Deflection from her own feelings.

'But did *you*?'

'Most have given up on the dream by their late twenties.' She's in lecture mode, still deflecting the question. 'Hopes and dreams don't pay the rent.'

'So, you did you hope to be an actor?' Never give up on a question.

'I was in a bed advert once, on telly, paid well.'

'Congratulations.'

'I was sleeping soundly, with a smiling partner, which was ironic. My sleep is appalling and my partners have never smiled. But that was it as far as the acting was concerned.'

'So, what did you do – to pay the rent?'

'I do have a trust fund.' Richardis looks coy; it's clearly considerable. She is the endless victim, hoping for someone to come and save her; but with private means, which the abbot imagines she has kept very private.

'So that must help.'

'But I worked as well.' *Little girl justifying herself to the grown-ups.* 'Jolly hard, as it happens. Admin, systems analysis, you know.' Peter didn't know. 'I'm quite good at that sort of thing.'

'Richardis re-joins the world!'

'And in the evenings, I got involved with a homeless project that my boss knew about. He was really amazing, such a great guy; and after a while, I decided to live homeless for a year myself, to make it more real.' Tamsin looks quizzical, which Richardis picks up on immediately. 'People said I was just another rich girl trying to make myself feel better – so I wanted to show them that I genuinely cared.'

'But how would that actually help anyone?'

'What do you mean?'

'How would you being homeless help anyone else who is homeless?' asks Tamsin. 'You'd be taking their food, wouldn't you?'

'I'm raising awareness.'

'By living in a tent by the sea? Perhaps you *are* just a rich girl trying to make yourself feel better.'

'It's not a crime to be upper-middle class, Detective Inspector.' Richardis smiles winningly. 'I don't actually think it's illegal yet.'

'So, the tent in the convent grounds?' says the abbot easing away from Tamsin's disdain and the social guilt of Richardis. Guilt closes people up; it wouldn't help them here.

'Yes?'

'It seems an odd choice of home, in a way.'

'I don't see why.'

'Don't they say, "Never go back"?'

'Who's "they"?'

'Well, Hildegard said it. She did not envisage the prodigal returning. Or encourage it.' And then a thought strikes him. 'Did Hildegard know you were here?' The shrug again. 'The shrug is back, Richardis, but still not helpful.'

'She didn't need to know.'

'She didn't know?'

'I'm not technically on the convent land anyway, though people often think it is, because of the path that runs by it. The garden shed is the boundary, and I am just beyond it – or rather, just behind it, to protect me from the wind.'

'You have chosen the windiest place on earth to pitch a tent.'

'And you know no reason why anyone might wish to kill Hildegard?' Tamsin is bored of the tent; bored of empty gestures from needy rich girls. 'Apart from yourself, obviously, now that you regret leaving.'

'I don't regret leaving.'

'Perhaps the tent and the "homeless" thing is a way back to the convent? What is it called these days – virtue signalling?'

'It isn't.' She shakes her head in disbelief at the suggestion.

'And is your toilet the sea?' New line of police inquiry. 'How does that all work? You obviously don't use the convent facilities. Or do you?'

Richardis breathes a little deeper, as if to make a confession. 'There is an outside loo and downpipe nearby.'

'Where?'

'Behind the cottage.'

'Which cottage?'

'Louisa's cottage. Here.'

'There's an outside loo?'

'It used to be a servant's cottage.'

'You mean the cook's?'

'The cook's cottage, yes.'

'And what would a servant want with an indoor loo?' asks Tamsin. It's rhetorical.

'And that's where you were coming back from last night?' says Peter. Richardis nods.

Tamsin: 'And you can confirm that you weren't in the convent on the night of the murder.'

'I can.'

'Where were you?'

'Reading – in my tent.'

'Alone?'

'There's not room for a witness, I'm afraid.'

'So, alone on the coastline, just canvass between you and the big sky.' Richardis nods. 'As opposed to alone with someone else?'

'As I said, there's no room. How could I be with someone else?'

'Not in the tent, no.' Richardis looks puzzled. 'But you know how people sometimes say, "When can we next be alone?"

Have you heard them say that?' Richardis is still confused. 'It's usually said by those conducting a hidden relationship, away from public gaze. Alone with each other, is what they mean.' The former nun now looks uncomfortable, like a child who's bored of this game and wants to go and play elsewhere. 'But that's not you?'

'No, I hardly think so!'

'Then that's quite enough for now.'

And after leaving via the back door of the cottage, and taking note of the outdoor loo – 'that's rough,' says Tamsin – they walk back towards the convent.

'That didn't quite add up, did it?' says Peter.

'No.'

'Because if she *is* the prodigal daughter, who was it who welcomed her home? Someone must have.'

'Precisely. And I've borrowed a clue.' Tamsin removes something small from her pocket.

'A photo?'

'I think Richardis is being rather selective about the truth.'

# Louisa sits crossed-legged

Polite and attentive. She's wearing jeans, dressing down and a different persona from her power-house Westminster look. Tamsin notes the shift and Louisa is aware.

'One can't always be in uniform, Detective Inspector. Though you clearly like it, Abbot. The dressing up – is it psycho-sexual?'

'Isn't everything?'

'But still odd,' beams Louisa. 'I remember we noted it in the interview at the retreat house. So much good about you, but we were concerned about the dressing up.'

'These chapel plans,' says Tamsin.

'Which chapel plans?'

'I mean, they'd certainly have got some tongues wagging, wouldn't they? And put the Community of the Holy Fire centre stage in the news cycle.'

'And I,' says Louisa, 'have no idea what you're talking about.'

'I'm talking about the Green Chapel.'

'I think we've discussed this mystery item before.'

'And Hildegard so ill beforehand,' says Peter. 'Before she finally wrote the revelations down.'

'Oh, she was always ill. We called her *Illy Hilly*. And while she claimed it to be so, I'm not sure revelations had anything to do with her illness. I mean, really. Stomach complaints of one sort or another; that was Hildegard.'

'She blamed herself for holding back the truth,' adds the abbot.

'She was a self-punishing soul. It can have the same effect.'

'She blamed herself for not speaking of the light given to her; as if she was holding back God.'

'I'm no doctor, but an anti-depressant might have been more to the point.'

Tamsin takes over. 'And the *Viriditas* festival, Louisa – which would have accompanied the opening of the chapel.' Louisa looks blank. 'Quite a day for the convent! No question the world's press would have been there, with young Greta pencilled in to open it.'

'As I said ... '

'Yes, we know what you *said*, Louisa.' Tamsin holds up her hand to pause the politician's reply, to stop it in its tracks; to save wasted words and time. 'It just doesn't match with other things you've said, so now we're confused – confused as two lost drunks at midnight with a map in their hands of somewhere else!'

'Again, I'm struggling ... ' The smile is getting politer by the minute.

'And we wouldn't wish you *struggling*, Louisa – God forbid! If he exists.'

'He does. As one day you will discover – Oh happy day!'

'And to explain our confusion,' says Peter, 'here's an email you wrote to Hildegard six weeks ago.' He notes her shock; but how did she imagine an email would remain silent? Emails hang around, with no loyalty to their author. Like a cheap whore, they'll display themselves to anyone who asks. He puts on his reading glasses. 'Here we go then, an email chosen at random: *"I have seen the plans for the Green chapel, Hildegard. Don't ask me how, but I have. They are no secret now. And let me be clear: a greater monstrosity I have not seen in my life. Have you no thought for the aesthetics of this wretched scheme? We shall be the laughing stock of Sussex, and mocked to kingdom come.*

*But more important than that, Hildegard, and a great deal more pressing, is the direction you seem set upon. So, the Community of the Holy Fire is to be the green hub of the south, a beacon of environmental integrity and challenge? All very well – but not a call I heard from the mouth of Jesus. Are we still followers of his here? Or is it that attention-seeking Scandinavian teenager who now demands our worship and assent?*

*Assist with food banks if you must, the poor are with us always, so no harm done; and Jesus himself fed the five thousand. But the convent as a shrine to Greenery? Really?? When Jesus said, 'Do this in remembrance of me,' he spoke of bread and wine – not of saving ice caps; not of re-planting the forests of Costa Rica! Not of ridiculous net zero targets!*

*In short, Hildegard, this is not my vision for the convent, not at all; and more crucially, it is not a vision that will be funded by me or by any who I have dealings with. So here is what I suggest:*

*Plans for this Green chapel must cease.*

*Plans for the Viriditas festival must cease.*

*And the invitation to that attention-seeking teenager, who was to open it, is to be withdrawn. She and her friends can get back to their school books.*

*I hope these proposals are acceptable, Hildegard. I have always supported your leadership here and will continue to do so, as long as we hear no more of the blasphemy that is the Green Chapel.*

*Yours in the love of Christ,*

*Louisa*

'And if that's the love of Christ,' adds Tamsin, 'God help anyone who gets on the wrong side of him.'

Again, Louisa smiles. 'Well, if you want the honest truth ... '

'And traditionally, we do. It's so much more helpful.'

'The honest truth is that I am very happy you know about this.'

'Really?' The tone is mockery.

'No, it's a great relief, actually. A great relief. I'm the world's worst liar anyway!'

'Your qualification for government, I'd imagine.'

Louisa is suddenly serious. 'I'm not so happy if everyone *else* gets to know, obviously, I don't wish for it to be public knowledge, mainly for Hildegard's sake, of course.'

'Of course.'

'I wish for her to be remembered kindly. But if it does leak out into public view, I'll fight my corner and win.'

'So, you lied to us.' With an amused shake of her head, Louisa indicates this is a ridiculous idea.

'I have merely withheld certain information to protect the community – information that has absolutely nothing to do with the investigation.'

'I'm not sure that's your call.'

'And I strongly suspect history will judge me kindly, Detective Inspector, as a defender of the faith, *fidei defensor.*' The abbot remembers the old maxim: 'Argument weak? Use Latin.' 'Yes, when this green obsession has passed, I think the faithful will be grateful to me.'

'Those who haven't starved to death, burned to death or drowned,' says Peter.

'Yet Hildegard was a remarkable woman, surely?' says Tamsin. 'You did tell us that.'

'A remarkable woman *in some ways,* Detective Inspector.' A condescending smile. 'But in other ways, remarkably wrong. And it pains me to speak in this way, to speak ill of the dead; it is not behaviour I condone, in any manner whatsoever. And – let me say – something I would never have done, unless prodded and poked by you ... when I naively imagined you were here to solve a murder.'

Tamsin: 'You must be pleased she's gone though, Louisa. *Surely?* You must be thinking Christmas has come early!'

'I'm not a huge fan of Christmas. Bad memories.'

'And thank you so much for the use of your cottage earlier, by the way. It was really very helpful. And amongst all the political snap shots, what a lovely photo of Richardis! Do you keep photos of all the homeless you meet?'

∿

Peter walks by the sea, beneath a clear and starry sky which means he has to think of Vincent. How could he not think of Vincent? On reflection, Van Gogh had regretted the size of his stars, leaping out from the canvass like wild things. He'd reprimanded himself, a theme in his life, feeling the famous stars were something in his life he should have done differently. *Well, we've all been there, Vincent.* But really, can a star be too large, when they possess eternity? Sometimes the abbot is almost lifted out of himself; though until now, he has always returned.

The water tonight is quiet; choppy this morning, but a mill pond now, disturbance is passed, lapping quietly against the shingle; a clean mirror for the creamy moon. And it was almost without noticing that Peter had become one who lived by the sea.

'Was it a life-long ambition?' people ask, as if he must have been planning it for years, holding on to the dream; when, in truth, there had been no plan and no dream; when the truth was that the sea had been the last thing on his mind as the years passed in the desert.

'Happy by the sea, happy in the desert' was his awkward reply when people raised the matter. And they never listened and never believed him.

'Yes, but there's something special about the sea, isn't there, Abbot?' At this point, he'd step off the conversational treadmill.

Did everyone wish to live by the sea? In England, apparently so. But he'd never thought of it in the desert where he'd imagined everyone wanted to be. Who would not wish to live amid the timeless rock and sand of Middle Egypt, by-passed by fad and free from the noise of the world?

But in England, it seemed everyone wanted a sea view; in England, there persisted the enduring dream of a cottage on the cliff – a dream undimmed by coastal erosion which threw cliff homes into the water; and untouched by storm winds of increasing brutality. Yet here he is, beside the seaside, beside the sea in the strange unfolding drama of his life.

And now, as he enters the convent grounds, he's thinking again of the Green Chapel – a small cry for sanity, while there is still hope. Though there's more clucking than crying as he walks past the convent hen house, with a nun on her knees in the dark, mending some of the netting.

'Intruders?' he asks.

'No, escapees.' It's Sister Rowena and she moves with grace, even in the mud. 'The hens got into Sister Roisin's vegetable garden today and wreaked havoc.'

'Oh dear. Is there any way back?'

'For the chickens or me?'

'I was thinking of you.'

'She's not talking to me – and I can quite understand.' Peter nods. He knew that the silent treatment had power even in a monastery where silence rules. There are different sorts of silence. You can feel them all. 'I mean, I wouldn't be talking to me either. But I do my best; and yes, more aware of intruders than those trying to escape.'

'Foxes?'

'Foxes, of course; and rats. They're so clever; you rarely see them, but you know they've been. Rather like our undiscovered intruder here in the convent.' Peter feels the jab. 'Any closer to finding them?'

'Not as close as we'd like; but nearer than before.'

'But how would you know that?'

'As the guru in the forest once said, when a traveller asked the way out, "I can't tell you which path will take you out of the forest. But I can show you many paths that won't." The possibilities are fewer than they were.'

'You might be very close, of course.'

'We might. I think we are.'

'Yet you're still on their side?' She remembered their earlier conversation when Peter had declared himself 'on everyone's side.'

'Always. So, who do you think it is, Rowena?'

'I'm not sure it's for me to say. I'm just the keeper of the chickens.'

'No one is just anything, as you well know. I believe you were a choreographer in the theatre. And before that, a ballerina?'

'I could dance and create movement, yes.'

'Do you miss it?'

'Sometimes. But not enough.'

'A whole land of knowledge and experience now put aside.'

'I know all about the body in space, yes, about proprioception.'

'I'm sorry?'

'Forgiven. You just need a better dictionary.'

'Proprioception?'

'It's awareness of the position and movement of the body. Yours tends to be awkward, Abbot. Your head is not well related to your body, there's an absence of physical flow, as I'm sure many people have told you.'

'No one has told me.'

'Ever thought of Pilates?'

'Not often.'

'Never say never. But that's me done. Unravelling the twisted skeins of evil; that wasn't my training.'

'Well, never say never.'

'I have enough on my plate with the hen house.' The abbot sees no hens. 'They're all in bed. They take themselves to bed at dusk. They're like nuns, they don't need telling.'

'A different knowing from your previous life.'

'Maybe. But what I do know is that we need a convent cock.' It sounds like a line from *'Carry on up the Cloisters'* and the abbot is saying nothing. Will the schoolboy ever finally pass through him and leave? Maybe he doesn't want him to. 'And I do see how that sounds, Abbot.' She smiles. 'You've done very well not to laugh; most men would not have managed it. But the truth is, the cock is good at looking after the hens; and we've lost ours and we miss him.'

'What's lost?'

'Oh, well, he'd be first out in the morning, checking the lie of the land; and then he'd go back to get the girls up if they didn't follow promptly.'

'The cock brings order.'

'It's not just order. He also protects. When you introduce a new hen, the others can be really quite beastly to the newbie – similar to ballet school, in fact.'

'Beastly *how?*'

'Not letting them near the food, that sort of thing.'

'No, I mean the hens.'

'Very funny – but not so far off the mark. The cock makes sure this doesn't happen. A cock makes sure the newcomer isn't pecked, he won't allow it; so, the poor newcomer can get to the food. The cock is very powerful; so it's important they are good.'

That was probably enough about cocks. He didn't know this woman well and it could get awkward. 'Well, God bless them, cock and all, Sister Rowena – though you still haven't told me who the murderer is.'

And in the moonlight, she looks at him strangely; as if he really doesn't understand.

'Have I not?'

~

The abbot bids her good night and walking across the lawn, discerns movement ahead; or rather, a sobbing – and then movement. A silhouette is stumbling forward; away, it seems, from Louisa's cottage. He walks towards the figure, a woman, solid – it's Daisy. He slows, not wishing to alarm.

'Hello, Daisy – is everything all right?' He is trained in foolish questions and this one will get him a professorship.

'It's nothing,' says Daisy, offering a stupid answer in return. 'Just me being, well, ridiculous. I'll get over myself.' And then she starts crying again.

'I don't think tears are ridiculous.'

'My mother would say, "Snap out of it, girl, you're not a bloody sponge."'

'I think tears are wise.' He offers her a hanky. She takes it.

'Who has a hanky these days?'

'I do. And tears have a voice, they're telling us something.'

'Look, it's nothing, Abbot, really nothing. As I say, I've just been stupid and yes, I just need to get over myself and snap out of it.'

She returns the sodden hanky, well used around her face, nose, cheeks and eyes. 'Why I ever thought that ... '

'Thought what?'

'It don't matter; really, I'll be fine, Abbot. So, get on with whatever you're, like, doing, though God knows what that is at this time of night. I'm fine.'

'OK. Where are you going?'

'And what's the point of crying, eh? It don't change nothing.'

'It can change everything. Who told you it won't?'

'My father.'

'Such inspiring parents.'

'I won't start on my father. There ain't time.'

She proceeds towards the convent. They walk together.

'So, what needs changing, Daisy? You said it doesn't change anything. What doesn't change anything?'

'Nothing needs changing. I'm happy as things are. I was just ... '

'Do you want a cup of tea?'

'I want to go, to be honest – goodnight, Abbot.'

And left alone on the path, as Daisy walks towards the convent, Peter notices the lights are still on in the cottage.

Perhaps Louisa can help. She has a heart of gold, apparently; so maybe a quick call. Daisy is a mess. He approaches her home and rings the bell. The door is swung open by Louisa in a luxurious bathrobe and some face cream amply applied.

'So sorry to bother you,' he says.

'But not sorry enough, Abbot, or you wouldn't be here!' She's quite angry in a jokey sort of way. 'It's rather late for a cold call. And it is cold.' He's not welcome and there's a slight pause. 'But really, no bother, no bother – how can I help? Have you run out of sugar?'

'It's about Daisy.'

'Daisy?' Surprise – as if that was the last name on earth she expected to hear.

'She seemed very upset when I met her just now – and I wondered if she'd been here?' He knew she'd been here; but always give space for the lie.

'Oh, poor girl, I felt terrible, yes, she was here – but what was I to say?'

'About what?'

'Would you like to come in for a moment, Abbot? Heat is leaving the hallway at an indecent rate and what with the price of fuel ... '

'Paid for by the community, I'm told.'

'That's hardly the point.'

'To those who have, more will be given. It does seem to be the way of the world.'

'Or perhaps it's just the reward for bloody hard work; and whoever's paying, we do need to be mindful of the planet.'

'Quite.'

'I'm not a fan of the Green Chapel, but I *am* a fan of the cause.'

'You didn't really give that impression earlier.'

They remain in the hallway, which is a half-hearted welcome, especially as Louisa leaves the front door ajar. He is clearly not staying long. On the wall, there are photos of political friends, one of Louisa with the PM; another of her skiing somewhere cold and expensive.

'And Daisy?'

'I can't give her what she wants, she must know that.'

'And what does she want?'

Louisa sighs. 'How much do you know?'

'About what?'

She takes the plunge. 'Hildegard did not like the classes mixing.'

'I'm sorry?'

'It may not be very 'woke' and all that nonsense – and God help us if it ever gets out – but she didn't like the classes mixing.'

'School classes?'

'Social classes.'

'I feel a time warp coming on.'

'So, Daisy could never be a nun, it wasn't going to happen, because she was, well ... '

'Let me say it for you ... working class.'

'Well, quite. I prefer "low-skilled", but it all adds up to the same, bless them. And Hildegard – may her soul know the resurrection of all true believers – was always very clear about it.'

'About what?'

'That the Community of the Holy Fire should be for those of a higher social standing; from the top drawer, so to speak.' The abbot had a sudden picture of his stepmother; that was a phrase she used. 'He's very top drawer,' she'd say, as if the fortunate soul came from another planet entirely. 'While Daisy, sad to say, was from the bottom drawer, from Tide Mills stock. Rather rough language, predictably. I mean, Hildegard was all for helping the poor and that sort of thing; but she was not for having them as part of the community; she felt it wasn't right for anyone.'

'And so, Daisy, a girl of humble origin, simply didn't fit in.'

'There's nothing humble about Daisy!'

'You know what I mean.'

'She was an excellent cleaner, mind; very committed. She absolutely found her calling as a cleaner; but not as a nun. Clearly, she could never be a nun.'

'So, you agreed with Hildegard.'

'We don't have to speak of it in public, obviously; people can misunderstand; social media is actually *contracted* to misunderstand – as any government minister will tell you!'

'Perhaps ministers just lie a great deal and that's the problem.'

Louisa will ignore this tedious jibe and return to the separation of the classes. 'So, yes, there is a great deal of sense in what Hildegard did.'

And now Peter pictures Daisy standing in Hildegard's study with the computer. What was that about? Was she really just a very committed cleaner? Or planning some sort of revenge?

'And she was here tonight because she wanted you to help her, now Hildegard is gone?'

'Very astute, Abbot. That cassock you wear ... '

'Habit.'

'It clearly hasn't sucked the brains out of you yet. But, of course, I can't; I can't help her, it's not within my power.'

'Really? He who pays the piper ... '

'Abbot, it's not my decision and I told her so. I told her that's for the new abbess to decide. "And it won't be me, Daisy!" But it wasn't good news for her, poor girl; hope is a terrible thing.'

'And probably knocking on the wrong door coming to you. She was forever a servant in your eyes too.'

'Now that's just mealy-mouthed, Abbot. And I completely forgive you! And if it's any consolation, the man we chose over you for the retreat house, was a complete disaster and left after nine months. You would have been a much better choice.'

'That's true.'

'So, *mea culpa.*' There's a sadness in the abbot. He would have liked the job and done it well. But life is not like that; some things are given, some things are not. 'And I've answered all your questions, I trust.'

'Indeed, you have.' She hasn't answered them at all. 'You have been most helpful.'

'So, if there's nothing else ... '

She has moved towards the door, wrapping her bathroom robe a little more tightly around her. It's chilly standing here, so best if he leaves quickly, this is the message.

'Well, thank you for your time, Louisa.'

'All very sad. But we wish Daisy well, don't we? We absolutely wish her well.' *You and the king?* wonders the abbot, who says good night and leaves with the strong impression that Louisa, on his arrival, had been expecting someone else.

~

He starts up the stairs towards his bedroom, but then a change of mind; a mind saying one thing and then saying another. Who knows how these things happen – which neural pathways will spark and fire and when? But a decision is taken, eternity shifts: he will turn around and go to the prayer chapel instead of his bedroom; and there, he will say the night office of Compline. It will be good for him, he feels; and also good for the chapel, re-establishing prayer, rather than murder, as its reason. Recovery of the space will take time, like the land around Chernobyl. Recovery can take a great deal of time but must start somewhere. He makes his way along the corridor, past the stone saints, and then down the steps to the chapel. And as he pulls open the door, a strange smacking sound can be heard. Peter pauses. It comes from within the chapel itself. Smack and gasp. Smack and gasp.

He steps inside and realises that Compline must wait.

'Is there something you're not telling me?' asks Margaret, putting the plates in the dishwasher; but not the pie dish. The pie dish will not concern the dishwasher again. She's been in court all day, listening to lie after lie and she wants no more of them tonight. Lies should cease on returning home. One may be cold but one should not lie.

'They just have more questions,' says Stephen. 'It's all routine, they say.'

'They have more questions for *you*?'

'Yes.'

'That isn't routine. And a fact you wouldn't have told me unless I'd heard you cancelling both a school assembly and a Fairtrade lunch tomorrow.'

'They're talking with everybody.'

'And they've already talked with you and want to talk again. That isn't normal. Do you understand?'

'Could you just let the case rest, for God's sake?' Sudden anger. He needs a break from all this.

'No.'

'Look, may be the defendant's had enough, all right? May be the prosecution needs to take a fucking break, make some coffee or something.' He never swore, it wasn't him at all; but living with a lawyer, everything becomes a trial, everything a point of order, and frankly, he's sick of it. 'The case is ongoing.' No, that was weak.

'Are we playing "State the blindingly obvious" Stephen?"'

'New issues arise, you know all this; fresh lines of questioning, I don't know. But it's fine.'

'What's fine about it? Which particular aspect? The murder itself? The fact that they are pursuing you?'

'It's fine that I am *not at all concerned* – and neither should you be.' He will play the man; play the strong man, the rock in the storm, everything's in hand. But Margaret sees only the boy, the frightened boy, with eyes dreading blame. She moves towards him, she's left the court and holds his shoulders still, so she can look him in the eye, with compassion.

'Stephen.'

'Yes?'

'Are you sure everything's OK? You can tell me if it isn't.'

'Everything's fine.'

'I'm familiar with the mistakes people make, sometimes terrible ones. And you seem worried.'

'Everything is quite OK, really. I didn't kill Hildegard.'

'I didn't imagine you did, Stephen.' *But it's strange you feel the need to tell me.*

Jason had spent the day attempting a cartoon about broken promises. The government was knee-deep in them, believing the positive promise renders actual delivery unnecessary: 'They'll forget, they won't remember.'

He'd started with the idea of a tsunami of broken promises crashing across the UK, leaving devastation in its wake. He might pitch that one, it was a decent drawing, but bleak, savage and nasty – a cross between a Hogarth and Scarfe. It might put punters off their breakfast, which no editor wished for.

'You have to be nice over breakfast.'

'But rude over elevenses – that's OK?'

The safer drawing, inspired by his meal with Tamsin last night, concerned incineration and was looking good on the page. He'd never felt more of a parasite, obviously, leaching off a real-life murder. But what was he to do? And really, was there such a thing as an ethically-sourced idea? He imagined the eulogy at the funeral: 'And let me reassure you all, that Hildegard did *not* die in vain. A tragic waste of a life, of course. We know that, absolutely terrible. But on the *bright* side, she gave Jason the idea for a cartoon, which may make it into one of the Sunday editions.'

He really must get a proper job; but he did like the cartoon before him. It was a picture of a steam train from the Wild West, travelling fast and furious towards a town called Oblivion, sign posted ahead, with the train fired and fuelled by the PM, shirt off and laughing, throwing endless wood-shaped broken promises into the furnace. "This weeks promise" "Last week's promise." "A promise you may have long forgotten about" etc. The passengers sit quietly reading their books or doing their make-up as Oblivion is approached at speed.

But his day had not been entirely filled with satire. It had also been filled with the detective inspector. She kept appearing, wandering through his mind, though not in a law-keeping capacity; and really, there wasn't a great deal he could do about it. The mind turns no visitors away and this can sometimes help the cartoonist, but not necessarily the man. The trouble was, he didn't know what he wanted, and never had, though maybe he did. Maybe at last he knew! And so, he'd decided to ring her, feeling as nervous as hell, feeling like a teenager, which in love, is what he was, though this wasn't love, because what was love anyway? Though maybe it was ... and so his mind continued. If he didn't ring her, at least he'd not have any bad news, which was at the heart of much of his decision-making – an avoidance of bad news.

But in the end, like a man possessed, like a mad impetuous fool, (who he'd punish later with self-recrimination) he *had* rung her, because she gave him her number. They'd had a nervous exchange yesterday about how little this all meant, and lots of 'I'm not expecting a phone call tomorrow or anything!' ... but it was tomorrow and he was making a phone call, because sometimes you have to.

'This is a bit sudden,' she said.

'Oh, just thought I'd say hello, you know.'

'Well, I suppose there's no law against it.'

'So, no need for the hand cuffs then!' No, that sounds pervy. Why, in situations like this, do you say things you've never said before? He had literally *never* said that before. *Change direction, Jason.* 'What have you been doing?' Too nosy. 'Been policing?'

'Pretty much. Cartooning?'

'Pretty much.' And now a joint smile is shared over the phone. And he wants to ask her if she wants to see a film, because it's safer than asking if she wants to see him; the film can stand in for him, ease the pressure, and maybe help with the disappointment as well. 'And I was just wondering if, er, you wanted to see a film?'

'A film?'

'*The Depot* here in Lewes is an excellent little cinema, comfy seats, not like those ... '

'What's on?'

'What's on?' He really should have checked that. He doesn't know what's on. He's asking the film to stand in for him and he doesn't know its name. *And* he has never actually been to *The Depot,* though he's heard good things. He hasn't really thought this through.

'I've never been to a cinema,' says Tamsin, thinking it has got to be 'no'. What she's never done before she doesn't like to do. 'Sounds good,' she says. And when did she last say that?

~

Blood was spattered on the stone floor.

The flagellant, oblivious to the abbot's arrival, had been busy for a while, smack and gasp, smack and gasp, naked from the waist upwards, a blood-ripped back still receiving the metal talons of the flicking whip. And the abbot's first thought is to leave, this transaction too private for public gaze. He has no wish to embarrass and everything has its reasons. But really, was there anything good in this self-assault, anything kind or true? Peter doubted it. And if goodness was absent, what was gained by his exit, by his quiet turning away? Was goodness sometimes staying where it wasn't welcome?

'Daisy.' She swings round in shock, dropping the whip, covering herself as best she can with her hands, though she can't, and Peter moving forward to give her the discarded coat. 'I'm sorry, I ... '

'What the actual fuck? Get out, you shouldn't be here, you never saw this!' She has now covered herself. 'Get out!'

'I understand.'

'No, you don't understand. You bloody don't. Just go!'

'I can't go.' He shakes his head to suggest it is quite out of the question. 'We need to talk, Daisy.'

'I don't need to talk.'

'We need to talk about what happened at Louisa's cottage this evening.'

# 'I want answers!'

Michael's distinctive voice bellows down the hushed convent corridor; the abbot is in search of breakfast. He has discovered this includes a boiled egg every other day, so it's good news this morning ... though the marmalade is poor, whichever the day; and this is disappointing. Cut costs by all means – they could ease up on the heating for a start; no nun needs to be this warm. But cheap marmalade, that's not the way to proceed, it's the path to hell ... though his mind leaves breakfast as Sister Patience appears, walking alongside the shouting Michael, little and large, but with little in charge – 'I want answers, Sister!'

'Come with me, Michael.'

They hurry towards her small office. At least she *encourages* him to hurry, her firm hand on his back, propelling him forward.

'All's quite well, Michael, you must believe me,' she says to his face, mouthing carefully as they walk. 'Daisy is OK.'

'Then where is she?'

'She's here, with us, safe in the convent sick bay.'

'Then it's *not* well, is it?' Is the woman stupid or something? Daisy didn't come home last night, the police wouldn't do anything, said she was an adult, told him to wait and see what the morning brought; and now he discovers she's in the sick bay. That's not *well.* Sometimes this place really pisses him off.

They arrive at her office and Patience guides him firmly inside. She closes the door, relieved – though unsure as to what she faces or how much to disclose? Michael's concern is all very touching – but beyond that? He shouldn't be getting involved. He's the gardener. She's the cleaner.

'She fainted, Michael, and so we kept her overnight.'

Michael is puzzled; he's not sure about the word. The sub-abbess mimes a faint and then he understands, irritated with himself, because he picks up most things from the lips and sometimes at a distance. The abbot follows them in – breakfast must wait - and for once, the Jackal is pleased to see him.

'The abbot will explain events,' she says, off-loading the intruder into someone else's care; though how the abbot is to handle this, he's unsure. He knows why Michael is here; but Patience will not.

~

Memories of the previous evening are still fresh in his mind; and had inhabited his dreams. It had been with some difficulty that Louisa and himself had taken Daisy to the sick bay, with the Snake particularly disturbed by events. He had left her to settle Daisy before informing Sister Patience, who had then taken charge, evicting Louisa promptly from the sick bay.

'The community will take charge now,' she said briskly and without thanks. How Louisa was regarded in the community, he was learning. She had been helpful in this crisis; hands-on help appreciated by the abbot. But clearly, in the eye of the storm, when all is revealed, she may raise the money for the place – but she wasn't one of them. She would always be an outsider.

Meanwhile, Michael is angry because no one told him. But then why would they? No one knew that Daisy was the gardener's brother. The abbot knew; Daisy had told him in the chapel. But before that, it had been a secret. He'd never said; she'd never said. So, what did he expect?

'I should have been told!' shouts Michael, and Patience is furious at the deceit.

~

The previous evening had been a worry for Michael. It was always a worry when routine broke down.

Daisy said she'd be a bit late for supper but that was two hours ago and she still wasn't home, which was unusual, because she didn't hang around that place longer than was necessary. And why would she, when every day in the convent was an insult, a rejection, a reminder of what might have been; a reminder that what you most want, you cannot have; and that *was* all that Daisy had ever wanted, silly girl; she'd wanted to be a nun in a snob-shop. They trampled on the dream, pissed over it again and again and again ... and still she dreamed her dream.

But that was Daisy for you. Always longing, never finding. And probably if she did find, she wouldn't want it anyway.

So, she'd be on her bike pretty sharpish at the end of the day, and hardly more than a mile to their flat in Denton. Because, well – you just had to get on with things, when your grandmother was born in the Tide Mill cottages. These were no ones' choice of home, with nothing to pass on, no nest egg for those who follow; no helping hand, no bank of mum and dad. So yes, you have to get on, make do and mend, as his mother used to say, or at least make do, and hope to get lucky, hope to win the Pools, hope to trip over one million pounds when out for a walk.

And, in a way, he had got lucky, bloody lucky, with the gardener's job at the convent. He had never gardened in his life, he'd had to blag that bit, but it wasn't so hard – he'd spoken about 'the sanctity of the seasons', which was something he'd heard Daisy say; and said, when asked about his experience of gardening, 'There's a lot I don't know, a lot I must learn – but when I see a garden, I want to cry.' They had liked that, he could see, and they never asked what he meant, thank God, because he certainly didn't know. He never cried.

And they liked the deaf thing obviously; employing him made them feel good about themselves. He could see it when he passed them in the corridor; he could see it in their eyes – 'That's the deaf person we employ; we're very good like that.' *Good? That lot?* But it meant he could keep an eye out for Daisy, get close to her again, like when they were growing up, like the old days.

Only now they knew. Now they knew he was her brother, which was none of their business. 'Michael don't tell you anything,' Daisy would say, and he'd reply, 'Why would I when information is power?' So, he'd never show his hand unless he had to; and he never had, he wasn't stupid. But now they knew, because of last night, because of Daisy in the chapel, Daisy being an idiot with the whip, she'd told the abbot. And he'd have to have told them anyway, if he wanted to see her, and he was angry about that as well. She'd forced his hand.

He'd always protect Daisy; and he wanted Daisy to be happy. But she made it hard sometimes and she'd need watching now. And sometimes you have to look after yourself.

He must speak with her.

~

Meanwhile, with the morning sunlight falling across the snug, Tamsin and the abbot are reading; and it's all a bit of a shock.

Bancroft had found the file in one of Hildegard's cupboards, hidden away beneath the kitchen accounts. Here was a secret, out of sight and not spoken of in public. The Community of the Holy Fire was largely oblivious to what was round the corner for them; largely but not completely. It was a secret with sieve–like qualities, unable to contain itself in the convent – like middle-age spread, it spilled a little, and with consequences.

Tamsin and Peter had heard rumours and surmise. Here in their hands was the real thing.

## The Green Chapel
### Why it must be built

*'Let me speak, dear friends, of* Viriditas, of Greenness – *the divine life force infusing the natural world. And if that offends you, glance at the sun, my friends, See the moon and the stars! Gaze at the beauty of earth's greenings here on the coast! I contemplate these things each morning. We all should!*

*And now, think – think hard! Think what delight God gives to humankind with, and through, all this growing, all this thrusting life. We behold nature in awe and wonder. Yet all nature is at our disposal.*

*It is given to us, dear friends, not just for delight and sustenance, but also that we might care for it. We are to work with nature, not against it. For without it, my friends, we cannot survive, we will not survive!*

*The Divine reveals itself in nature. Do you not know this? Nature itself is not the Divine, just as clothes are not the person. Yet the natural world clothes our God, gives proof of the Divine, exists because of the Divine, and daily gives him glory.*

*This is why our convent must protect nature; must work with nature. What else can we do? For in doing this, we work with God.*

*So, in all our buildings, in every structure, for God's sake and ours, we need to change! We need to 'follow the science' as people say, listen to the experts, who tell us – and with some urgency – that we need, well, where to begin? We begin with our buildings. We need improved levels of thermal insulation, we start there; we need better than normal air-tightness; good levels of daylight; glazing oriented south for light and heat. We can do this! Thermal mass to absorb that solar heat; minimum north-facing glazing, to reduce heat loss; and heating powered from renewable sources, heat pump or biomass; photovoltaic panels, small wind turbines ... or electricity from a 'green' supplier, we must investigate, I have started! And natural materials, of course — and the avoidance of PVCu and other plastics; triple glazing, yes! We know these things! We can do these things here at the Community of the Holy Fire!'*

The abbot looks up from the text.

'She wasn't playing games, was she?' He puts the folder down for a moment. Their interview space has become like the reading room in a gentleman's club – paper everywhere, Hildegard's paper; Hildegard's plans for a green revolution on the south coast.

'We're a little beyond virtue-signalling,' says Tamsin, duly impressed – less with the plans, and more with the vigour, with the brazen honesty of her approach. 'She was going to rip the guts out of the place.'

'So, what are the police doing, out of interest?'

'About what?'

'About all this.' He indicates Hildegard's green vision so passionately explained. 'What are the police doing for the environment?'

'We're a crime agency.'

'Well-disguised.'

'We had a meeting about it last week, since you ask.'

Stirred by national protests and government initiatives, there had been a 'Green' meeting in the Lewes nick, and Tamsin had been there, in error. Called 'Future Cost,' she'd thought it was about pensions, when in fact it was about environmental threat.

'And did the meeting go well? Can the planet breathe more easily now?'

'Chief Inspector Wonder did address the issue, so you can stop being pompous – especially with your wood burner.'

Why is she defending the police? It never happens; it's defending the indefensible. Yet somehow she feels compelled, in the face of the self-righteous abbot.

'And what did he suggest?'

'You've never been interested in anything he has ever said before.'

'Harsh.'

'Apart from when he praised you once.'

'Again, harsh.'

'So why now?'

'Why now? Well, mainly because, as a race, we're about to destroy ourselves. We need everyone on board ... even the police.'

'He says everyone has an opinion on the matter, obviously; and that everyone's opinion must be respected.'

'Here we go.'

'It's a fair point.'

'It's not a fair point. It's avoidance. What if some opinions are dangerously wrong? Must they also be respected? Must we now respect Hitler? Must we agree Fred West had a point? When did you ever respect bullshit? In what universe is that a good idea? All opinions must be allowed; but that's different from respect.'

Tamsin doesn't want this discussion. She is not that bothered to be honest; and more important, it has nothing to do with the case. She's caught out by the abbot's ferocity; but still can't quite back down in a tussle for supremacy.

'He says it's all well and good this eco stuff ... '

'"All well and good?"' Oh, the disdain! But Tamsin goes on.

' ... but warned us not to throw the baby out with the bathwater.'

The abbot pauses with eyebrows raised. 'And what does *that* mean?'

'I have no idea.'

'You must ask him.'

'He'll have no idea either.' She should never have attempted to defend the police, and particularly, Chief Inspector Wonder. Why would she do that? 'Though he's dropping in later, so you can ask him yourself.'

The abbot sighs. 'Well, unlike the chief inspector, Hildegard *was* doing something about it. And thanks to Bancroft, we have her plans for the Green Chapel here.' The abbot hands her another sheet of A4. Again, the room goes quiet, as Hildegard speaks from the grave.

*It's not often you hear architects talk about demolishing a building that they are designing. You do not often hear it! But that is how it will be as they plan our Green Chapel. For our chapel shall be different, designed and built on the principle of circularity. Have you heard of this? The principle of circularity demands we consider what happens to the building beyond its intended lifetime.*

*So, we shall challenge the conventional "build, use and dispose" method of design, by using components that can easily be taken apart. It is like with children's LEGO – you know this? The same principle applies. You build your structure; then take it apart to build something new! Is this not the way forward for construction?'*

She then goes on to consider the practicalities of both the building and dismantling of the chapel, including concrete panels, bolted together, and stone wool insulation, which can be re-used. She also notes that circular building construction is much more flexible should adjustments need to be made to the building.

*'Moving walls and roofing is both easier and cheaper. When the community here is four times the size, it will be no problem! The Green Chapel will grow with us!'*

And then, hand-written at the foot of the page, are Hildegard's notes:

*Louisa is appalled by the idea of a chapel that is constructed out of recycled items, and which could then have another use afterwards. She comes at me all gun's blazing.*

*'The house of God must be a building of majesty,' she says. 'It must be built to last for a thousand years – not some LEGO construction that can be taken down as quickly as it has been out up!'*

*She misunderstands and I have replied to her:*

*'I suppose some would say that that is its majesty, dear Louisa. The majesty of the chapel is to be in harmony with our planet rather than opposition. How can we praise God and at the same time ransack his creation? Green is not a hobby for fanatics as you suggest. Neither is it a distraction from God's gospel, as you seem to imply, but the warp and weft of all that is, the very texture of life, the conduit of belief. God is in the sun,*

*in the moon and the stars! How therefore can we not look after God's habitat? God shows himself in the sea and the sand, in the verdant green of existence, the pulsing plant life. Every day he arrives to bless! We feel God when we feel the breeze. The green shoot reminds us of resurrection! Yet every day, we crucify him anew! Every day, we hack down his home. We kill him in the sky and on the earth, in the sea and in the air.*

There is a joint sigh in the room as Peter and Tamsin return Hildegard's work to the folder.

'Quite a vision,' says the abbot and Tamsin nods, reluctantly. 'But if this is what she wanted, is it also what she died for?'

'I think it's time to ask Volmar about Satan. I have so many questions.'

~

'So, the abbess cast you as Satan in her new musical. Is that right?'

'She did, yes.'

They sit in the snug, Volmar is hunched.

'And how did you feel?'

'I wasn't overly pleased.'

'You were furious by all accounts.'

'Hardly that!'

'And is that why you killed her?'

Tamsin wished to get straight to the point with Volmar; and it was Sister Patience who had given them the point to get to.

'They had the most terrible row,' she'd told them. 'Hildegard had written a morality play, well – it was a musical.'

'She wrote a musical?'

'She did all sorts of things.'

'Full of surprises, our Hildegard.'

'She often wrote music. We sang some of her liturgical settings in our services. Very competent.' The praise is faint; as when people say the evening was 'fine' to indicate it fell some way short of expectations.

'And the musical?'

'Well, while the nuns could play all the other parts, each representing a virtue, Hildegard said that Volmar must play the part of Satan.'

'Why?'

'Because he was the only man available.' It was almost too obvious to state; convents are short of men.

'And Satan's a man?'

'Of course, Satan's a man!' Sister Patience is clear.

'What about Michael? He's a man.'

'He *is* a man.' Patience confirms this. 'But the wrong class, so not a man, if you know what I mean. More of a *bloke* than a man. There was no way he was appearing in the community production. He's a competent groundsman, but hardly ... '

'Not very inclusive,' says Tamsin, as if she cares. Patience just smiles because that is the way it is here; or the way it was. These were decisions taken by someone else. She can hardly be held responsible. 'And Volmar wasn't happy at the casting?'

'Furious. He was absolutely livid.'

'When so many performers would have been delighted with the part.'

'Volmar is our confessor. He did not see himself as a performer.'

'But everyone wants the dark role, don't they? Virtue is considered uninteresting for performers.'

'None of us had ever heard Volmar shouting before; but he shouted then. He always seemed so quiet, so accepting. And, of course, he worshipped Hildegard.'

'Until the worship stopped? That can be a moment,' says Peter, 'the moment worship is disappointed, which can send things in a very different direction.'

'It was during evening prayer. We were all in the chapel trying to say the psalms. But their voices down the corridor rather drowned them out. Volmar was volcanic. The nuns just made surprised faces at each other, eyebrows raised all over the place. But they kept singing. The show must go on.'

And so, Tamsin had to ask Volmar about the Satan episode. And Volmar pauses before answering, breathing heavily; disturbance is passing through. Will the volcano explode again?

'Maybe I smothered her. I hope I did not.'

'Smothered who? Hildegard?'

'She was a difficult one to smother, even if I had wished to; for she always had a sharp and separate spirit.' Tamsin invites him to continue. 'She claimed obedience was everything' – he smiles at the memory – 'but would always pursue her own way. Always. Perhaps other people's obedience was everything; she herself could never be shackled by it.'

'You knew her from the very start.'

'Oh yes, I was given an eight-year-old girl to protect; and I remember her delight on arrival – perhaps rather determined delight. I was not sure if I believed it. But I think she was glad to be free of a father who was embarrassed by her visions. "I have visions, you know," were almost her first words to me.'

'You clearly did a great deal for her.'

'I did my best.'

'I'm sure you did, so it must have been, what – heart-breaking when you fell out?'

'We never fell out.'

'You sort-of fell out. And quite loudly I hear.'

'I could never fall out with Hildegard.'

'A lot of shouting during evening prayer.'

'It was nothing.'

'But as nothing goes, it was one of the noisier examples.'

'I may have raised my voice a little.'

'You may, yes. "Volcanic" was one description. And in her final letter to you, written on the night of her murder, she called you a ... ' – checks notes, unnecessarily – "The Worm."'

'Well, that's Hildegard for you!'

'Isn't it just.'

'Her reactions were – how shall we say? – visceral on occasion. She would often react strongly, as I'm sure you've heard. And not always wisely; not always wisely. She could cause offence.'

'Which is why I mention it, because now she's dead. And someone said your fall-out was something to do with Satan. Can you enlighten us?'

Volmar sighs deeply.

'I shouldn't have reacted as I did. She meant nothing by it.'

'By what?'

'Hildegard wrote a musical.'

'We heard. Unusual.'

'Oh, she was a good composer. Someone approached her about an album. She didn't say no exactly. And some of her settings for the psalms, we still use in the chapel.'

'But you didn't want the part of Satan.'

Volmar is remembering the conversation. He can still feel it in his body, how she announced it at the weekly gathering on Monday, quite without warning, and certainly without asking.

'And we will ask our visiting confessor, Volmar, to play the part of Satan. He will need our prayers, girls!'

Everyone had thought it funny, looking across at him, while he sat there and attempted to smile, burning with shame, feeling such anger – and profound betrayal. Had he not nurtured this girl into womanhood? Had he not been with her every step of the way? And now, out of the blue, she announces he is playing the part of Satan in her new musical! He had always encouraged her music making, when others might have questioned it. But that did not mean he wished for a part in any production, the idea made him feel ill. And when that part was the embodiment of evil on earth ... no, this really couldn't be; he would have to have words; strong words.

And her response when they were alone? She said he was making a fuss about nothing.

'It is just acting, Volmar. It is not you, of course, just acting. You are *pretending* to be Satan.'

'I do not wish such pretence. It makes me feel ill. You should have asked me.'

'I am asking you.'

'You should have asked me in private; not in public. That's not asking – it's telling.'

'It's just a morality play, Volmar, like the parables of Jesus. Why should I ask you? All morality tales must have baddies!'

'And *I* must be the "baddy", as you call it?'

'You're a man!'

'I did not know Satan's gender was a matter of record. Do we also know his favourite film, the name of his dog and his most treasured possession, in the event of a fire?'

The abbess shakes her head in dismay at this ridiculous outburst. 'This is a fuss about nothing, Volmar. I expected better from you.'

And from that moment, from that shake of the head, he knew he could no longer be her confessor. He walked out of her office, a hailstorm of confusion and rage. He was raging.

And soon after, with feelings still running high – and his sleep a mess – he attended the meeting in the summer house, which now seemed a terrible mistake. But not one he could mention to the Detective Inspector; or to her absurd assistant, a man in a habit – but with no community. You cannot be a freelance monk. It is simply not possible. And he was using his bedroom.

'I did not wish to play the part. I do not like acting.'

'You became angry.'

'Maybe the abbot here should have played it.'

'Oh?' says Tamsin.

'He clearly likes acting.' And now he looks at Peter. 'I am told you are not a member of any religious community – yet still dress for the part.'

'I suppose I do.'

'So did you kill the abbess?' asks Tamsin.

'She should not have died.'

'Not really an answer.'

'I did not kill her – and she should not have died!' He is shouting at them. 'She should not have died!' And now he bends forward, clutching his face, his body jerking with emotion, sobbing.

'Let's leave it there for now, Volmar,' says Tamsin calmly. She looks to Peter for assistance, who moves closer to him, puts an arm on his heaving shoulder. He tells him it's OK.

'It's not OK, it's not OK!' They allow the sobbing to ease a little. Tamsin doesn't like it but the abbot stays, his hand on his shoulder. He feels the heat from the Worm's body, and asks him where he needs to be now – and can he help?

Volmar shrugs him off, with some aggression; and makes quickly for the door.

'Not a happy man,' says Tamsin. 'And still angry about you taking his room.'

'"She shouldn't have died." Why would he feel the need to say that?'

'Aren't "should" and "shouldn't" at the heart of all religions?'

'Maybe the poorer sorts,' says the abbot. 'But he's a man on the edge. Something has brought Volmar very close to the edge. And there's more here than the play.'

'I suggest we find Daisy.' Tamsin does like to move on, after displays of raw emotion. 'She's another one who's a bit edgy at present. Why do people whip themselves?'

'I don't understand you! Why did you do it?' Michael is distraught at her bedside, rocking backwards and forwards on the small chair. This tiny sick bay is no place for a big man in large muddy boots. 'There is no need for you to whip yourself, Daisy. No need! What have *you* done wrong?'

He pleads with her; he is angry; and then to make things worse, Tamsin and the abbot arrive. The convent sick bay was previously Sister Rosa's room. She died earlier in the year of various illnesses, the list starting with sepsis and pneumonia but not ending there. Though maybe at the top of the list was her loss of the will to live; this can often prove fatal. At the age of ninety-four, Sister Rosa had simply felt it time to go.

The sub-abbess, however, wanted clarity on the matter, because she liked clarity and had to keep records. Everyone – as well as posterity – needed to know exactly how Sister Rosa died. People would ask and she would need an answer; and the doctor was being evasive.

'So, what was it that actually killed her, doctor?'

A weary smile. 'Not one thing, but a conspiracy of things. I'm putting "TMB" on the death certificate.'

'TMB? Is that what I am to tell people?'

'If you wish.'

'And which illness is that?'

'Too Many Birthdays. It is a terrible killer.' Patience is not impressed with his levity. There's a time and place.

'This is no time to jest, doctor.'

'I do not jest. I tell the sober truth.'

Her body was removed with the undertakers suitably discreet. This was not easy in the convent's narrow corridors with sharp-turns, hidden statues and uneven floors. Rosa had twice nearly gone flying. But a month later, her room became the sick bay for the community because it was further from the kitchen than the previous one, which was thought to be a good thing; separating food preparation from disease. But the two sisters either side of the new sick bay had complained. They had preferred Rosa as a neighbour, as she was quieter, and generally less ill than the new ones; and also, because the sick tended to have visitors, which disturbed private prayer.

And so, with communal pressure building, it was possible the sick bay would move again.

For now, though, it housed the flagellant Daisy. Her back is a mess but she's sitting up, dressed and looking ready to go.

'Sorry to interrupt,' says Tamsin, 'but we do need to speak with you, Daisy.'

'OK.' She's not enthusiastic. 'I've got nothing to say.'

'Is here a good place to talk?'

'As good as any. I mean, I'm not sick or anything. I don't need to be here.'

'And she's got nothing to say,' adds Michael, in case they'd forgotten.

'We've just got a few questions. Nothing huge. And Michael, you will need to go.' She doesn't bother to look at him.

'She's my sister.'

'Precisely. That's why you'll need to go.' She is enunciating clearly and looking him straight in the eye. 'A sister is a different person to you, an individual with her own voice – a voice which deserves privacy.' Now she looks at him. 'As will yours, Michael, when we speak with you. Do you understand?'

Michael understands but he's not happy and he rocks in his chair again, looking at Daisy.

'She hasn't got anything to tell you.'

'That may be true. We'll see, won't we?' Tamsin smiles the smile of goodbye, and after a few heavy breaths, Michael's large body ups and leaves, creating sudden space for the interview team.

'Don't keep her long,' he says, turning in the doorway. This feels like a terrible defeat and one he cannot accept. But the abbot closes the door behind him, and then, after a while, opens it again, to make sure he is gone.

'How are you feeling?' says Tamsin.

'All right.' She's cautious, still watching the door.

'Good. And as I say, this won't take long.' Daisy offers nothing. 'I suppose our first question, Daisy, and one which won't be a surprise, is what you were doing with the computer in Hildegard's office, the morning after her death?'

'I've already said.'

'Remind us.'

'I was going to clean it.'

'Why?'

'It's good to keep things clean.'

With a sigh, Tamsin indicates how patient she is being. 'It's evidence, Daisy. *Evidence.* You must know its evidence. And you're taking it away, removing it from the crime scene.'

'To clean.' She is blushing, rattled.

'So, where are we now?' The sick bay feels incredibly small. 'You know that's not true and we know that's not true. So, according to my maths, that's everyone in the room who knows it's not true. Which leads me to wonder just what you're prepared to do to be a nun?'

'I don't want to be a nun. I did once.'

'You certainly did.'

'But not now.'

'So Hildegard was right. It never would have worked. You're too working class to be a nun.'

'Maybe.'

'Too "low-skilled". But now you have found your true ... what's the word?'

'Calling?'

'Calling, that's the one. Trust the abbot to know. The mop and bucket is who you are.'

Empty look from Daisy. 'I suppose.' Peter watches this slow death with sadness; like a cat with a mouse, and the mouse carrying on, not giving up; imagining somehow, it's going to be all right. 'Is that it?'

'Why did you visit Louisa last night in her cottage?'

'Who's to say I did?'

'The abbot here – he's one witness.' Daisy looks at her betrayer.

'Perhaps he got it arse over tit.'

'That's possible; wouldn't be the first time either.' She smiles in feminine collusion. 'But the other witness, the one that sort-of backs him up, as in *absolutely confirms his story*, is Louisa herself. Did she get it wrong as well?'

'What did she tell you?'

'Enough.'

'You can only ask. So I asked. Nothing wrong in asking.'

~

And Daisy had asked before. She remembered when she first inquired about becoming a nun, meeting with Hildegard in her big office, full of hope and excitement, her life and calling before her. She knew this was what God wanted from her, so Hildegard would know it too. And then the conversation she'd never forget; the conversation with her hero. She was never her hero again.

'Is it true your grandmother was born in the Tide Mill cottages?' Hildegard had asked.

'She was, yes!' said Daisy. 'So, I'm nothing if not local! Local girl, me!' Before they fell into ruin after the war, and became a hang-out for foxes and drunks, the mill cottages had been homes to a community less than five hundred yards away from the site of this convent.

Hildegard had smiled, in a kindly way, as though trying hard to understand; though from where she was sitting, the poor girl was entirely missing the point.

'But they were workers' cottages, Daisy. Workers at the mill.'

'They were, yes ... originally. Three generations of my family worked there.' She feels proud. 'They were tough in those days. I feel dead proud of my family. *Workers*.' Hildegard smiles again. Can this girl really not see?

'But how will that work?'

'How will what work?'

'And the answer is, dear Daisy, it won't, it simply won't.' Daisy is struggling for some solid ground.

'I'm not quite seeing what won't work.'

'We cannot mix the social classes.' There, she'd said it. It did need saying sometimes. 'We all know it doesn't work. And it's not that there's anything wrong with you, far from it. You have your place, of course. But mixing doesn't work.' Daisy didn't know this. Daisy didn't know she was in a class, 'in a social class', it hadn't been explained to her in the priory school. 'So, let's put aside all talk of a calling, dear Daisy. It isn't going to happen. It simply *can't* happen.'

'I don't understand.'

'You will do. And I think you'll be grateful.'

'But I am called to be a nun. I *know* it.'

'No one can know it for themselves. A calling must be validated by the church otherwise it would be chaos. Everyone declaring themselves "called"!' Daisy is beginning to cry. 'But we do have a small property in Denton, a flat on the Brownsall Estate, very decent I'm told, which we can offer to a cleaner here, for a small rent. Perhaps it is like the one your grandmother lived in down the road. Rather sweet.' But Daisy is confused.

'I still don't understand.'

'I'm asking, Daisy, if you'd like to be a cleaner for the Community of the Holy Fire. That's a calling too, you know. As John Milton reminds us, "They also serve who only stand and wait."'

'You don't stand and wait.'

'Too busy! Oh, that I could!'

'A cleaner?'

'As indeed your mother was, I believe. And I'm sure a very good one.'

'What's my mother got to do with it?'

'We all serve the Lord. We just serve in different ways. The disciples, however much they wished it, could not be Jesus.'

'Whereas you can?'

'One must not be bitter, Daisy. No one likes *bitter*.'

And so, Daisy, like her mother, had served the Lord as a cleaner and almost convinced herself she was happy; until other possibilities arose ... no shame in that.

'So, I asked Louisa – so what? Hildegard isn't here anymore, so perhaps the rules have changed – as Michael said they would.'

'How would he know?'

Daisy shrugs. 'So, I asked if I could join the novitiate.'

'The beginners,' says Peter, translating for Tamsin.

'I mean, Louisa has some clout round here, we all know that. She pays the bills, doesn't she? And you know what they say, ask and it shall be given; knock – and the door shall be opened.'

'Quite. Only it wasn't, was it?' Daisy doesn't understand. 'I mean, it wasn't given when you asked ... and the door wasn't opened.' Daisy shrugs. 'Louisa wasn't your fairy godmother, waving a spiritual wand and declaring all your dreams shall come true. It didn't happen.'

'Well, that's not police business, is it? It's nothing to do with you. It's between me and her.'

'With a lie ratio as high as yours, Daisy, I think everything you touch is police business.'

'I ain't lying.'

'I'm not sure you're telling much truth either.' More silence.

'So, why the whip?' asks Peter.

'Maybe I'm not happy with myself.'

'I'm not happy with you either,' says Tamsin.

'Well, there you go.'

'But I wasn't going to hit you. I mean, *why?* What have you done, to turn on yourself in that way?' It would help if she simply admitted to murder and then they could all go home. The abbot wanted to get home. He didn't enjoy sleeping away and the convent had reminded him why he left his monastery. As Brother Andrew had once said to him in the desert, 'Religious intensity can turn sane folk mad.' And the abbot felt the intensity here.

'I ain't done nothing,' said Daisy, ruining everyone's day.

'So why reduce your back to mush? It's a bit extreme, don't you think?'

'*Exactly.*'

'Exactly *what?*'

'Maybe purification *needs* to be extreme – or what's the point?' Daisy is happy now, as if truth has dawned and everything makes sense. 'More extreme the better, I'd say. Has to be extreme.'

'Are you OK, by the way?' asks Tamsin.

'What d'you mean?'

'We should have asked, really; we should have inquired after your health before all our pushy-pushy questions – so, both of us on the naughty step for that.' She looks at the abbot to confirm his presence there. 'Your *back,* Daisy. It must be very sore.'

Daisy nods, her eyes water – vulnerable now to the attention given; so needy of it, any attention; the abbot is almost moved. 'Sister Patience, she gave me pain killers.'

'Clever Sister Patience,' says Tamsin. 'Access to the drugs cupboard, of course. We must hope they don't lessen the purification.' Daisy looks worried. 'I mean, I don't know how these things work, but I'm presuming the degree of pain determines the degree of purification? So, I suppose we don't want too much of the pain to be killed.'

Daisy's breathing is unsettled. Tears break down her cheeks, tearful words.

'You're fishing in the wrong pond, you know that?'

There is a pause, broken by Peter.

'Why do you say that?' he asks gently, before Tamsin attacks her again; before her glare peals the yellow paint from the convent walls. Daisy will not be served by further ridicule. 'Which pond *should* we be fishing in? Perhaps your knowledge of the convent, your knowledge of events here, both public and secret, can point us to the *right* pond?'

'I know everything.'

'Everything? We have a god in our midst. So, give us a glimpse inside this remarkable storehouse of information, Daisy.'

And so she does; from her heavenly heights, Daisy gives the common folk a glimpse. 'Ask the bishop why he asked to meet the abbess in the chapel? Ask him that. Ask him why he asked to meet her there and at that time? And then ask him why he didn't turn up. Ask him about that as well. Why he didn't turn up to the meeting in the chapel. 'Cos *she* turned up and waited for him, worse luck.'

'How do you know about this?'

'And then ask him about the summer house, about meetings there. Bad things were done in the summer house.'

## 'Well, here we are again!'

Says the bishop with tense cheer, in purple shirt and dog collar. He wears a smart suit, a man used to chairing meetings himself – brisk and firm, firm but fair, he'd like to think. He 'suffers no fools' obviously; but funny as well, he believes in a joke to lighten the mood, preferably one of his own. Other people's jokes can rather miss the mark sometimes.

And today he hopes to draw a line in the sand, a clear line, because he is not a murderer; no reasonable person could say that of him. So, let's face the day hale and hearty, and a brisk opening line to set the tone, 'Well, here we are again!'

He finds them waiting for him in the snug, with the arched windows and a gorgeous stone floor, like a cathedral. And he won't be intimidated; he will be jolly; or at least brisk and firm, firm but fair, suffering no fools, that sort of thing.

Tamsin looks up at him as he enters. He doesn't knock, hardly the need, only servants knock; and a late smile arrives on her face.

'So good of you to carve out the time from your busy day, bishop.'

'It was no problem at all,' he says, perpetuating the myth that he actually had a choice. Though to be honest, he wasn't sad to be missing the school assembly. This sort of thing was good for PR and paid lip service to the idea that kids are great. But, in truth, he felt like a stuffed dummy when he was with them, exposed to their keen and innocent gaze. Every clever construction of words was somehow dismantled in their presence, rendered empty and useless, which left him feeling terrible. He was better with adults, who appreciated 'clever', who knew the rules of engagement in a way children did not. He needed the rules to function and to shine.

'And there's nothing too complicated this morning, bishop.'

'Glad to hear it, I'm a simple man!' Self-deprecating comedy, timeless.

'In fact, just two questions, really.'

'Sounds like my sort of agenda, short and sharp! Not a fan of long meetings!'

'It was just two, wasn't it, Abbot?' Peter nods. 'Unless there's any other business of course.'

'Always beware of the A.O.B!' says the bishop. 'That's where the knife is hidden.'

'Your meetings are obviously more exciting than mine,' says Tamsin and he smiles.

'Church meetings are some of the most savage, tactical minefields, believe me.'

Tamsin smiles in return but can't quite leave it there. 'Well, we won't believe you to *order*, bishop.' The jollity stops. 'We might believe you if you tell us the truth.'

'Of course.'

'And in particular, why you arranged to meet Hildegard in the prayer chapel on the night of her death – and then failed to turn up?'

Silence. It was the silence after a cannon ball has struck; as the dust slowly settles. And then from the wreckage, from the devastation and the rubble, the bishop appears.

'Who told you this?'

'Does it matter?'

'It matters a great deal! And I ask again: who told you?' No answer. 'And I have no idea what you're talking about.'

'So, for the benefit of the recorder, because it does like clarity, you didn't invite Hildegard to meet you in the chapel on the night of the bonfire.'

'No.'

'With your hand on the bible – metaphorically, obviously, I'm afraid the abbot has forgotten his – you are denying that.'

'Look, let's be clear.' He sits forward, which is always the sign of a rear-guard action. 'I have many conversations, many meetings.'

'So, the answer might be "yes".'

'No. I mean I can hardly remember every one of them. You know what it's like. But to the best of my knowledge, that's not something that happened; or at least not something I remember. What matters, surely, is how I have supported this place. And I want to get on with supporting it!'

'So again, you're not denying it?'

The bishop jumps up, like a jack-in-the-box released. 'I came here in good faith. I came to provide any assistance I could.' He is pacing around. 'And all I hear are vague insinuations about things that may or may not have happened, by people who may or may not exist, quite frankly; and with what motives, who can say? I mean, who is this person? I think I have a right to know, an *absolute* right to know, so if this is all you have to say ... '

'It isn't – so *sit down*,' spits Tamsin. The bishop is like a man too close to lightning, a man in shock and the abbot indicates it would be a good idea if he obeyed the D.I. and parked himself back on his chair.

'Tantrum politics doesn't work here, bishop.' The abbot speaks gently but firmly. 'It's not a stunt that solves anything.' The bishop was known for his tantrums in the diocese. It often got him his way. An angry bishop can make people cower. His previous P.A. had resigned 'for personal reasons'. But no one here is intimidated by an angry purple shirt. And the bishop hates no one in the world as much as the abbot right now.

'If you'd prefer to continue the interview at the police station?' says Tamsin, politely. 'Would you prefer that?' And slowly the bishop sits down, rigid as a crab, though the abbot sees mainly the terror. He sees a man who is terrified to his bones and ponders the old therapy mantra:

'Beneath every behaviour is a feeling.

Beneath every feeling is a need.'

They'd had the tantrum, felt the fury. So, what about the need?

Meanwhile, down the corridor, the Jackal handles the arrival of Wonder. She found him wandering aimlessly around the cloisters, which wasn't good. There does need to be order. You can't have strangers wandering around the convent.

'Can I help you?' she'd asked, with the friendliness of sniper fire. 'I'm sub-abbess Patience. And you are?'

'I'm a chief inspector ... Chief Inspector Wonder – from Lewes.'

'So shouldn't you be in Lewes?'

He shouldn't be here now, he knew that. He'd turned up early because he'd been bored in his office and thought the convent might be a bit of fun. But the nun facing him hasn't got the memo about that; and she's black, which is a bit of a surprise because he didn't realise there *were* black nuns.

'I'm here to meet DI Shah,' he says. 'And the abbot. But I'm a bit early.'

'Yes, you are a bit early.' He was meant to arrive at 11.00am; she'd been warned. It is now 10.15am.

'The early bird catches the worm, eh!' he says.

'But the second mouse gets the cheese. They are presently with the bishop.'

'Well, if you just tell me where they are ... '

' ... and they'll not wish to be disturbed.'

'Oh?' Wonder is irritated. Who does she think she is? And the answer is she thinks she's the boss and Patience does enjoy being boss. She notices this more and more. She is born to it;

An Inconvenient Convent

she knows how things should be done and likes the power
which ensures that they are. It's no good knowing how things
should be done if one can't then do them. That's just the path to
frustration. So, the chief inspector's attitude is disappointing.
He has turned up early and imagines everyone else will adapt.
Why would they do that? His leadership appears lazy, concerned
mainly with himself.

'Maybe you think nothing of interrupting important meetings
in the police? For myself, that doesn't seem right. It's not how
we do things here.'

'Oh no, well, I mean – I'm sure I can wait.' *Bloody hell! Hadn't
expected the third degree.*

'And they'll not be long, Chief Inspector. I believe they were
expecting you at 11.00am. So, a short wait only.'

'And perhaps some coffee and sandwiches while I do?' He's
smarting a little; he feels like he's been mugged. He hadn't
expected to be put in his place by a bloody nun. *But let's have
some tucker at least*, he thinks. Aren't convents meant to be
places of hospitality for the weary traveller? A jug of home-
brewed ale or something? And he's not exactly just *anyone*.
He's a chief inspector, for God's sake!

'I'm afraid we have lost our cook.'

'Ah, well, you never want to lose a cook.'

'No, an unfortunate business – which surprised us all.'

'Most important member of the community, the cook. "Good
canteen, happy staff."'

'She proved ... well, disappointing.'

'The scrambled egg, was it?'

'No.' Is the man a fool? But he appears to be on a roll.

'That's the true test, I think.' He's settling in, sitting in one of
the large windows, which opens onto the sea. 'Scrambled egg for
large numbers is tricky. For one or two, it's not such a challenge,
but for a larger crowd – well, there's a Premier Inn not far from us,
not a word of a lie, and very decent in many ways, but ... '

'And so, her famous secret leaves with her.' She'll not join him
on the window seat; and she doesn't have time for the Premier Inn.

'Oh?'

'Yes, she always claimed to possess a cook's secret, Chief Inspector.' Wonder wants to get back to his story of the Premier Inn scrambled egg disaster, which is a good one. He's told it several times. 'But she left here in disgrace, so we'll never know. People do disappoint.' *Is she referring to him?*

'Well, sorry to hear that, of course. If there's anything the police can ... '

'And I'm sure we can manage some coffee, Chief-Inspector.' She will keep the rest of the story in-house. She has no wish for police involvement in Gemma's departure and the accusations made against her. Her behaviour had surprised everyone, quite out of character, but she was probably unwise to mention it now. Gemma is gone and that's the end of the matter. And what's her secret worth anyway? Every cook thinks they have a secret. 'You can wait in my old office. Follow me.'

They walk together down the corridor.

'So, seeing the bishop, are they?' says Wonder as they pass some alcove saints.

'Yes. Seeing him for a second time, as it happens. I don't know if that is significant.'

'Could be.'

The Jackal is happy that the bishop is put through the wringer again this morning. She has no wish for the wringing to be interrupted. *Wring on!* Until this moment, she hadn't realised how little time she has for the man; or her disdain for his manner towards her. If a patronising attitude could kill, she'd be with Hildegard's ashes in the morgue.

'Very happy to wait,' says Wonder and Patience smiles. 'And you are?'

'As I said, the sub-abbess'

'The sub-abbess, yes.' As with a foreign name or complex travel directions, he repeats in order to remember. 'Sounds a bit like ... '

' ... a naval rank, yes, people do say that.'

They are in Patience's cupboard office, with Patience behind the desk, and the large policeman wedged uncomfortably on a chair too small for his bulk.

'And I'm sure we'll have this all this sorted in no time,' he says by way of something to say. He hadn't been ready for small talk. I mean, what was there to say in a place like this apart from a heartfelt 'Hail Mary!' 'The abbot is here, is he?' He wonders what she thinks of him.

'He is, yes.'

'He must be like a pig in clover, with all these nuns.' And then, in case he is misunderstood, 'I mean their *habits*. I don't mean anything rude. It's just that normally, he's the odd one out, by about a thousand years – but not here, eh? Blends in like a native.' And then he's wondering if that's the wrong word to use. Is it racist? He has a sense it might be, and he's feeling uncomfortable. But the sub-abbess seems unconcerned, her interest elsewhere.

'He does not belong to a religious order, I'm told.'

'The abbot? I wouldn't know. He did once, I think … ' says Wonder, weak on the abbot's personal history.

'But not *now*.'

'Not my bag, I'm afraid. He might do. Who knows where he belongs, frankly?'

'Indeed.' The smile is frosty.

'Bloody good detective, mind, 'scuse my French.'

'We must hope so.'

'I sometimes think he belongs in the desert, really. I'm not sure how obedient he is, though; and I suppose obedience is rather important here. I mean, in a place like this. Obedience, Poverty and Chastity, isn't it? All obedient girls, are we?'

'It is not such an odd idea, Chief Inspector.' This man needs educating and she is happy to oblige.

'But not very 21$^{st}$ century.'

'On the contrary, obedience is everywhere. Everyone is obedient to someone or something – money? Prejudice? Bias? Self-image? Family? Anxiety? The government?'

'Well, I suppose ... '

'In the words of Bob Dylan, "You've gotta serve somebody."' Wonder has heard better American accents; but he won't be saying. 'No doubt you are obedient to your superiors in the police force?'

'Now and then – but not always, mind, not always; very much my own man.' He manages a devil-may-care chuckle. In the presence of this woman, he somehow feels the need to be the maverick cop he has never been. She's right. Obedience had been his chosen way; it's how you get on. 'And poverty?' he asks. 'I mean, you don't exactly go starving here.'

'How do you mean?'

'Sister Rose met me at the gate.'

'I hope she was helpful.'

'Helpful, yes – but I mean she certainly hasn't gone without.' *Pretty face – but she was a size.*

'Poverty, in our order, is not starvation, Chief Inspector. That would be very shallow, would it not?' Her smile is not reassuring. 'No, our poverty is a great deal more challenging – the poverty of non-attachment; of letting go of our attachment to attitudes and possessions. It's poverty of spirit. Blessed are the poor in spirit. Attachments, whatever shape they take, can have a considerable hold over us.'

'Like power, I suppose.' Patience questions him with her eyebrows. 'I mean, you seem to be enjoying it.'

'My present power, as you call it, is not a matter of enjoyment; but a matter of duty. We do need to be free from *all* attachments, Chief Inspector.' Though she feels the emptiness of her words, even as she speaks them.

'And celibacy?' Well, he has to ask because she's an attractive woman underneath her head gear. 'Tricky one, eh, Sister? Your chance to defend the indefensible!' Truth be told, he's quite enjoying the banter. She's a feisty one, this Sister Patience. And she isn't scared.

'Are you celibate today, Chief Inspector?'

'What do you mean?'

'Have you enjoyed or will you enjoy sex with someone today?'

'Today?'

'Or recently? How about this week?'

'That's not the point.' Why did he start this conversation?

'Well, it sort-of is, Chief-Inspector.'

'And none of your business.' This wasn't the intended direction.

'Do you save it for Sundays, some do, later in life – or perhaps Christmas Eve?'

'Should a nun be asking these things?'

'Should a policeman? We all see the news. The uniform seems to attract sexual predators.'

'A few bad apples.'

'An entire orchard, Chief Inspector, many now in prison.' Wonder is fumbling for a reply. 'So, be careful when you mock celibacy. It's not the worst of traits. And, of course, most people, like yourself, are celibate most of the time.'

'I didn't say that I was.' Though he might as well have done; the bedroom department in the marriage, like Debenhams, had closed down a while ago.

'I'm afraid that's my intuition at work. But most people don't have sex most days. Celibacy is not so odd.'

'Seems bloody queer to me!' *Keep fighting, Wonder! Keep going with the heavy artillery!*

'It's the loss of intimacy that is the hardest aspect for me.'

'Oh?'

'That's the greatest loss in celibacy; not to have that *someone*.' How does a policeman answer that? He'd normally give her a hug and say 'There, there' but that isn't going to work here. 'There is a gap, a definite gap in our being, which I believe others must fill. Celibacy must make you more loving towards others or it is nothing.'

'So, you really are a virgin for Christ?'

'It depends what you mean. I once had a secular life. I worked in the city, earned more than you, with a partner who also earned more than you. We enjoyed sex often. I was hungry for it.' *Bloody hell, how had they got to this?* thinks Wonder. 'But then the call comes and what can you do?'

'What did you do?'

'I left him and my bank balance behind.'

Wonder is shocked.

'That's pretty ruthless.'

'Sometimes we have to be ruthless. I've always regarded "*ruthless*" as a compliment, Chief Inspector.' Tamsin knocks, walks in and sees the relief on his face. He is glad to see her apparently.

'You're early,' she says.

'Change of plans, can't stop too long. But the, er ... '

'Sub-abbess'

'The sub-abbess, yes – we've been talking about London, and er, related topics. Any news?'

~

'To be honest,' says Wonder, 'she seemed more bothered about the loss of the cook than the death of Hildegard.'

Back in the snug, with tea and biscuits provided by Sister Agatha, Wonder recounts his time with the sub-abbess, selected highlights, which don't include the Debenhams thing.

'She knows what she wants,' says Tamsin, in a complimentary tone. 'And Hildegard was in the way.'

'In the way of what?'

'Of her becoming abbess. That's obvious, isn't it? She stood in the election but Hildegard beat her.'

'And she still feels sore? Well, it can eat away at you.'

'She pretends great calm on the matter; "*God's will*" and all that. But how well hidden her ambition remained, we don't know. Hildegard referred to her as the Jackal.'

'The Jackal? That's not kind.'

'So, maybe it wasn't that well hidden. Mind you, she also calls Volmar the Worm, Louisa the Snake, Daisy the Darkness and the bishop, the Ego. So, no one's left out.'

'Apart from Richardis,' says the abbot. 'And Michael. But I suppose they weren't in her orbit like the others were. She may not even have known Richardis was here.'

'So it's all up in the air, is it?' says Wonder, who is just hearing names he doesn't know.

'Not at all,' says Tamsin, instinctively. The five continents could be up in the air and in considerable turmoil – and she'd still say, 'Not at all'.

'Sounds like you're half-way to nowhere, Detective Inspector.' He's half-joking but there's also some malice, which he can't always keep in. He's had enough of women this morning.

'Why *did* the cook leave?' asks the abbot, shifting the scenery.

'The cook?'

'You said Sister Patience spoke of the cook leaving.'

'Oh, something about her being disappointing. I wondered if it was the scrambled egg.'

'Well, we know she lost her cottage to Louisa,' says Peter. 'Louisa told me. Maybe good fund-raising trumped bad cooking. And so, Gemma was out, a traveller again, begging for spare rooms in Peacehaven.'

'Which must be the very definition of hard times,' says Tamsin.

The abbot felt for the community in the face of this loss. It had once taken two years to replace a cook in the desert. Brother Bertrand had been the worst cook on the planet; really very poor. Yet better than the monks who filled in for him before a replacement could be found. 'Bad can get worse,' as his step-father would say to Peter. Not a hopeful man; but right on occasion.

'And especially a cook with a *secret*,' says Wonder. Tamsin and the abbot offer quizzical looks in unison. 'She took her secret with her, apparently. That's what the nun said.'

'What secret?'

'Well, I don't know *what* secret. Would hardly be a secret if *I* knew. But the sub-abbess definitely told me the cook had a secret. Surprised you didn't know.' And delighted.

'A buried body in the grounds?'

'A special ingredient, more like, that's the traditional chef's thing, to which they attribute their culinary success.'

'Not something much spoken of here,' says the abbot briskly. Praise for the convent food had been sparse among nun's he'd met.

'My secret's to follow the bloody recipe,' said Wonder. 'But that does rely on me finding my glasses. Could the print be any smaller on food packets?'

'We need to get on,' says Tamsin. The chief inspector is settling in when he needs to be leaving. He shouldn't be here anyway; he's crossing a boundary and over-staying a welcome that wasn't there in the first place. He probably just wanted to see inside a convent; there are weirder bucket-list choices. But he's done that now, had a good nose around and even met a sub-abbess – 'You wouldn't mess with her, matey' – which will keep him in banter and chat for a while. And this, as the abbot observes, 'is really all he needs from life: fuel for banter and chat and a bit of self-promotion.'

'Well, I'm glad my interview with Patience was helpful to you both,' he says getting up. He won't be dismissed without some credit.

'Moderately,' says Tamsin. 'We'll keep you informed.'

'Feels to me like you're struggling.'

'We're not struggling – we're investigating.'

'No suspect.'

'Lack of a fixed suspect at this stage is quite normal.'

'If you say so, Detective Inspector. And enjoy your lunch! God knows what's on the menu today!'

He takes the remaining biscuit and leaves.

Lunch was eaten in silence at the Guest Table in the refectory; and was perfectly acceptable. A thick leek soup, tasting mainly of flour was accompanied by rolls; the abbot took two, and treasured the butter available. This was then followed by rhubarb crumble and custard. The crumble was more evident than the rhubarb; and the crumble comprised mainly of sugar. Tamsin ate hardly anything.

'So, staying positive, plenty of energy for strenuous afternoon activity,' says the abbot.

For him, it was standard fare. He was trained, in his desert years, to eat anything that arrived on his plate. Sometimes it had been best not to ask, particularly with the meat. It was why he became a vegetarian. Less taste; but fewer questions; a more certain provenance. Tamsin's training was different, however. And her mood was not improved by Sister Maria's long reading on temptation from one of the Desert Fathers.

'Spiritual readings at mealtimes are traditional,' explains the abbot. And afterwards, he tells Tamsin he's just off to find the chef.

'And when you do, warn them that a prison sentence awaits.'

'I was actually going to say thank you.'

'Why?'

'I'm told Sister Maria cooked as well as read – so *two* strings to her bow.'

'They call her "No-strings Maria".'

And soon after, the abbot finds No-Strings by the metal kitchen basin where large pans are washed.

'I am not really a cook,' she says.

'I beg to differ!' says Peter. 'I enjoyed it very much. As did my colleague who imagined you were a professional.'

'It's just my week on kitchen duty, even though I ask *not* to be given kitchen duty, because I have never cooked, never in my life, *ever* – we had a housekeeper you see, mummy couldn't cook either. But the sub-abbess says we must all help out, until we can find a new cook.'

'And so sad that the old one had to leave.'

'Grotty. Total swizz, actually. Because cooks are very hard to find, good ones, anyway – mummy always said that: 'If you find a good cook, never tell your neighbour.'

'Otherwise, they'll steal them?'

'They stole Thompson.'

'Your neighbours stole your cook?'

'Offered him more money.'

'Perhaps your cook here was offered more money.'

'I don't think so, I can't imagine that.' She giggles at the idea. 'No, something happened with Gemma – but no one knows what. Just smuggled out the tradesmen's entrance one day and never seen again. So here I am.'

'And doing your best. Was she a good cook?'

'She was better than me,' says Maria. 'But I think that's what they call "faint praise". A bull with a limp would be better than me in the kitchen. And I know I put way too much flour in the soup, so we won't pretend otherwise; but it's a cold day, and I wanted to thicken it.'

'As I say, very tasty.'

'No, it was wallpaper glue, an utter shit-show, but there we are. Now, I better be tottering on. Sister Rowena wants me to drop off the leftovers for the hens.'

*Poor hens.* But Peter has one last question.

'The old cook, Gemma – she had a secret, I'm told.'

'A secret?'

'Someone mentioned it and I just wondered if you knew what it was. I'm always looking to improve in the kitchen.' *Oh, the lies, the lies.*

'Well, I did hear Sister Rose talk about it ... I'm not sure, I wasn't that interested to be honest; and she was a terrible cook anyway, so how valuable was the secret? It couldn't be the secret of her magnificent roast potatoes because they weren't.'

'They can be tricky.' He too has failed with roast potatoes.

'But was it something to do with forty-five seconds? That's what comes to mind.'

'Forty-five seconds?'

'Yes, that just came into my head. Forty-five seconds. But that would be a pretty runny egg, so it can't be that.'

'Maybe it wasn't about eggs.'

'I'm sorry, that may all be absolute nonsense. Daddy told me I was always speaking nonsense. In fact, that was his name for me, "Nonsense". And then it became my family name. They all called me "Nonsense" after that, and thought it very funny.'

'I'm not laughing.'

'Though as I reflect on it all – I haven't seen him for seven years now, which is a lot of prayer and reflection – I tend to think Daddy spoke more nonsense than I did.'

'I think we can be fairly sure of that.'

'And that I'm well away from him.' She smiles. And then eyeing his clothes, she can't resist the question. 'Are you a member of a community, Abbot? Well, you must be! Which one?'

'I'm not a member of a community,' he says. 'Not now.'

'Oh!' Maria is surprised. And it was the surprise that hurt.

~

Michael catches them in the corridor. As ever, he is unaware of the silence which he smashes with his hectoring words. He moves quickly alongside them, just beyond the image of St Cecelia, stooping in pain.

'What did she tell you?' he demands. He's a big man in a small space speaking in harsh tones.

'You need to come in here,' says Peter, indicating Hildegard's study, where Sister Patience now sits. She looks up with displeasure from the large desk.

'I'm sorry, Patience, but we need this space,' says the abbot.

'I'm not sure it's yours to take.'

'We'll make the whole convent a crime scene if you wish,' says Tamsin. 'And you can all go and have a take-away in Stormhaven.'

'Every cloud,' says Patience, with fine comic timing, but the threat does the trick. Patience sweeps out, with dark looks, and returns to her broom cupboard office. Tamsin indicates that Michael should sit down. He doesn't want to sit down; he shakes his head. 'Sit' says Tamsin. He sits but he's not comfortable.

'So, what did she tell you?' he asks.

'What did who tell us?' asks Peter, trying to calm him, though nothing will; certainly not words. You can't still a storm with verse.

'Daisy.'

'We can't tell you what she said, Michael. It's private.'

'She's my sister!'

'We've spoken about this, Michael. She *is* your sister. But she is *not* you.' She offers hand and head gestures to support the words.

'Did she tell you about the summer house?'

'What do you know about the summer house?'

'What do I know?' He laughs. 'I know their plans.'

'Whose plans?'

'She didn't tell you, did she? You're faking it.'

'Didn't tell us what?'

'It wasn't just Volmar you know.' *Volmar?* What had he got to do with the summer house?

'Who else was it?'

'I'll tell you tomorrow maybe.'

'No, tell us today.'

'I can't tell you today. I'll tell you tomorrow.' How could he tell them? He'd never put Daisy at risk; he wouldn't do that. And maybe she would still get her dream. It doesn't matter how long you wait, if you get it in the end. He'd done his best for her, done his best for her dream. He wouldn't throw it away now.

'We could take you to the police station.'

'I don't mind. I like police stations. They're warm.'

'Let's speak tomorrow,' says Peter, smiling. And Michael gets up and walks out.

'Why did you say that?'

'Because he's not desperate enough yet. He still thinks he's in charge.'

~

'And Louisa, thank you so much for the use of the cottage – for our interview with Richardis.'

Tamsin starts brightly, with brisk and polite formalities. But with everyone settled, there is the shared desire – you can feel it – to crack on. None of the assembled enjoys wasted time.

'Not at all,' says Louisa. 'Anything I can do.' She has arrived prompt for her 3.00pm interview in the Tudor snug; one of the few interview rooms in England with two sofas, three alcoves, two virgins and a Norman window from a wine cellar in Kent. Comfort, devotion *and* history. 'You have to wonder where they found that?' she adds, admiring the ancient stonework of the arches. 'They scoured every ruin in England to create this marvellous fake!'

'Then let the truth of our words make up for the architectural lie,' says the abbot with a smile.

'Amen!' says Louisa.

'Richardis seemed very relaxed in your front room,' says Tamsin. 'Wonderful to behold, how a room can feel so safe!'

'I want people to relax there. Especially the homeless.'

'Of course, you do – your virtue is an example to us all. And shame on me, and probably the abbot, but I'd not let the homeless in. They might never leave. Yet Richardis – it was almost as if she lived there.'

'What can I say?'

Tamsin's wondering the same.

'And two toothbrushes in the bathroom.'

'Oh, father's to blame for that!'

'Is he staying?'

'No, no, that wouldn't work – but "Morning Brush" and "Evening Brush" was one of his strange quirks. And it has somehow continued, a family tradition, I suppose. Like soaking sultanas in water overnight, before putting them on his cereal. And I still do it! People live on in our lives, do they not? And sometimes in the strangest of ways.'

Tamsin nods; though no one lives on in her life; there are no traces of anyone; not that she can think of.

'And as with the toothbrush, I'm sure there's a reason for this photo of yourself and Richardis in your front room.' Tamsin holds it up to show her. 'That looks like a picture of two very good friends.'

'And what of it?' Louisa smiles again. 'Richardis is a fine young woman. I'm not sure about friends. That may be pushing it. But huge respect, obviously. And who would not wish to support her? Is care for the homeless now a crime, Detective Inspector? If so, we must close our community food bank immediately. Will you tell them, or shall I?'

'Richardis calls it a relationship.' Louisa is silent. But she's smiling again and the abbot watches the game. When it comes to power struggles, he is learning that smiles are an important weapon in her armoury. They give time to think, those crucial few seconds; they pretend a jovial air, as if all this is a rather comical misunderstanding and all quite unnecessary; and they declare that whatever you have on me, or *imagine* you have on me, it will never be enough ... .because I am power, and you are nothings. 'Truth does struggle to escape from your mouth, Louisa.'

'Have I lied?'

'In your own way, yes. You hold back the truth, which is the same.'

'Maybe you're asking the wrong questions.' She smiles again. 'Because I've done my very best to answer them.'

'We're done with you, Louisa.' Briskly spoken by Tamsin. 'Thank you for your time. But we're done.'

Louisa is unfamiliar with such a dismissal; as though she's been spat out. No one spits her out. No one should try.

'You people do need to get your act together. Sinking at the moment.' She smiles again and leaves.

'When did Richardis admit to that?' asks the abbot.

'To what?'

'To a relationship with Louisa.'

'She hasn't.'

'No, I felt it might be a stretch.'

'Doesn't mean it isn't true.' She waves the photo at him.

'But it does mean we need to speak to Richardis. If Louisa gets there first ... '

'She won't.' Her phone rings. 'Could you leave, Abbot?'

'Your cartoonist?'

'Go and find Richardis.'

~

'It was just an idea,' says Jason, by way of explanation. He is trying to diffuse the silence on the phone.

'But it didn't stay as one.'

'How do you mean?'

'It's become a phone call.' He's lost.

'Well, yes.'

'So, it's not just an idea. If it was just an idea, it would be in your head still and we wouldn't be talking about it and I wouldn't be disturbed in the middle of a case.'

'Yes. Or No.' He's unsure where this is going. 'I mean, you can *say* "no". It was just an idea.'

'Which became a phone call.'

It shouldn't be so hard. 'Let's leave it,' he says and rings off. He hadn't expected the hostility; and hostility is the last thing he wants. Hostility has no place in a relationship; he has no defences against it, which is why it's been so hard to find one he wishes to be part of. The way people behave towards those close to them! Everyone's friend at work and a nightmare at home; as if they can get away with it there. And he's sad, he's very sad – no, he's angry – because he really felt it was otherwise with Tamsin. He felt it was somehow meant to be, them meeting like that at his talk – what were the chances? It was definitely meant to be, if he believed things were meant to be, which he didn't; because that wasn't how the world worked. And clearly it wasn't meant to be, or she wouldn't have been such an awkward cow just now. Had he really thought that thought?

He returned, distracted and unsettled, to drawing the prime minister's arse.

~

'That's two packets of pasta, four tins of tuna, two Bolognese sauce, three packs of cup-a-soup, two tinned steak and kidney pies and a large jar of instant coffee.' Richardis, sleeves rolled up, is packing boxes for the convent foodbank. 'Just lending a hand,' she says as Peter arrives. He wouldn't mind that box himself.

'I need a word,' he says.

'What about?'

'Could we find a quiet spot?'

'This is important work,' says Richardis.

'I'll mind things,' says Sister Rowena.

'Will you be OK, Sister?' asks the abbot.

'If you can look after chickens, you can look after anything. Pasta is reassuringly stationary.'

'And we won't be long, Richardis.' But she's still sulky.

'We need to help the poor!'

'Indeed, and meanwhile, the abbess is dead, burned alive, you may remember; and sadly, the ripples of murder reach even the food bank. There's no sanctuary for anyone until all is made well.'

'I know nothing about all that.'

'About what?'

'About her death.'

'Shall we go outside?'

'It will be fine,' says Sister Rowena who often wonders about the Dead Angel's Society and whether to mention it. It had been notorious. And ghastly. But everyone beats a path to this woman's door and she appears to contribute so much. And people change, sometimes. So, she won't mention it for now.

'Your relationship with Louisa,' says Peter, once they are alone, with only sea and sky for company.

'What of it? There is no relationship.'

'It's important to tell the truth, Richardis. We have spoken with Louisa.'

'What did she say?' She had always told her to say nothing.

'The truth is, you don't always sleep in the tent, do you?'

'I don't know what you mean.' At the age of ten, Richardis had written to her teacher to say that she wished to save the world – and nothing had changed. She still wished to save the world, though this whole business was not helping. Why could it not just go away? She could expect only misunderstanding from the abbot and that nasty detective woman.

'Your toothbrush is in her bathroom and your picture on her sideboard.'

And now Louisa is striding across the lawn to meet them. It has never really worked as a lawn, laid on the sea stones – as if somewhere in the universe there's a law that a convent must feature a lawn. It was always patchy, like a golf club in Egypt; but now it is angry, and carrying a storm towards the abbot.

'Say nothing,' she says to Richardis, taking charge. 'Have you said anything?'

'There's nothing to say,' says Richardis.

'Precisely. Nothing to say. And Abbot, if that stunt back there was designed to delay me – well, it failed. *Pathetic.*'

'What stunt?' He had no idea.

'That idiot sergeant.'

'You'll have to be more specific.'

'He of the cheeky-chappy brigade,' *Bancroft?* 'Asking me to fill out a ridiculous questionnaire in the library.'

'A questionnaire?'

'Who knows where he got that accent from?'

'The west country, I believe.'

'Sounded like he was ill.' *Definitely Bancroft.*

'I can assure you, I know nothing about this ... whatever *this* is.'

'Richardis, I suggest you leave us.' And Richardis is not sad to go, nodding her farewell, for she's not a fan of the firing line. She disappears into the descending gloom, hurrying along the sea path, having, it seems, forgotten about the food bank. The poor must wait. 'And we need to have a chat,' adds Louisa, looking at the abbot with a smile, while the earth spins and transactions in Stormhaven accelerate.

While Tamsin, for instance, is driving into the night, away from the convent, feeling unlike she has ever felt before; and about to *do* something she has never done before. No one need ever know.

While the bishop is standing in the kitchen at home, working out what to say but knowing he needs to respond. The words will need careful crafting; the shit he stands in is deep. Margaret's one-word question hangs in the air: 'Well?'

'It isn't as it appears,' he will say. To which she will reply, 'What isn't as it appears?' And then he will need to tell her.

While Daisy sits in her favourite chair in Denton; it was bought from the cancer charity warehouse, an absolute bargain. But she can't find a comfortable position, everything is pain, emotional or physical; there's no comfort to be found tonight. She's aware the lashing has achieved nothing, neither peace nor joy – a bloody waste of time, quite literally; and, if anything, she's feeling worse than before and fearing the worst, displeased with her actions and her alliances. She has been stupid. Though she is visited now by a new fear; and one which doesn't wish to leave ... a fear that is very close to home.

While Michael, in the room next door, with headphones on, plays his new video game, which is all about strategy. He is no longer a convent gardener but a Mongol commander. He loves their armour, he thinks it's amazing – 'really cool' – and he'd like it for himself. With that armour, he'd be invincible. And he plays on 'Lethal mode', the highest difficulty level, according to the brochure, 'putting an emphasis on the player's timing during combat'. He's playing against some toe rag in Canada, and he will win or he will abort. It is so important that he wins, and he will do anything necessary; or destroy all evidence of defeat.

While Volmar weeps in the summer house, the scene of the crime, and cries to the stars for forgiveness, determined upon confession before anything else; before what must be done, for there is no other way.

While Sister Rowena tidies up in the food bank store. The deliveries have been sent out into the world, food on poor tables, steaming steak pies on a cold night – and all despite the disappearance of Richardis. 'Not a completer, that girl,' as she has previously observed. 'Loves to start, struggles to finish.' While Sister Rowena is a completer, she always completes; though she struggles to complete a 'thank you' to Sister Maria for her help this evening. Rowena hasn't forgotten lunch and no one should make soup that badly. They walk in silence to evening prayer.

While the abbot – buffeted by internal currents of considerable force – walks with Louisa back to her cottage. No, he is *led* by Louisa back to her cottage, wondering if this might be all about the succession. If Hildegard was blocking someone's path, whose path was she blocking? Do convents experience succession battles? Or is that too simple? And why has he never felt himself to be such a fraud as he does today? Like nausea, this thought keeps returning.

While Sister Patience is kneeling in the prayer chapel. It is preparatory prayer, for she is not worthy, 'I am not worthy, Lord.' She is definitely surprised at the request, it came out of the blue; and like Tamsin, she is about to do something she has never done before. It is breaking the rules; the Order does not allow it. But the man is desperate. She'd never seen such pain and confusion in human eyes. It is breaking the rules but surely not a sin? She has most certainly never done this before.

But Louisa has done this before, frequently. She's about to take control.

# 'Let's be absolutely clear'

~

S he says, with them both seated in her front room.

'That's what politicians say as they dive down a rabbit hole of obfuscation.'

'Really ... '

'No, I find it's a remarkably accurate signpost of intention. "Let's be clear" means "Let nothing be clear".'

'So, there is a relationship between myself and Richardis. So what?'

The abbot nods as another truth emerges from the slime of human terror. 'A relationship?'

'I won't be showing you photos, Abbot. I wouldn't want you blushing.'

'I've already seen a photo. I don't remember blushing.'

'And yes, she stays here sometimes.'

'Quite often.'

'Yes, quite often. She wasn't born to live in a tent.'

'Who is – apart from the bedouin?'

'Quite.'

'So why the lies?'

'Because it has nothing to do with anything other than ourselves. There's no crime in closing a door, if there's nothing to see inside. And there *is* nothing to see.'

'And the Community of the Holy Fire are quite happy about this relationship?'

'I refer you to my previous answer.'

'So why not move out and live your happiness together in the open? Why tie yourself down with secrecy and subterfuge? Why not just give a straight answer?'

'Because I care very much for this community. As does Richardis.'

'She cares so much she left it.'

'She left the abbess. She didn't leave the community.'

'She went to London.'

'She never left the community in her heart.'

'Why did she leave the abbess?'

'She has told you why. Hildegard was getting obsessed.'

'A love rival?'

'I think you can cross that off your detective list. I hardly knew Richardis at the time. She only came to see me when she was struggling to know what to do. I said I would help her if she decided to leave and well, things developed from there. Hildegard was no rival.'

'What about the summer house?' It was worth a punt.

'What about the summer house?' As calm as the Greek sea. 'I have very fond memories of the summer house in *Scotland*, if that's what you mean.'

'It isn't.'

'A rather large affair, I should say, including the most comfortable sofa in the world and a grand piano that needed frequent tuning. And plenty of glass, so necessary to catch the little sun that was available. It's where I received my first kiss, Abbot.'

'And the summer house here?'

'The summer house *here*? It's not somewhere I go. Why would I? A rather pokey little dive. Michael probably uses it as a toilet.'

Tamsin is driving towards Lewes and for now, the death of Hildegard is of no consequence; and this is new. What is of consequence is the phone call; the excruciating phone conversation with Jason this afternoon, when she behaved in a way – well, in a way she'd behaved a hundred times before; only this time, somehow it wasn't allowed. *She* didn't allow it; unable, on this occasion, to nod it through as quite justified behaviour. Instead, she declared herself some sort of a criminal, she felt bad, when Tamsin never felt bad, not in that way; guilt had long been a stranger, never once allowed in, it hadn't come close ... until now.

The address is in the sat nav, the instructions are clear – 'In two miles, take the second exit.' She is aiming for Thomas Street, and has tried to ring, but it was engaged, and she's glad, in a way; because this didn't need a phone conversation, with awkward pauses – 'are you still there?' No, it needed something more real, something face-to-face ... with awkward pauses, obviously; but at least you could see them. And it's true, she's never done this before, never apologised to anyone, never wished to apologise, never felt the need to apologise, never feared something lost ... but she does tonight.

She remembers her therapist; not often, but she comes to mind now. Her name was Lorna and they'd only had two sessions before Tamsin declared it a complete waste of time. But as she drives to Lewes now, she remembers Lorna speaking about the crazy self inside, who both saves and destroys.

'Think of the alcoholic, Tamsin.' That was most police officers she had met.

'Just one?'

'The booze is saving them from their pain; but also destroying them.'

'I suppose.'

'The crazy self both saves and destroys. So, what's yours doing?'

'Mine?' That was rude.

'We need to begin negotiations with the crazy self. Its advice can kill us.'

And perhaps that's what this is about. The crazy self is protecting her; and ruining everything. The thought strikes her as she enters the womb of the Cuilfail tunnel, dark and close – a therapist's dream – and then out into the light and a small roundabout. 'Take the second exit', says the sat nav and then suddenly it's here, Thomas Street. It's a left turn, a sharp one, into a small road of two-up, two-downs, cheek-by-jowl. 'A street with character,' the estate agents would say, 'secluded yet central.'

'You have arrived at your destination,' declares the sat nav with enormous pride. She gets out the car and approaches the door of No.18. It is white but peeling and could do with some attention; and maybe she could as well. Is she really beginning negotiations with her crazy self? And more pressingly, what will she say to Jason? And then the despair, which is quite overwhelming; despair her crazy self worked so hard to keep away: 'Don't leave me, Jason! Can we go back to how things were before?'

She gathers herself in the chill night. She has to prepare for the worst. And it may all be too late, 'bridges having been burned'. She says it out loud, sounding like a Latin primer. It was the sort of thing Caesar did. He burned bridges.

'Bridges having been burned,' her creepy old Latin teacher would say – he probably taught Caesar as well. 'It is the past participle form, and used to emphasize that a first action has been completed before the second action begins.'

'Like "bridges having been burned, Caesar marched on Rome," sir?'

'Precisely, Shah. Very well done. See me after class. Shah is an example to you all. '

But Tamsin had been an example to no one in her phone conversation with Jason. Her first action was tragically complete: bridges having been burned. But could the second action save the day?

Peter is tired and only slowly extracts himself from the force field that is Louisa; a force field of reasonableness and calm, though it could be a black hole, destroying everything that comes too close. It is sometimes hard to tell.

He has decided to walk to Splash Point. He needs the exercise, a mile walk there, with the westerly wind behind him, and then the wind in his face on the return, smacking him hard, the sea churlish and disturbed, no friend tonight. 'Never imagine the sea cares,' as a fisherman had told him. 'It couldn't care less.' After three days in a convent, Peter enjoys the lack of concern.

And Richardis for abbess? He had broached the subject with Louisa.

'Oh, we joked about it, of course!' *Of course.* 'I mean, I'm sure she'd be brilliant. She'd sort the place out in no time!' *Really?* 'And infinitely better than Sister Patience.'

'What's wrong with Sister Patience?'

'She likes things as they are. Whereas Richardis ... '

'A more restless soul?' *And not a completer, as Sister Rowena observed.*

'More adventurous, I'd say.'

'She's not actually a nun.'

'Things can change.'

'But not for Daisy apparently. Perhaps you have to be rich for things to change here?'

'As I said to Daisy – "that simply isn't in my power". I know my limits!'

'Yet you discussed Richardis becoming abbess?'

'Don't be afraid of change, Abbot. You sound fearful, but there's no need. It was Cardinal Newman, a hero of mine, who said, "Life is change. And to be perfect is to have changed often."'

'Hildegard was for change. It was you who was against it.'

She pulls back. 'What happened to Hildegard is terrible and tragic. What do you want me to say? It's simply awful! But the story goes on. The bills keep coming, the community keeps praying, the years keep turning, opportunities keep presenting, the story goes on.'

'She's your lover.' He didn't wish to sound prudish, but it perhaps needed a mention. 'Your candidate to be the next abbess. And she's your lover?'

'You sound like a tabloid, Abbot.'

'And you sound like someone not answering the question.'

'Who knows the future, certainly not I! But what isn't seen, isn't known; what isn't known, doesn't harm.'

'Every liar's charter, Louisa and it does sound good; though it doesn't work for cancer.'

~

Volmar thanks the sub-abbess as she carefully lifts her hands from his head. It had been hotter than she expected, pierced with sweat; she feels she must wash her hands, but refrains from wiping them on her apron. He remains kneeling; she remains standing, in a scene of strange intimacy in the prayer chapel. They could not be closer.

'As you know well,' she says, 'we do not call it 'confession' at the Community of the Holy Fire.'

'No, Sister.' She steps away from him, suddenly uncomfortable with their physical closeness, and with the deed now performed. It was not something she was quite ready for.

'We call it the Sacrament of Reconciliation; reconciliation with God and with yourself.' He nods, still staring at the cross on the altar; now freed from Hildegard's terrified grasp. 'May such reconciliation be yours, Volmar, this day and forever.' The Jackal likes the final flourish, 'this day and forever'. But the Worm remains kneeling, as if he needs more.

'Thank you,' he says, and, to Patience, it sounds merely polite, as if something about it all disappoints him. Had her performance been inadequate in some way? This is her first thought. It is always her first thought. She had tried to make it sound as if this was something she did often; as if she frequently heard confessions, and was quite at ease with the process. When in truth, she had never done it before.

But what did that matter? Her first spiritual director, now dead – six-feet-under near Ramsgate – had always encouraged her to try new things and perform them with confidence. 'When conducting liturgy, Patience, whatever it is, you fake it until you make it.' But what did that even mean? And had she made it yet? Or was she still faking? The Sacrament of Reconciliation had been performed; but Volmar did not look reconciled with anything.

Hildegard had occasionally played the role of confessor in the community, some had asked for it; but the unspoken tradition had been for a male to play the part; that only a male, as Jesus' representative, could properly forgive; and this, of course, had been Volmar. It was he who held the secrets of so many in this community, sending sin away with a blessing. Only now, in the prayer chapel, it was different; he was the sinner, Volmar was the supplicant; the confessor had need of confession. And who was there to help but the sub-abbess, Sister Patience?

As for his confession, it had been a little difficult to understand, if she was honest. Something about the summer house, some incident there, 'We sinned, we sinned!' Had he been intimate with a nun? Summer houses did have this reputation; a place for private liaisons. But she couldn't say for sure, she hadn't heard everything; he would often turn away, mumble, whisper or speak into his sleeve. And it didn't feel right to keep asking him to repeat what he'd said; he might get angry and ask if any other confessors were available.

And perhaps incoherence didn't matter. It mattered not that *she* didn't hear as long as God heard. And perhaps the ashamed are deliberately incoherent, fearing clarity above all things, embarrassed by their acts. They wish to name them but do not wish to hear of them; hiding them from themselves, even as they speak.

And presumably God is familiar with this practice and clearly hears the crime; one must hope so.

The absence of light in the windows of No.18 does not bode well for Tamsin. Perhaps he has gone to a pub to get drunk, if that's what rejected cartoonists do. And for God's sake, it wasn't as if he wasn't trained in it. Cartoonists know all about rejection; this she had already learned.

'Nineteen out of twenty ideas are dispatched down the toilet by the editor,' he'd told her.

'Not literally?' she'd asked and then felt embarrassed when he laughed.

'Not literally, no. Mind you, it used to be forty nine ideas out of fifty, when I was younger, so it's progress of sorts. I'm failing better than I used to. Do you ever fail?'

'Not as far as I'm aware.' And he laughed again which unsettled her.

But how was she to know about these things? She knew nothing about the world of the cartoonist. And it was quite possible she was not going to learn anything more. The house was a blank, shadowy and closed.

'Hello,' he says. The door has opened and there he is, standing in the doorway, a dark room behind him, a street light revealing his face.

'I thought you were out,' she says.

# The next day

~

Tamsin is driving along the A27. Radio Sussex is playing the Carpenters.

'I'm on the top of the world,' sings Karen, 'looking down on creation ... '

There's hanging mist across the fields, obscuring the cows, swallowing the sheep; a low sun rising over the downs, autumn chill, glistening dew; the moment the photographers call the 'golden hour'. Tamsin agrees; and for the first time in her life – so many firsts recently – she's singing along with Karen and her perfect voice, which is best simply listened to and admired; one cannot compete. Yet today, perfection be damned! Tamsin has to join in; it feels compulsory, her body and spirit insists. And it's not as if Tamsin can't sing, she can sing well, a husky alto and pitch perfect. But that really doesn't matter, because the call is not for quality, nor even performance; the call is simply to sing and to sing and to sing.

And as she turns onto the A26, full of pleasing bends, there's a feeling of progress at the convent. They are not there yet, obviously. But stories are beginning to crack; alliances starting to crumble. They'd let the questions do their work and all would become plain. It was proving one of the more painless cases; though not for Hildegard obviously. Who can imagine incineration? And Tamsin didn't even try. Hildegard's pain was not her business; her business was the cause of the pain; the one who made it so. And who knows? Perhaps today is the slime ball's last day of freedom.

She turns left onto the A259, which will take her to Tide Mills and the convent. A police car passes, driving unnecessarily fast. Give a traffic cop a blue light ...

She hopes the abbot has got some rest and looks forward to their 8.00am meeting. She's brought a jar of expensive instant coffee to help things along. And events always became clearer when she and the abbot meet. That isn't something the abbot needs to know, obviously. But it is still true. She'll hear how things went with Richardis and where things are with Louisa right now. She's ready for the day.

But then all thought is halted by the chaos in the convent entrance. There are at least four police cars; and high viz everywhere; forensics in white, and a very strained Sister Patience arguing with someone. What on earth is happening?

She parks up, grabs her bag, moves quickly towards the entrance, and for once she's glad to see Bancroft.

'What's happening, Bancroft?'

'You haven't heard, ma'am?'

'Haven't heard what?'

'You need to hear about yesterday evening.'

# Yesterday evening

~

T he abbot is tired. He hopes Tamsin is having a nice time with her cartoonist friend in Lewes. He's sure that's where she has gone, though she said nothing.

And whether there is anything else to be done today, he isn't sure. He will go to his room and sit quietly with the loose ends. Tamsin has suggested an 8.00am meeting tomorrow morning, which will be a good place to start. But for now, he climbs the stairs, solitude drawing him forward with indecent power. It had been a slow learning that nothing could draw him like the gift of being alone. Perhaps Rosemary had once; filling his thoughts for a while. But longing is not the same as commitment, and while Rosemary excited the first, solitude enjoyed the second; and simply to be alone for a moment was all he wanted now.

Like Jesus in the temple, the abbot found the convent rather *busy;* busy with people being purposeful, whether at prayer, or at dinner, or at food packing or with the cover up of murder. And people were work for Peter – as his spiritual director in the desert, Brother Andrew, observed. 'You must understand Peter, that for you, to be in a room with one other person – even if they are asleep – that is work. It may be work you want;

it may be work you love even; but it is work nonetheless, work rather than rest. Rest for you lies in solitude.'

And now rest beckons, as he pushes open his bedroom door; though he's falling immediately to his knees in shock. He isn't alone; Volmar has joined him with a vacant stare, twisted from the struggle for life. He is hanging from a beam, the chair kicked over, taut garden rope eating into his wrenched head and neck, and Peter is up and trying to hold him, to lift him, to save him – but there is nothing left to save; no life to revive. The soul of the Worm has gone; only his body remains, the struggle over and Peter steps back and sits down on the bed.

'Oh my God.' His heart beats hard; his breathing deepens. What to do now? Maybe nothing. Maybe the calling is to sit. It is good to sit with the living; and good to sit with the dead; the communion somehow continues.

'So why here, my friend? Why end it here?' Was he angry with Peter for stealing his room? This was his first mad thought. Or was this Volmar reaching out, Volmar leaving a message? He looks at the limp figure. 'What do you want, Volmar? Partnership or war?' It felt like a request for partnership.

Volmar will have known he'd be found by Peter; and no one forgets such a discovery. Whether the body swings in the garage or the bedroom, for those who find it, the image loiters, long after it is taken down and carried away; it remains forever a disturbed companion in unguarded moments, a visitor of dreams.

But was this murder? The thought strikes him. It was possible, forensics would know. 'But if it looks like a suicide, it probably is a suicide,' a paramedic had told him.

And then the abbot sees the note sitting on the mantlepiece. Is this from Volmar? It hadn't been there earlier; he didn't think so. Peter holds back from picking it up (Bancroft has taught him something) and looks around the room. There is a box of tissues by his bed. He takes one and gingerly lifts the paper, which he assumes he is intended to find. He hopes it won't be the standard suicide note. 'It is better that I do this.' It is a line which always makes him angry. 'Better for whom exactly?' would be his reply.

And then he begins to read:

*'I am so sorry. Let it be on my head. I die guilty of foolishness and rancour; but I die absolved. I would have preferred your absolution, Abbot, I liked your spirit but Sister Patience did her best. There were others in the summer house. Does that matter? I don't know. My path is run and my case is closed – but maybe theirs is not. And who locked the door? I still do not know. It wasn't one of them. I would like you to find out, Peter. Can you do that? And cremated, not buried.'*

No mention of Tamsin; but then he didn't like Tamsin. Did he like any women? He had once liked Hildegard, watched the child become a woman, supported her at every turn; but she had let him down; she had humiliated him. She had cast him as Satan and not noticed the offence; she had just told him 'to snap out of it'. So, he'd given the case to the abbot. He'd wanted Peter to find him in his despair; and then to continue the search – but what was Volmar confessing to?

'You could have been clearer, my friend.' Peter speaks to the body hanging lifeless from the beam. 'You really could. But I'll do my best. And presumably the door you speak of was the prayer chapel door on the night of the killing? Yes? Someone locked it in some way?' He looks to Volmar. 'Hildegard could get in, but she couldn't get out. Was that how it worked? And that, you say, was nothing to do with you. So, what, in God's name, *was* your part in all this?'

Volmar remains silent; absolved, free but silent. He has offered as much help as he can.

~

Within the hour, forensics are busy in white, taking Volmar down and dabbing, scanning, photographing and bagging everything which doesn't move.

'Someone has sat on the bed,' says one of the team, an unrecognisable male beneath a tight hood.

'I sat on the bed,' says Peter, in the doorway. There is quiet exasperation from Tight-hood. 'It's my bedroom.'

'It's a crime scene.' The abbot nods, regretting his attempts at self-justification.

'I'm sorry. Hopefully not too much damage done.'

But Tight-hood is dismissive. 'Forensics is mainly about dust, fluff and fibre, Abbot. I mean, blood's nice – but sadly not always available. The fluff and fibres from your dress are a shit-storm.' Professional sniggers.

'He wasn't murdered.'

'How would you know?'

'Nous.'

'That'll play well in court.' More mirth.

'Doesn't mean it's not true, of course.'

'I prefer the quantifiable myself, reverend.'

'He left a note.'

'Which couldn't, of course, be left by a murderer to deflect attention.'

'It wasn't.'

'But what you were doing spilling yourself everywhere, God only knows. What's the opposite of helping the police with their inquiries?'

'I suppose someone has to discover the body.'

'What?'

'Someone has to walk into the room, all fluff and fibre – otherwise you'd never hear of it.' Tight-hood stops and glares. 'So, discovery tends to be a physical event, that's all I'm saying, rather than an angelic announcement. And if it doesn't involve an angel, dust, fluff and fibre are more likely.'

'Are you laughing at me, monk-face?' Tight-hood is rigid.

'Crying maybe.'

'Fuck off.'

'Bitterness all over the crime scene. Sad day.' The abbot closes the door, raging. 'Probably a cross-dressing paedo,' says Tight-hood and laughter breaks out among forensics.

'I call them "space invaders"!' says Bancroft when he meets the abbot on the stairs.

'Who?'

'Them lot!' he points up towards the suicide room. 'That's how they look to me. Like space invaders! You know, that old video game!'

The abbot doesn't know what he's talking about. 'Sadly, they're from Mother Earth,' he says.

'And everyone's ready, by the way.'

'Oh?'

'Yes, *everyone*. All waiting with extreme interest. It's like before the show starts at the theatre. And you're the star, Abbot!'

'Thank you,' says Peter. He remembers now. He has called for a meeting and Bancroft has made it so. 'You've done a fine job, Bancroft. In every way, you have done a fine job.'

And he has needed him. Peter has been unable to make contact with Tamsin, which is highly unusual. She may be with the cartoonist fellow enjoying cagey conversation in a restaurant – but with the phone off? Since when did a relationship come before work? Since never.

And now for the waiting nuns.

∼

'Thank you for coming,' he says, as if it was his wedding. But the Community of the Holy Fire had been summoned and then harried, Bancroft discovering his inner sheep dog. Sister Patience was not pleased that the chapel should be used in this way again and had made this clear.

'It is not an annexe of the police station, Abbot. It is for the worship of God.'

'All truth worships God, Sister.' Her eyebrows seek explanation. She is used to simpler conversations when it comes to right and wrong. 'All truth, whatever its shape or colour, sings God's praise. It can't help itself. And truth is what we are after here tonight.'

'Very clever, I'm sure.'

'Volmar is dead.

*'Dead?'*

'Yes, he's dead, quite so – and now, we need to inform the community.'

'But ... '

'A great shock, Patience, I know. I am very sorry.'

But Patience and her heaving body can think only of her absolution in the chapel. Did it fail him in some way? Is she to blame for the death of Volmar? She had only done what he asked. And then Michael and Daisy arrive in some disarray, clearly at odds with each other. It was Bancroft who had rung them.

'You need to get down to the convent. There has been an incident.'

'What sort of incident?'

Had Michael taken the call there might have been an argument. Phones make him angry, playing with his weak hand; no lips to read. But he hadn't taken the call because he was still in game mode, still a Mongol warrior, very much his strong hand, empire-building with fury. So, Daisy had spoken to Bancroft – but had been unable to discover more.

'You'll find out when you get here.'

She'd broken into a sweat, wondering if it was about the computer. She'd been waiting for Louisa to confess; perhaps she needed to get in first, if it wasn't too late. But Louisa is here in the meeting and apparently untroubled. She sits next to the bishop, each a study in calm, each ignoring the other; and each choking on the humiliation of being summoned by a man like Bancroft. And then the bishop turns to his neighbour, discreet hand over mouth.

'Are you aware of the purpose of the meeting?' he asks her and she tells him not to worry himself – 'or indeed soil yourself, bishop. Not a good look.'

But he is worrying himself, to be honest. And still wondering how anyone could know of his meeting with Hildegard – the one that never was. Just who was 'the chatty pig'?

He has the greatest respect for Louisa, a powerhouse of a woman; but he does wonder a little sometimes. Or perhaps Volmar was the leak? He looks around but can't see him – just the nuns who sit in their normal seats, each to their own and always the same; because everyone needs certainties in life and a seat in the chapel – one which you know will be yours – is one of them. When a new nun arrives, they do have to learn this.

Meanwhile, the bishop notes the sub-abbess on manoeuvres, moving among her flock, reassuring everyone, telling them that Compline is postponed and that 'there is no cause for panic, really none at all' – though maybe she speaks more to herself than the nuns, who are more excited than anxious.

'Thank you for coming,' says Peter, who has dragged them from the 'Quiet Hour'. The Quiet Hour is time given over to the devout reading of the spiritual classics, as initiated by Hildegard. 'I want you reading Thérèse of Lisieux, Brother Lawrence, Julian of Norwich and so forth! Thomas à Kempis if you must, but none of his self-punishment, please!'

And then the line from Hildegard that no one had expected. 'So, you will all hand over your phones to Sister Patience at 7.00pm, and they can be collected from her office at 10.00am the following morning.'

This was all well and good. But she had not briefed the sub-abbess about this new scheme, and Patience was angry at not being consulted; though hardly surprised. Hildegard did just go ahead and do things without much reference to others. And Patience was obedient in response. Phones were duly dropped in the basket in her office; but not all phones. Not every nun's obedience had extended to losing their phone and now, with the law of diminishing returns, perhaps only six phones would be awaiting collection. No doubt Brother Lawrence still featured in some Quiet Hours; but so did Facebook, TikTok, Instagram and Twitter. She'd heard at least two nuns had Twitter accounts, one called 'Nuntooobvious' and the other 'CrazyConventPerson'. They offered prayers for the world, highlighted little known saints' days and slagged off the government. There was also a rumour that five of the nuns had staged a dance routine in the kitchen – Sister Rowena doing the choreography – which had appeared on TikTok. Sister Maria would later say, 'It was just to show we know how to have fun.'

Should Patience become abbess, if God willed it so, this was a matter she would have to attend to. If you had a rule, it needed to be observed, with no blind eyes turned, no special pleading, no favourites excused. This had been a flaw in Hildegard, her attachment to Richardis. All very awkward and rather embarrassing; but those days were gone. There would be changes in the Community of the Holy Fire; it was getting lazy.

'And I have some very sad news to share with you,' continues Peter, in glorious isolation at the front of the chapel. 'Shocking news, in fact.' All devout reading has been forgotten. They have seen the space invaders and are fully aware of the uniformed presence at the chapel door. 'Volmar, so greatly loved in the community, and its servant for so many years, has been found dead.' There is a communal gasp. The sub-abbess looks particularly troubled.

'How?' asks Sister Maria, the first to regain consciousness.

'Volmar was found hanged.'

'Did he kill himself?' Sister Rowena is matter-of-fact. Her father had killed himself; another inadequate man. 'I don't think he ever recovered from being cast as Satan. He was different after that.' Some around her nod; this was well known.

'And we must hope they are not together now,' says Sister Agatha, with feeling. She causes some shock in the room but everyone knows she never liked Volmar and the role he played. Why bring in a man to take confessions in the convent? 'Gender colonialism has no place in the 21st century. We are actively choosing to perpetuate patriarchal norms of the 17th century.'

'I think we can be quite sure he isn't with Satan now,' says the sub–abbess, who agrees a little with Sister Agatha – the girl has a point – but does not like the image of Volmar in hell.

'This is not the place for speculation,' says the abbot knowing that it was. A closed community is held together by prayer and speculation. 'But he did leave a note; or appears to have done so.' Never in his life had he felt so listened to; never with such intensity of attention, and the brief power made him smile.

'It's a hardly a comic moment,' says the sub-abbess, quiet but firm. Though in a way, it is; for when had the nuns ever been so gripped, so caught in a seventh heaven of excitement? The church has always struggled to make virtue more attractive than sin. And sadly, this hanging was more enthralling than Christmas.

'All I can say presently is that the note mentioned the summer house, which you will be familiar with.' *Let's bring that into play.*

'The summer house' is muttered and murmured round the room. 'So, if anyone has any information' – he pauses to quieten the animated chapel – 'if anyone has any information about *why* Volmar might have been troubled by events there, of whatever sort, please come forward and speak with either me or PC Bancroft. He will be in the interview room and everything will be heard in the strictest confidence. In the meantime, if you need emotional support, don't hesitate to approach Sister Patience here.' The sub-abbess looks surprised and pleased. 'We'll gather tomorrow morning when we hope to know more and have more to share with you. For now, though, we will let the police do their work and I suggest Compline is said, remembering the soul of Volmar, now departed this vale of tears.'

Louisa and the bishop are locked in conversation, the intensity clear; while the abbot also notices the slight frame of Richardis, standing in the shadows, near the door. She is uncomfortable, as if she shouldn't be here; but she should be here, Bancroft having found her crying in her tent.

'If you've got something to tell the abbot ... '

'I've got nothing to tell the abbot.'

And now she disappears, exiting the chapel, before she is noticed, as Daisy approaches Peter. She's well aware of Michael behind her, left standing, watching and deeply disturbed.

'We need to talk,' she says. 'I'll talk to you now, if you want. Right now. We need to bloody talk.' She's pushy but, mainly, she wants to cry because this isn't how things should be.

'What are we talking about?'

'Well, it ain't the bloody weather.' The abbot waits as the chapel empties, though Michael remains, holding the back of a seat, rocking forward and back, forward and back . 'A confession, if you like. We're talking about a confession, all right?'

'Let's meet in ten minutes, in the kitchen.' The kitchen would be quiet. Daisy nods and walks away and the abbot indicates to Bancroft that he needs a word. Bancroft is talking with Sister Maria who is saying that Volmar would never kill himself, how his theology would never allow it. This throws Bancroft, because he isn't absolutely sure what theology is – is it like archaeology? But he feels that whatever it is, it can hardly be important. When you are desperate, you are desperate ... 'ologies' don't count for much then.

'We'll know more soon, Sister Marcia.' Bancroft speaks kindly and he quite fancies her as it goes, the unobtainable dream. 'We'll not sleep better for guessing.' But Marcia will not sleep anyway because she loved Volmar ... from a distance.

'Bancroft, I need you to find DI Shah.'

'Any clues?' *Clues?*

'Start with Hove. Then expand the search – ports, airports, hairdressers. Sorry, I have no idea.' He really didn't know what she did with her time. She never told him and he hadn't asked. 'Possibly Lewes. She may have a man there, a cartoonist. Try restaurants, expensive ones.'

'A cartoonist?'

'And wherever she is, she's never far from her phone. She needs to be *here*, though.' Peter liked their partnership. They were like tag-wrestlers; and presently, he had no one to tag and the fight was about to get rougher.

'I'll do my best, Abbot.' Bancroft is delighted. He enjoys a problem to solve. Though another thought occurs. 'Or perhaps you and I will solve it, Abbot.' He offers a conspiratorial wink. 'Perhaps we'll solve it!'

Peter smiles. 'Perhaps we will, Bancroft; but we will need the luck of the lottery winner and the calm of a mill pond. We'll stay calm, Bancroft. And calm will carry us home.'

'Calm as custard, Abbot!'

~

And now Michael is in his face again, with urgency.

'I have information, Abbot.' He looks around.

'What about?'

'The summer house.'

Peter ushers him out of the cloister and into the small chapel vestry, where robes and candles are stored.

'Do you know what happened there?'

'It was Volmar, Louisa and the bishop. I saw them.'

'You saw them doing what?'

'They were talking.'

'It isn't a crime.'

'About Hildegard. They were talking about Hildegard. Not nice things.'

'How do you know?'

'Read my lips,' he says. It's a joke. 'Because I can read yours.'

'You read their lips in the summer house?'

'Not everything. But enough.'

'And you're telling me now because ... ?'

'Volmar. I mean, why do you think he's done that?'

'Quite. I mean, are you saying they planned to kill her? You're saying Volmar killed her?'

'I'm not saying anything. I'm just saying what I saw. And now Volmar's dead ... '

'Yes?'

'Which makes you think, perhaps he couldn't handle it.'

'Couldn't handle what?'

'The consequences.'

'Volmar got drunk that night, didn't he?' This quiet and unobtrusive fact suddenly seems more interesting.

'He did, yes. Too much wine.'

'And not a drinker, I'm told.'

Simon Parke

'Explains everything. Couldn't handle it, like I said – if you listened.'

'Well, thank you, Michael. Thank you. A lip reader is a dangerous man in a community with secrets. You must be careful.' And Michael snorts which could be agreement or derision. He's a big man in a world of women. Maybe he thinks he doesn't need to care.

He certainly knows he needs to speak with Daisy. He needs to know what she said to the abbot.

～

Daisy hasn't arrived and should have done so by now.

Peter is waiting in the kitchen and the Darkness is ten minutes late, which is strange because she'd been keen to meet. She said she had a confession to make; they'd agreed on the kitchen, with the smell of cabbage strong in the air. Everything is washed and put away; but the smell of cooked cabbage remains and probably will do after the apocalypse, the single legacy of human residence of planet earth. Not perhaps the highpoint of civilisation, thinks the abbot, nor even the strongest smell; but the most durable, the most resilient – and the abbot must draw on its stamina. The luck of the lottery winner; the calm of the mill pond – and the stamina of cabbage. There's a self-help book in there somewhere.

But these remain dangerous times and he's wasting moments here; it feels so. He'll give it another five minutes.

～

And Richardis also waits, having knocked on Louisa's front door.

She could let herself in, she has a key; but she is frightened by events and wonders who is watching – she has seen police around. She has done nothing which anyone could call a crime, that's what Louisa had said; she called it all 'so much piffle and nonsense'. And now Richardis just wants to hear it again, to

196

be told it will all blow over and another future will emerge, a better one. She just wants Louisa to look after her, because Louisa is indestructible, she's her rock. How could Hildegard call this woman the Snake? Louisa believes in her ... and that makes all the difference.

~

While the Jackal believes in order; in the maintenance of good order and in rules that are conducive to that. This is what true leadership brings to the community. Hildegard had not brought order; she had brought force – the force of her personality. This imposed something that looked like order, but was more a cowering and an anxiety. One always wondered what would happen next. So, life was never dull, for who knew the direction of things from day-to-day? No one – because it all depended on Hildegard; and this wasn't order. Order was quiet and consistent; it had no favourites and didn't change its mind and mood. People knew where they were with order; and in this sense, Hildegard's death was helpful. People had to understand that.

~

And, having spoken with her brother, Daisy is drifting, half-awake; though she can't be sure. She may be asleep. The floor is hard, stone-hard; she knows that. And she can see the familiar face – the face of the *The Scream*, the only picture on her bedroom wall since the age of fourteen.

'She's a weird one,' as her father said and she feels the 'gust of melancholy' now, it is inside her; it always has been inside her, life lived through this face on the bridge, a stranger to joy; a companion of despair.

Munch never married, never had children; he never really left his studio. And Daisy identifies with all of that – if you swapped 'studio' for 'convent'. No one understood her, like they never understood Munch. Reaction to his painting had been hostile. In a public debate, an art student called him a 'madman' to his face, which hurt him deeply; he often referred to it in his letters. And so, a year or two later, as infra-red inspection reveals, he wrote eight words in the top left-hand corner of the painting: 'Can only have been painted by a madman'.

And Daisy knew why. Daisy knew exactly why he wrote it. He was taking back control. He took the abuse and made it part of his work; it is part of him.

And Daisy too had been trying to take back control. She'd tried.

But stone is cold and it was Michael who did this. Or was she imagining that? She'd been taking back control after years of drift. Taking back control with Louisa as a friend, or rather, an ally. She had helped Louisa, or tried to; because Louisa would give her back control, allow her to be who she wanted to be. But what was happening now? Her mind is a fog and the stone is hard, and she's tied in some manner, with tape over her mouth.

It is Michael standing in the doorway.

'What are you doing here, Abbot?'

'I'm meeting someone.'

'A secret meeting?'

'Not for those invited. But you will need to leave.' Michael shows no signs of leaving. 'It's confidential. You can't be here when they arrive.'

Pause. Michael looks hard at Peter. 'They're not going to arrive.'

'How do you know?'

'Daisy found something better to do.' How does Michael know who he's meeting?

'That sounds unlikely. She was keen to meet.'

'I know. She told me just now.'

'What did she tell you?'

'How she was going to confess. So, I've come in her place, Abbot. She agreed it was for the best.'

'Best for who? I'd like to know where Daisy is, Michael.'

The abbot needs to get to the door. He's trapped. And Michael follows his eyes.

'I'm afraid I am the door, Abbot. I am the door and the door is closed, you're not going anywhere.'

'Let me through, Michael.' He stands up.

'It's me who needs to confess, Abbot, not Daisy.'

'And what do you need to confess? I hope it won't be to wasting my time.'

'I'm afraid your time is up.' Such sudden movement towards the abbot, hands across his nose and mouth, the cloth of chloroform, Peter wrestling, he knows the smell, but the sheer force of the hold, he cannot compete, the gardener's strength, and he's going, he feels himself going with mad eyes looking down at him. 'I confess to poor judgement and violent assault.' The abbot feels the spittle on his face, and then ...

Michael lifts the abbot onto his shoulders.

∼

'Hello,' says Jason.

'I thought you were out,' says Tamsin. 'No lights on.'

'I'm just the prince of darkness.' It's a cold joke; Tamsin doesn't feel the warmth as she stands outside No.18 Thomas Street in silence, no script available in her psyche. 'Do you want to come in?' Does she want to go in? Nothing is obvious.

'I was just passing.' She doesn't move forward. She doesn't know what to do.

'The thing is, Tamsin – and cutting to the chase, and all that – I don't want a high maintenance relationship.' He speaks in a matter-of-fact way; but he might as well have shouted. *High maintenance?*

'And you're so perfect?' The return of fire is instant.

'If attack is all you've got, Tamsin, perhaps you need to see a therapist. Attack is no help here.'

'Or perhaps I'll save money and just go home to my fantastic flat in Hove and continue to enjoy life alone without the judgements of crayon man.'

'"Crayon man?"' Jason starts laughing. It is good he has discovered early that Tamsin is just another damaged little girl, pretending to be free. This will save him later pain – pain he knows well; and which he has no desire to return to. His previous relationship, which he'd been too lazy to end, involved maintenance costs of the emotional variety and left him bankrupt of both energy and joy ... .though it's a shame, a massive shame, that this is how it ends. Tamsin made him laugh, she was smart and with looks that were way out of his league. 'Trust your instincts,' he says, to the figure in the road. 'Whatever your instinct says right now, Tamsin, do it.'

And it sounds like a good idea, trust her instincts, and she turns round and gets into her car because she can't live this moment, it's annihilation; and she won't beg, and she won't plead, like some loser – because she isn't a loser, she's in control. And control is not being vulnerable, control is getting in her car, and driving away from the tin-pot town of Lewes, which thinks way too much of itself, like certain of its residents.

Bancroft can't find the abbot, and he's looked everywhere; though he hasn't quite looked everywhere, because he hasn't thought of the prayer chapel. It is the one place unvisited, because this really isn't the time for prayer; and knowing the abbot, he'll be doing something more practical than gabbing away to a god who doesn't exist, no offence – and the abbot must know that, surely?

Bancroft has never thought of the world as kind. It is more of an assault course, a place to be negotiated with extreme care. The world for Bancroft is a lot of struggle and only occasional elation ... *very* occasional.

So, he managed it as best he could, controlled what he could control which wasn't very much, and tried to be kind, because kindness doesn't cost anything, and it does make life better. Cynicism was his more natural home; a strong belief, when the accounts are drawn up, in the ultimate value of nothing. But cynicism unplugged makes the present day worse, as he'd discovered with that little breakdown episode. And he didn't want to go back there, so kindness must rule.

'I'm looking for the abbot,' says Bancroft, reduced to knocking on the bedroom door of the sub-abbess. He imagined they all slept in a dormitory, like in the films, and perhaps the others do – he wouldn't be checking. But here is Sister Patience in her night gown – and something underneath. They almost look like jeans, but that can hardly be. And she looks somehow different, younger, female; and it's all a bit embarrassing, no question about that. But it's only 9.30pm, so hardly the witching hour.

'Constable, you should not be on the premises. Let alone at my door.' She finds this careless male presence insufferable. It feels like violation; standing here at her door with neither apology nor shame.

'It's not my choice, sister, but there was a death here tonight.'

'And we've had deaths before, constable; we do not fear death.' Does he really imagine death to be such a big thing? 'Death is baked into life's cake.'

'But two deaths in forty-eight hours ... '

'What do you want?'

'I'm looking for the abbot.'

'Well, he's *not here.*'

'No, I didn't think ... ' He can't help smiling.

'I have no idea where the abbot is. Probably in bed in Volmar's old room.'

'Which he'd be sharing with the forensics team.'

'They're still around?'

'They've barely started.' And the Jackal doesn't reply; she simply stands in the doorway, for what is there to say? And Bancroft can see, just for a moment, how intrusive he might appear. He'd imagined himself a friend of the convent, but can see how he might be the foe – just another big-booted policeman trampling on the sensitivities of others. 'I'll leave you to your, well, whatever, sister.' Are they jeans? 'Sorry for bothering you. But if you do see the abbot ... '

'I won't. Sleep well, constable.' And she firmly shuts the door. One just needs to keep calm, she tells herself. The policemen will soon be gone and order restored ... holy order.

And he didn't notice her jeans. He was too all over the place. But perhaps he did? He did seem to find something rather funny. Perhaps he is telling everyone now. Oh God, this has got to end! This had really got to end.

The sofa had belonged to the bishop's parents and possessed sentimental value. He probably felt more for the sofa than he did for them. It had been their last purchase, before the care homes had taken them in; life's epilogue, which did not include personal furniture. It needed replacing now, of course; it was looking scruffy. But there were other priorities. Margaret wanted a conservatory, if permission was granted by the church commissioners. It didn't seem much to ask but the church could be utter bastards over the homes they owned; more hoops than a hoop-la. They had had to apply for a 'special housing measure'; but really, there wasn't a great deal of hope. Not their gaffe – so not their rules.

But the sofa would do Stephen for tonight. It would save waking Margaret, who would only have more questions, which Stephen couldn't answer. Well, he *could* answer them, and kept trying; but he was aware his defence changed every time. He had started by knowing nothing about the whole wretched affair. He then moved to some vagueness of memory; he couldn't remember exactly who had said what to whom and when. After that, it all became an unfortunate misunderstanding. And where had he got to now with the story? Would he finally admit to a minor misjudgement on his part – 'one anyone could make, surely?' – but which he now regretted? That would be his line.

He regrets the incident though believed it to be quite harmless at the time. Establish intention. Now *he* was becoming a lawyer! His memory was mistaken – but he intended no harm. A little slap on the wrists but integrity maintained. He could do it.

And now Margaret is standing in the doorway. She switches the light on. The bishop is in his vest and underpants. It is vest weather.

'What are you doing?'

'I just didn't want to wake you, dear. I know you're busy at the moment. I didn't want you falling asleep in court tomorrow!'

'What's going on, Stephen?'

'Volmar – you know Volmar, you met him at the convent. The odd one.'

'Which odd one? There were so many. The sane would be a shorter list.'

'He was the male one.'

'I know Volmar.' A gentle man; repressed but gentle. You always felt that if things got nasty, his anger could do all sorts of damage – but gentle in the meantime.

'He killed himself this evening.'

'He *what?*' Another death at the convent? Margaret is shocked.

' Well, he *probably* killed himself. We can't be sure yet.'

'"*We?*"'

'Well, the police ... the abbot.'

'Someone else you don't like.'

'We don't always see eye-to-eye, but a perfectly decent ... '

'I told you, you didn't like him. And the bodies are adding up at the convent.' The bishop shrugs. 'Did he leave a note?'

'He may have done.' He couldn't leave it there, though he wanted to. 'I think so, yes.'

'You *think* so?' Oh, the barrister is working late today! 'So *did* he leave a note or didn't he?'

'He did, yes.'

'And why was that so hard? The note seems to be making you uncomfortable. Should it be making me uncomfortable?' If he was a witness in court, she would tear him to merry shreds; but he was her husband of twenty something years. 'I'll give you one chance, Stephen – one chance to tell me what you've done. *One chance.*'

And when he had finished, he sat quietly on the sofa, the evening chill but he was somehow hot in his vest and underpants, as if over-dressed. Though maybe the sweat was the sweet sweat of relief, for this was his strongest feeling … more than shame, relief.

'I did it on behalf of the church.'

'You did it on behalf of your ego, Stephen. And on behalf of your pathetic infatuation with Louisa.'

The Snake hugs Richardis. She found her standing hunched at the door, and so thin, like a waif in a Dickens tale; and somehow reduced in size by fear. She'd looked up into Louisa's eyes and said, 'I'm frightened,' which was rather touching; and useful, in a way.

'There's nothing to be frightened about,' she says and holds the waif in the salty darkness. And she remembers when she held her little sister, in exactly the same way, a place of reassurance in a stately home, some way from stately. 'A fine place to behold; but not to live in, not if you were small.' And she'd been Lydia's protection; she'd had to take control. She'd always taken control.

'I shouldn't have done it,' says Richardis.

'You meant no harm.'

'You said it was a joke.'

'Life is a joke!'

'Death isn't a joke.'

'You were just doing the cleaner a favour.'

'The cleaner?'

'No muddy footprints while it was wet.'

'But there wasn't any cleaner. Hildegard was in there.'

'Tragic, I know; absolutely tragic. Who could have known?'

'She thought I was Bishop Stephen, I think.'

'It doesn't matter now. *Really.* It doesn't matter. What matters is that we sort out your future.'

'She called out his name. She thought I was Bishop Stephen. There were no cleaners.'

Louisa is becoming impatient. She has no time for scrutiny; nobody had that right. 'Richardis, you're all over the place.' She gives her a silly-old-thing smile. 'Come inside and let me make you a cup of hot chocolate.' It will include a sleeping tablet to help the girl rest. 'It will all look better in the morning, believe me. Remember Gloria Gaynor's advice.'

'Who?'

'"I will survive". You know it.' She starts to sing.

*"Oh no, not I, I will survive*
*As long as I know how to love … "*

Richardis begins to smile, swept along by the woman's bravado. Louisa really is indestructible.

'And we won't mention the chapel door, because it just isn't important to anyone, dearest. It's a distraction, in a way; and the police don't need those right now, not when there's a killer on the loose.' Richardis nods. It makes sense as the chocolate soothes and the warmth of the cottage envelops her. 'And how *wonderful* – how simply wonderful! – if you were to become abbess of this convent, eh? Imagine it!'

Tamsin is driving out of Lewes, following her instinct and feeling a fool. What *was* she thinking when she went round there? She didn't want a relationship, so why was she pretending she did? A relationship was the last thing she wanted, particularly with some airy-fairy cartoonist. And what did they actually do? Glorified joke writers of the Christmas cracker variety … hardly a proper job. And as she accelerated into the darkness, she was suddenly suspicious of Kate, whose idea it all was. It was like it had all been managed between her and Jason; and she'd believed it. She'd have words with her.

She approached the roundabout, first exit back to the historic town of Lewes – *boo!* And the third exit to Brighton and then Hove and safety at last – *hooray!* It wasn't a difficult choice.

She took the first exit.

~

Peter is looking up into the big eyes of Daisy; eyes made bigger by fear.

She pulls back when he wakes. She'd been saying 'wake up' for a while, gently patting his face with her bound hands. But through the tape, the 'wake up' was just a noise, Neanderthal grunts, as was his 'I am awake!' They needed to speak, to understand – somehow, anyhow.

Peter is up on his feet, with difficulty; bound hands make it harder to balance. Daisy helps him and he helps her. He tries the prayer chapel door, finds it locked and immediately, he knows – he knows what is coming. He can't see it but he knows – like those who hear the wave before the tsunami comes into view. They have to get out. They really do have to get out. The prayer chapel will soon be an oven, courtesy of Michael. He wasn't a man to cross.

And it was the cross that saved them; or at least gave hope, enabling them to remove their gags. 'The good news is we can now die screaming,' says Daisy.

The cross appeared to grow out of the stone altar, not separate but part of the whole and therefore strong and secure to rip off the face masks, inch by painful inch, cutting throat and chin. There was blood on his face and blood on the cross as Peter used its hard edges to rip the tape from his mouth.

'You've just got to do it,' he said, with appalling pain in his jaw. He had knocked a tooth. 'We need to talk.'

And Daisy was straight in there, kneeling on the altar – there's a first time for everything. She was quicker than the abbot, less careful of the damage done; bloody but smiling.

'It bloody hurts!' she said, with pain and delight.
'The door is locked. Is this how he killed Hildegard?'
'He didn't kill Hildegard.'
'So, why's he doing this? Did he kill Volmar?'
'No, that wasn't him either.'
'So why? Why this? Daisy ... '
'Is the floor getting warm?'

~

The bonfire was only slowly noticed by the community; though not by Richardis, who was in a deep sleep at Louisa's, led upstairs and laid down on her bed fully-clothed.

'I feel so tired,' she'd said and Louisa had said, 'That's because you are, Richardis; it's been that sort of a day. So up the stairs to Sleepy Town for a nice long rest. Does that sound good?'

'It does sound good.'

And with Richardis settled, Louisa sees the fire as she stands in her kitchen, looking into the night and seeing a flicker in the dark. Stepping out of her front door, she watches the blaze strengthening, at about the same time as Sister Patience opens her curtain. She is woken not by the light, but by the sound; the crackle and exploding matter. Who on earth is lighting a fire at this time of night? Well, it can only be Michael, as if there isn't already enough disorder here. You can't tell that man anything. He makes his own rules, and that simply isn't going to work here. She needs to talk with him; but this is hardly the moment and she returns to bed though how can she sleep? She is angry. She feels out of control, a rudderless boat in a strong current; as if everything is conspiring against her, when all she wants is what is best for the convent. No one can say otherwise.

And then, from somewhere outside comes the strangest noise, maybe an animal, but it could be a man, a cry to the sky, or a woman, hard to say, a wailing; haunting the night with their pain.

There's a knock on the door which is the last thing she needs. What's happening out there?

'Who is it?' she asks, sitting up.

'It's Bancroft again, Miss – I mean, Sister.'

She's out of bed, putting on her dressing gown again. She opens the door to find the constable subservient but determined.

'Yes?'

'You need to come down, Sister. You need to speak with Michael.'

'And why do I need to speak with Michael?'

'He's whipping himself by the fire.'

It is getting hot in the prayer chapel. The fire is passing the heat through the stone efficiently, just as the architect planned. He just didn't plan for the bonfire; and two people trapped inside. Perhaps he should have thought.

'Forgive me,' says Peter removing his habit. It leaves him in an old rugby shirt, boxer shorts and socks. 'And I hope this is not your final sight on earth.' He lays the habit on the stone floor. 'We can stand on it. We'll need to. It may give us time, until the cavalry ... '

'What cavalry?' Daisy is removing her overcoat; a further carpet. 'I'm told they were always too bloody late.'

'They're out there somewhere. We have to believe.'

'I don't believe. We're going to die.'

'We may die. But we don't give up.'

'I'm scared.' Daisy is crying and they hug in the heat.

'We must try and stay alive.'

'What chance of that?'

'Are you up for staying alive, Daisy?' The abbot almost shouts.

'Of course, but ... '

'I'm up for staying alive, one more day at least; and I want you to stay alive because your life is hardly begun.'

'I deserve to die.'

'No, you don't.'

'Yes, I bloody do.'

'No, you bloody don't.'

'Louisa asked me to take Hildegard's computer from her office.'

'I know.'

'You know?'

'Of course, I know.'

'She runs this place. Money talks.'

'She wanted the emails on the laptop.'

'She didn't tell me why. Just that she needed it on secret convent business. Should have guessed – never trust a posh bitch.'

'The emails were embarrassing for her, with all the Green Chapel stuff. While you, Daisy – you simply wanted to become a nun?'

'I really do deserve to die.'

'You deserve to live.' She shakes her head.

'It was Michael who gave Volmar the sleepy pill – on the night of the fire.'

'When he got drunk?'

'He wasn't drunk, he was sedated.'

'And why did Michael do that?'

'Because he heard them, didn't he? He heard their little threesome in the summer house. Well, he didn't *hear* them – he saw them, read their lips.'

'And that's what you were going to tell me tonight?'

'I wanted him to be free. It's getting hot.'

'I know.' His feet were burning.

'But he'd never be free until the truth was out. And nor would I. And now I'm thinking of bloody Gemma, don't know why!'

'Which Gemma?'

'Gemma the crap cook, from the Wormwood Scrubs School of catering. She had this secret.'

'I know.'

'We're going to die, aren't we?'

'What *was* the secret?'

'It doesn't matter. I can feel it coming. We'll be pigs on a spit.'

'Did she tell you, Daisy? Did she tell you the secret? Listen to me!' He is shaking her.

'OK, OK! Whenever it went pear-shaped in the kitchen, which must have been always, she said she could get to the prayer chapel, say three 'Hail Marys' at the altar, and be back in the kitchen, all within forty-five seconds.'

'That's it? That's the secret?'

'Yes.'

*Such disappointment.* 'Well, it can't be true. It can't be true.'

'Why not?'

'Why not? It's at least a minute walk from the kitchen to here. Could be more. That's two minutes without any hailing. Impossible.'

'It's what she said. Forty-five seconds.'

'It's impossible.' He's angry at the false hope.

'She was teasing, the old cow.'

'The secret can't help us, Daisy.' He says this to himself more than her. 'I don't know why, I thought it might, but – OK, so, we think again.'

'I sort-of knew it. She was full of it, Gemma was; absolutely full of it. Forty-five seconds to boil an egg more like.'

They sweat heavily and the habit beneath their feet is warming. It would soon ignite and there'd be no place to hide and Daisy would meet *The Scream*. And Peter is remembering; he remembers his words to Bancroft. *The luck of the lottery winner and the calm of a millpond.* He'd settle for any sort of pond right now; water to plunge into, any water. And as for the luck of a lottery winner ...

'What if Gemma was telling the truth?' says Peter.

~

Tamsin is back in the Cuilfail tunnel and ignoring her self; because her self wants to be back on the road to Hove, back to safety and away from this mad act of self-harm; away from doing something she has never done – and what will she say to him anyway? Let's imagine for a moment. Something like, 'I'm an idiot, Jason – will you let me in?' to which the only reasonable reply would be, 'You are an idiot, Tamsin, more than you know, and so *no*, I *can't* let you in. Why would I let you in? But do give my regards to your fantastic life in Hove.'

She's at the roundabout, the same roundabout as before; and she can't drive down the same road again, it's embarrassing. So, she takes a left and then a right, drives up towards the large Tesco's, and in the moonlight, finds a quiet spot on the industrial estate, where nothing industrial is happening right now; and she won't be long, after all.

From here, it is a short walk to Jason's front door, and after a moment of hesitation, she knocks. Again, out of the darkness, Jason appears.

'You again?' He looks tired, he may have cried, she can't tell. He has a coffee in his hand and half a digestive in the other. 'Wasn't expecting this.'

'Nor was I. And look, I'm an idiot but will you let me in anyway?'

'Have you got a warrant?'

~

'What the hell are you doing?' shouts Bancroft as he strides towards the bare-chested Michael, who is walking round the fire practising the ancient art of flagellation and shouting 'I am not worthy!' He doesn't care who knows. And he can neither hear nor see Bancroft.

'What are you doing, Michael?!' Bancroft is stunned by the raw passion in the fire light; never seen anything like it, though there was that farmer in Dorchester who did weird things on his land. 'Come away from the fire now ... *now!* – and put the bloody whip down!' Michael stares into the dark, he can't locate the sound.

'Unworthy, unworthy!'

'You're as worthy as anyone, mate!'

Bancroft realises he cannot be understood and steps into the light. 'You need to put the whip down and come over here.' He's a big man, Michael. You wouldn't pick a fight with him and Bancroft has to shield himself from the heat. 'You're as worthy as anyone, yes? You understand? Worthy as anyone!'

'It's too late!' he says.

'It's never too late!' Bancroft speaks with his hands as well; the body, his new tongue.

'Believe me, policeman, it is too late. You don't know. You know nothing.'

'Sister Patience will look after you, Michael. We can talk in the morning with the abbot.'

'No, we won't.'

'Come on, Michael,' says Patience, who emerges from the shadows. She fears he'll throw himself on the fire, which would be awful publicity, and under her watch. She grabs his sweaty arm. It slides from her grip and she tries again, as in the dancing light of the fire, his bloody back is revealed. They'd need a cover for the chair, if he sat down anywhere; she's thinking this as they walk. He is suddenly compliant, like a beaten dog. Perhaps the kitchen would be best for now. It's familiar with blood. 'It's going to be all right,' she says firmly, because it would have to be. It would have to be all right; the sub-abbess will not allow another possibility. Though Michael knows otherwise, for he has killed the thing dearest to him and nothing matters now. 'We're going to find you a room for the night. Have you seen Daisy anywhere?'

He starts to quiver but doesn't answer. Patience wonders if he doesn't understand. 'We don't think Daisy is here, Michael, so she has probably gone home. Would you like to go home? We can arrange that.' She's looking to Bancroft for back-up. A police car would be very helpful. It would save messing up a chair – but Michael is saying nothing. Whatever troubles him - and he seems in a trance – has left him very disturbed, she has never seen him like this. She has never seen anyone like this. 'We'll sort out a hot drink. There's a kettle ... '

'We go to the prayer chapel – *now!* We go there.''

'You want to pray?'

'Take me to the prayer chapel!' He looks into her eyes. She cannot turn him down. He is a frightened bull, all power and sadness. 'And bring the policeman.'

'I thought you handled that marvellously, Constable.' Louisa has been watching events and now moves in. 'Heaven knows what he was up to, but he has always been quite mad, of course.' Bancroft doesn't like posh people. Apologies and all that, but he really doesn't. They always arrive like they're in charge; like they have a right to be there, like their opinion is the most valuable opinion on earth – even if it's a piece of shit.

'I was always told there was mad, bad or sad, madam. Perhaps he's just sad.'

'Or perhaps he's just bad, Constable.'

She remains troubled by Michael's remark to her at the gathering in the chapel. Well, it was to her and the bishop.

'I see you,' he'd said to them, to which she'd replied, 'And I see you, Michael, even if I don't wish to.' And he'd just stared and walked away; and while Stephen and she had exchanged amused looks, the incident stayed with her. She had thought it through, before the wretched Richardis arrived. Volmar had told no one about the summer house; otherwise, why mention it in the suicide note? This was his big reveal. If he'd already spoken about it, why bother? Yet the police had an interest in the summer house before then. So, who told them? It wasn't Volmar; it wasn't her and the bishop was way too comprised of fear for him to be the whistle-blower. So, who? And then there was Michael standing in front of them, saying 'I see you' – words which, spoken by a deaf man, contain an extra layer of danger. She needed Michael to be bad; ideally, mad and bad. It would also be helpful if he were a sexual predator. It is a light-bulb moment. Yes, that could be advantageous. And perhaps Richardis can help with that. She can make herself useful at last.

~

'Tamsin, do you read poetry?' asks Jason, still in the doorway.

'Why would I read poetry?' She is genuinely mystified. She hasn't driven back here for an English lesson.

'There's a man, he's American, called Robert Frost.'

'I'm not warm myself.' She isn't dressed for this.

'He wrote a poem called "The death of a hired man".'

*Why is he telling me this?* 'I appear to have missed it,' she says. 'I can't think why.' Jason remains in the doorway. Should she go back to the car? Most of her wishes to. 'Is it relevant – the poem?'

Jason is now laughing. 'Relevant to the investigation?! Is that what you mean? And, well – maybe ... relevant to *my* investigation. The poem includes the line, "Home is the place where, when you have to go there, they have to let you in."'

'And what's that supposed to mean?' It was nothing Tamsin had ever known. There had been no going back for her; no place to go back to and no possibility of it, even if there were. And she's quite cold now and cannot believe she's still here.

'I was wondering if you wanted to come inside?'

'You mean you're letting me in?'

~

'I don't know why he wants to go there,' says Patience, still bemused by Michael's prayer chapel request. He had never shown any interest in the place before; really none at all. But they are going there just the same. 'He's insistent in a way only Michael can be. And no one's getting any sleep until we have done as he asks.'

'And we don't know why?' says Bancroft, who has caught up with them after dousing the fire, helped by some timely rain.

'We have *no idea*.' And even less interest, as far as Sister Patience is concerned.

And it's a big waste of time for Bancroft as well. There'll be nothing to see in the prayer chapel, that's for sure. And while he longs for sleep, he needs to find the abbot. Maybe he's gone home, thinking this business could be left to the morning. 'Calm as a mill pond,' he'd said and perhaps he is right now – asleep in bed and miles from danger. While Bancroft's here alone, when he doesn't like being alone. They're a team. *Where are you, Abbot?*

Michael is pacing up and down the corridor, watched by the largest policeman available. They'd asked him to sit and he had refused. 'I don't want to sit!'

'Shall we go now?' said Bancroft with a smile. He reckons things will be sufficiently cooled and leads the way along the corridor and down the steps to the cellar chapel. 'You want to say a prayer, Michael? Is that it? You'll have to be careful – because of the fire and that. We all know what fires do to the prayer chapel.' Michael starts to groan, as if shot. 'It's all right, mate, we'll be there in a jiffy.' The corridor is warm and he covers his hand with his hanky as he opens the door. It won't open. He looks down. There's a rubber wedge beneath the door.

'Shit!' he says as fear lurches through his body. '*Shit.* Michael, move away, move back!' He needs space – space to think. 'The door has been wedged again!' He calls out to anyone behind him in the corridor. 'I'm removing the wedge.'

But Michael is crying, he's wailing again, contorting himself and afraid, he's cowering, as if the door might now hurt him. Bancroft opens the door and is hit by the heat; it's still as hot as hell. He takes a step back, whacked by the burning air, takes ten deep breaths and then propels himself forward, covering his face, he must go in. Michael follows, silent at last, and then they both stop still.

What they see is an empty chapel, save for some ashes on the floor.

$\sim$

He had let Tamsin in. She had walked through in silence and he'd sat her down and made her a cup of tea.

'You sure know how to push the boat out,' she said, as he placed the mug in her hands; the tea hot and strong. But in truth, the boat felt well and truly launched. When she had to go there, he'd had to let her in.

'The thing is, Tamsin' – he sat on the arm of the sofa – 'I don't mind some damage.'

'What do you mean?' What is he talking about?

He's not in a hurry. He's searching around for words. 'I've reached that time in life when I am settled with my, well, inadequacies. I can accept them. I don't punish myself like I used to. But I'm not proud of them, this is the thing, and neither do I worship them.' Tamsin is wishing the abbot were here to help her understand this psychobabble. '"Fail but fail better", as Beckett said. And so yes, I see politicians, I see their faults – but only because they are me writ large. Yes?'

Tamsin is unsure what the question is. But says 'Yes' in reply, allowing Jason to continue.

'But what I'm *not* interested in – and this is my problem with yesterday and your behaviour on the phone – what I'm not interested in is those who worship their damage, do you understand?'

'No.' She really doesn't.

'People who make a virtue of their damage, who imagine it's *them*, imagine it's who they are, and it's all OK and everyone else must just get over themselves.' This is exactly what Tamsin felt. 'So – and here's the rub – if you wish to be an emotionally-crippled control freak, Tamsin, open to a relationship but only as long as you have all the rights and your partner has none, well, so be it. But I won't hang around to be shat on. I've been there and felt that.'

Tamsin sits quiet and in some dismay. It's a strange feeling, almost as if she doesn't exist; as if strong pillars collapse inside her, crumbling in dusty carnage leaving, well, she's not sure what. It's as if everything she is, *isn't*.

'Do you have any sugar?'

'Sure,' says Jason, probably glad of the walk himself. It had been a bit of a speech, and where it came from, who knows? But he goes through to the kitchen, which is the time for Tamsin to walk out of the door. It is the perfect moment. Let him return to an empty room, point made. Though surprisingly, non-existence is not the worst feeling in the world for her; especially when existence is so disappointing. She sees this for a moment – and now he's returned with the sugar, much too soon.

This is the trouble with small homes. They give no time to think. Stately homes are better. Large hallways, long corridors; they give plenty of time to think. Ask for some sugar and you've got at least half an hour to yourself.

'So, who taught you the grand art of welcome?' she asks.

'And who taught you the dark art of avoidance? This isn't banter, Tamsin.'

'I know.' And to think she could be home by now. But then she doesn't wish to be home. In some ways, she *is* home. 'No really, I do know.' Jason nods. He believes her. 'So, what happens now? Do you draw me or something?'

Jason can't help but smile but the smile fades. 'Just the chance to be real for a moment.'

'Real?' The disdain cannot be hidden.

'The chance to venture out from behind your shell, Tamsin – imagine that. Give up control.'

'Well, that's not going to happen.'

'No.'

'I mean, why would I do that?'

'Why on earth? Hell will freeze over and all that.' He gets up. 'So, it's probably time, no rush of course; but probably time you were on your way home. There's nowt so dull as a control freak.'

And now he's calling her dull! No one had *ever* called her dull! She absolutely isn't dull – though she can't actually move; as if her body has decided to stay, regardless. There was a moment of peace when she didn't exist; and maybe it remembers.

'I suppose – I mean, I don't know, I've never tried. But I suppose I could let go of control a little bit.'

'Which bit do you imagine you'll start with?'

'Will you kiss me?'

~

'Looks like someone's coat,' says Bancroft, surveying the chapel floor. 'Lucky it wasn't worse. Seriously lucky.' Privately, he's wondering why someone would leave a coat on the floor and then close the chapel door with a rubber wedge. It had been a night of odd happenings. 'Want to say a prayer, Michael?'

But Michael is in a trance. 'Where is she?' he asks, looking around and falling to his knees.

'Where's who?' says Patience, arriving behind him and troubled by the heat. 'Are you all right, Michael? It's very hot in here.'

'Never been better, Sister!' His happiness fills the chapel. 'Thank you, thank you,' he says to no one in particular.

'Let's get you to somewhere you can rest,' she says and Michael is happy to be led, 'like a lamb' she would later say – which was not often said of Michael. So, they left the chapel, Sister Patience now leading, followed by Michael and then Bancroft, who didn't understand any of that. It was the transformation in Michael which baffled him. Had he missed something? The abbot would know. But someone had definitely been there recently; and whoever it was would need a new coat.

~

'We're not lying, Richardis.'

'Really?'

'Really. Michael always made me feel uncomfortable; the way he looked at me. And anyway, haven't men been lying for years?'

'I just don't see why, Louisa.' Does this girl understand nothing?

'Because Richardis, he can hurt us, trust me.'

'How can he hurt us?'

'Trust me, like I said. Trust me absolutely. Do you trust me?'

'Of course, I trust you.' Did she trust her?

'And I'm mainly worried not for myself, but for you, my dear.'

'Why worry for me?'

'Your actions on the night of Hildegard's death.'

'We've been over this.'

'I'm merely saying that it could be spun in a particular way; which could end up very messily – for you. Do you wish to be abbess?'

'I'm not sure, Louisa.' Somehow, everything seems to be curdling; turning into something different. 'I'd prefer to be with you.'

'One day at a time, Richardis. We know what we want. But we do need to be very grown-up, because first of all, we have a problem to solve; or rather, a fire to put out. We wish Michael no harm, lovely man.'

'He was always nice to me.'

'Quite. But we do need to place some doubt inside the small minds of the police – some doubts about his, well, credibility. We need some scepticism concerning his motives.' Richardis doesn't understand. 'We have thwarted his sexual advances. That is what has happened.'

'But ... '

'It would be best for us if, just for a short time, he is regarded as a pervert.' She speaks firmly. This is an instruction. 'And God loves him, of course; God loves him so nothing lost.'

If we likened the convent to a train, then the wheels had come off tonight. Sister Patience is almost existing by numbers, trying to do the right thing, when nothing is right – and who knows what to do with Michael.

'We'll go to the snug,' says Patience, 'where you can stay with him, Bancroft.'

'I can't do that.'

'Or find someone who *can* stay with him. Would you like to rest in the snug, Michael?' He's not listening. He's excited.

'OK,' he says.

'I need to find the abbot,' says Bancroft.

'Well, he's not here, believe me,' says Patience. 'He's probably well asleep, as we all should be.' The abbot is not her concern, though when she opens the door of the snug, he is sitting on the sofa in a rugby shirt and boxer shorts.

'Abbot ... ?'

He is caught out and embarrassed. 'I can explain.'

And then Michael appears, pushes past Patience, takes in the scene, and, well – is it horror or happiness?

'Daisy!'

'Michael.' She speaks quietly. She has no idea what to say to him. How do they ever talk with each other again? And why does he have a blanket over his shoulders, stained with blood? What has he been doing? He stands before her in evident pain, and begins to rock, forwards and backwards.

'Can I be with my brother?'

'I'm not sure,' says Bancroft.

'We'll stay on site. Promise.'

'Of course,' says Patience, too quickly perhaps; but she's not sad to have him removed from her care. 'If you think that is best.' She knew Michael needed the outdoors. He was too big in body and spirit for walls and a ceiling. His restlessness needed space – high skies and generous acreage.

'So *do* stay on site,' says Bancroft, who is unsettled. 'We'll have someone watching you.' He feels protective of Daisy; but also aware that while he can see what's going on, he can't see what's going on at all. He probably just needs to get home, get some kip. The abbot nods his consent and brother and sister leave in awkward union.

'Good to see you, Abbot.'

'Good to see you too, Bancroft.' It *was* good to see him.

'Bit of a night, eh?'

'Bit of a night, yes.'

'I was worried about you.' It was an accusation.

'I can explain.'

'Not answering your phone and that.' Peter holds up his hands in acknowledgement of the crime. 'Didn't know where you were. And you appear to have lost your clothes.'

'Not all of them – and, as I said, I can explain.' He looks to Patience. 'Bancroft and I need to talk. But can we arrange a meeting of the Community at 9.00am tomorrow ... or rather, today. I need to speak with everyone.'

'Why?'

'Well, there's much we do know now; I have learned a great deal tonight. But also much still to be revealed.'

'Hardly reassuring.'

'What I *can* say is this: everyone is safe, Sister.'

'You're confident of that?'

'Barring a few minor jolts, the roller-coaster ride is over, yes. And very soon the truth will be out and you will have your convent back.'

'It would be nice,' says the sub-abbess, who moves to leave.

'So help the truth out now, Sister, and before you go, tell us this - is it true you knew of the plan?'

And soon after, sitting in the snug, Bancroft hears the abbot's strange tale. It is a brief version, salient points only, majoring on outcomes rather than the terror. And while Bancroft is careful with his language – 'That swearing is not clever,' as his nan said – he did think 'Bloody hell' a couple of times as the abbot recounted events.

'My habit saved me, Bancroft. But it couldn't save itself.'

'You'll need new togs.'

'I'll sleep at home tonight, and I suggest you do too. We'll need a guard on Michael's door – and not some idiot who gets distracted; someone with focus. Michael's night won't be easy. He may try something.' Bancroft nods.

'I know just the man. I'll sort that. And what's the plan for tomorrow? Or rather, today.'

'Bring a few friends with you. Be here for eight.'

'And you think it's all over?'

'No, I don't; far from it. There's another chapter; a dark heart here which hasn't been exposed. And I don't know if it will be.'

## And it was Bancroft's friends

Who Tamsin saw as she drove into the convent the following morning, still on top of the world and looking down on creation, with Karen Carpenter; but becoming aware that something was amiss, that things were not as she'd left them in the convent grounds. There were three police cars in evidence with Bancroft in happy command and Daisy looking like a lost soul at the front entrance.

'What's going on, Bancroft?'

'There have been some developments, ma'am.' He feels awkward knowing so much more than she does; because she liked to know everything first. But he feels joyful as well, like a coming-of-age moment, when you realise your mother hardly knows anything at all.

'What sort of developments?'

'We've been trying to get hold of you.' And she could not believe, as she arrived for their 8.00am meeting, that she hadn't checked her phone; that she had actually done what Jason asked and switched it off last night; and then forgotten about it until this moment. She blamed Karen Carpenter.

And who's this? It's him but it isn't him. 'I didn't recognise you.'

'They're my gardening trousers,' says the abbot. 'Gardening *shirt* and trousers.'

'You don't have a garden.' Tamsin has seen his small back yard. Only an estate agent could call that a garden.

'No, but if I did have a garden, I'd wear these.' They walk and talk like two intimate strangers.

'It's a shock, seeing you like this, when – '

'I can explain, but later perhaps.'

'So, what's happening? Why is the convent crawling with police?'

'What happened to your phone?' he counters.

'I can explain, but later perhaps.'

There is a loud wailing from somewhere inside the convent.

'What on God's earth is that?'

'It will be Michael.'

'Michael? What's he so unhappy about?'

'Himself, mainly. Yes, mainly himself.' And now they've arrived in the snug and he is able to recount events.

'Volmar is dead. Hanged.'

Tamsin is shaken. 'Suicide?'

'It looks that way. He left a note.'

'Why do people do that?' She needs a target.

'Self-justification. The need runs deep in us. We're about to destroy the lives of those we leave behind. But we still wish to *explain* ourselves, even though it isn't going to help ... though Volmar also confirms a meeting in the summer house which leaves him full of guilt.'

'A meeting about what?'

'There's good news and bad news.'

'The bad news?'

'He doesn't tell us.' And then the abbot starts to read Volmar's final words.

*'I am so sorry. Let it be on my head. I die guilty of foolishness and rancour; but I die absolved. I would have preferred your absolution, Abbot, I liked your spirit but Sister Patience did her best. There were others in the summer house. Does that matter?*

*I don't know. My path is run and my case is closed – but maybe theirs is not. And who locked the door? I still do not know. It wasn't one of them. I would like you to find out, Peter. Can you do that? And cremated, not buried.'*

He died in my room. He knew I'd find him.'

Tamsin takes it in but struggles; there's too much to catch up with. Why wasn't she here?

'This isn't sorted, is it?'

'No, it isn't.'

'And who locked the door?'

'I think I know.'

'Not a strong line for the prosecution.' The abbot smiles.

'And the good news?'

'The summer house three.'

'Volmar doesn't tell us.'

'But Michael has. He told us *all* about the meeting. Or rather, he told Daisy, who told me.'

'And we trust them?'

The abbot nods. 'Daisy and I had some time together last night.'

'Sounds very warm and cosy. What's wrong?' The abbot looks pained.

'It's OK.'

'It doesn't look OK. Are you breathing all right?'

'And as forensics will confirm, Volmar did *not* get drunk on bonfire night.' He resets himself, he needs to, time is pressing.

'He collapsed in the undergrowth, didn't he?' She's still trying to catch up, searching for facts she knows. She liked to know without being told.

'He was drugged. Michael spiked his drink.'

'Why would he do that?'

'So, now we're back with the summer house.'

Louisa knocks and walks straight in.

'Found you guys at last.' She has a broad smile on her face. 'I'm the cavalry!'

~

'Sister Patience, I wonder if there's a place we might talk?'

The bishop had been a surprise attendee at prayers tonight, and moved alongside her as they left the chapel. They had shared in Psalm 51 – David's lament after his infidelity with Bathsheba. It is a desperate plea for forgiveness. 'Be merciful to me, O God, because of your constant love. Because of your great mercy, wipe away all my sins, wash away all my evil ...'

It all seemed most timely for the Ego; and only strengthened his resolve for what was to follow. 'I have been evil from the time I was born; from the day of my birth, I have been sinful.' Like the bishop, King David knew how to turn on himself.

'Of course, Bishop,' says the Jackal. 'We can go to my office.' And now her heart beats harder because she wonders if he knows. She wonders if he comes to interrogate her; though she hardly needs help, for she interrogates herself daily and declares herself guilty every time.

'Can I make you a cup of tea – or coffee? I have both.' She has her own kettle in her cupboard office; mainly for guests. She has two cups of green tea a day, and that is quite sufficient for her needs.

'Tea and sympathy, eh, Sister?'

'Tea, certainly. Sympathy has never been my strong hand.'

'And I deserve none,' he declares. 'I deserve none. Because I took part in the most obnoxious – well, what shall we call it – charade?' Patience feels horrid tension in her chest. 'I mean, it was never a charade, really; never "a naughty little joke", as she called it.'

'Who called it that?'

'Louisa.'

'So, what was it?' *Please God, no.*

'It was a punishment. That's what it was.'

'A punishment of who?' Though Patience knew; she absolutely knew.

'Of Hildegard, yes. It was punishment of Hildegard – may she rest in peace.' The Jackal and Ego cross themselves. 'This has all been ghastly – but it was felt that she, well, needed punishing; or rather, warning.'

'Warning about what?' Patience can hardly speak.

'About the direction of travel, shall we say?' This rang a difficult bell. It was the phrase used by Louisa after Compline – and the moment the sub-abbess became complicit.

A couple of weeks ago, when leaving the chapel, Louisa had simply said to her – and it was not something they had ever discussed before – that Patience would make a wonderful abbess of this community.

'And it may be sooner rather than later, Sister.'

'Do you know something I don't?' she'd said. 'I believe Hildegard is our abbess.'

'But no one can be happy with the present direction of travel. I'm sure you're not!'

'Well ... '

'I have heard some are very concerned – very concerned indeed – and plan a surprise. So who knows what might happen? We all want what's best for the convent – as I'm sure you do.'

And Patience could have warned Hildegard. She could have mentioned the conversation with Louisa, mentioned talk of a surprise, when they met the following morning. It would have been a basic act of loyalty – to let her know of these rumours and shadowy plans. But she didn't. And she didn't because perhaps she thought Hildegard deserved some comeuppance. And perhaps she *did* want to replace her. Louisa may have sown the seed, but the soil was accommodating. So, she'd stayed silent. Patience had stayed silent. What harm done? And then the surprise – whatever it was – proved fatal in the most awful of ways. Was the bishop part of this surprise?

'And why are you telling me, Bishop?' Did he know of her complicity? She's sweating at the back of her neck.

'It's just that I've always wanted what's best for the community.' Echoes of Louisa again.

'Have you told the police?'

'Not as such. I mean, I could have offered more clarity on the matter.'

'And why didn't you?'

'Are you suddenly my confessor?'

'Why didn't you?'

'Fear. Shame. I was jealous of Hildegard.' It is like Patience is talking to herself. 'Hildegard rather dominated the scenery, you see. That's how she was. I would say I was the Bishop of Lewes. And all people could say, was 'Oh, isn't Hildegard wonderful!''

'Perhaps you should tell the police.' She has made up her own mind. It's as clear as day. 'Perhaps we're all going out to lie for someone who doesn't deserve our lies. She does rather rely on our weak wills and complicit hearts. It's all evil needs. And perhaps you and I deserve better, Bishop.'

Some winter sun spills across the floor, beautifully coloured by the small stained glass. The bishop has to shield his eyes. 'The sun always makes things better,' he says, tears in his eyes. 'It doesn't change anything – just makes them better.' He chokes a little. He's aware this is the end of everything.

'If only you'd told us the truth, Louisa.' The abbot offers her a sad smile as the cavalry stands in the doorway of the snug.

'I absolutely told the truth – the truth as I remembered it.' She is affronted.

'Your memory appears to be the servant of your ego.'

'I have done nothing but help the plods. "For I'm a jolly good fellow!" and all that! I mean, what do you want?'

'The truth would be nice.'

'What one cannot remember, one can hardly confirm or deny.'

'I see you've brought your inner lawyer with you.'

She looks at the tape recorder with a smile. 'And if Michael the pervert is all you have, you may struggle in court.'

'But what did you think you were doing?' The abbot asks in baffled amazement. 'Hatching such a hair-brained scheme in the summer house.'

'I deny that.'

'Remarkable. Any trouble sleeping?'

'None whatsoever.'

'Any trouble praying?'

'I will not listen to this buffoonery, Abbot! And I present myself now, determined *not* to join with you in the vague speculation of the damned.'

'There's nothing vague about it.'

'I mean, who said what and when and to who – does it really matter?

'Yes, it does.'

'We're never going to know. So, really ... '

'We will know, Louisa. In fact, we do know. I know.'

'And our main business is Michael, surely? I mean, thank God he has been arrested. We'll all feel much safer now. Certainly us women.'

'Not arrested, Louisa – he's helping the police ... '

' ... with their enquiries, OK, I'm happy with that. His inevitable incarceration can wait.'

'Would you like to sit down?' The abbot doesn't like her looking down at them; though she does that seated as well. 'And then you can tell us why you are here.'

'Happy to sit, but it won't take long.'

'Well, I'm all for brevity.'

'I'd like to report sexual harassment on the premises.'

'Who?'

'The victims? Myself and Richardis.'

'And the perpetrator?'

'Michael.'

'Michael?'

'We turned him down, of course, on several occasions – and I actively encouraged him to seek help, really I did. "Help is available," I said. I never give up on anyone, I'm afraid. It's a weakness of mine, I know. I'm too honourable for my own good. I *so* want the best for people. It's not a crime, is it?'

'The best for people?' The abbot shakes his head. 'You stitched up Gemma, didn't you? She was never a thief, she never stole anything, but you wanted her home. You were no Jean Valjean, Louisa. You took the little she had ... '

'And Michael?' says Tamsin. She wants to stay with Michael.

'He became threatening.' Louisa looks at them with *please-love-me* amazement.

'So why report it now?'

'Yesterday was the tipping point, for both Richardis and myself. No wonder he was whipping himself. So sad. I mean, I'm a big girl, I can look after myself; but to prey on Richardis like that ... ' She calls out into the corridor, the door still open from her own brisk entrance. Richardis appears in the doorway. 'I mean, why Hildegard ever allowed such a man into the convent? Richardis, do you want to tell them what happened?'

Richardis steps into the room, a nervous sparrow.

'We're speaking with you at the moment,' says Tamsin. 'We'll decide when the interview is over. Richardis, if you could just step outside and wait ... '

'Richardis, tell them what you know. About Michael. Tell them what that man has done to you.'

~

And later that day, sitting in a police car with a tuna sandwich, the abbot fills Bancroft in.

'Volmar simply wanted to give her a fright. He was still seething after the whole Satan thing. That struck very deep; and coalesced with his already ample self-loathing. We're only vulnerable to shame, if the shame is already there. If you feel there's something of Satan inside you, then Satan is the last thing you wish to be called. And we can imagine the fateful conversation, when Hildegard suggested the idea.

"Of course you must play Satan, Volly!"

"I don't see the need for it to be me."

"Well, it can hardly be a woman!"

"Perhaps an androgynous figure might be best, Hildegard – neither one nor the other."

"No, no, Satan is definitely a man, quite definitely; and as my father isn't here to play him, it must be you."

"But I don't wish to."

"I've always found men to be the more disappointing sex. The evidence is there, is it not? Do you really think the world would be as it is, if women were in charge?"

"And do I also disappoint, Hildegard?' The terrible thought strikes him. 'Am I just another disappointing man?"

"Oh, lighten up, Volly! You begin to drag me down with your long face."

"Perhaps I am hurt."

"When there's no need to be hurt. Why could you possibly be hurt? I think you will be splendid in the part. And it is a great honour we have included you."

"It's an honour that I am Satan?"

~

'So, it was Volmar's idea?' says Bancroft. 'I didn't see that coming.'

'No, it wasn't Volmar's idea. It was the bishop who suggested it to him.'

'The bishop? Bloody hell.'

'Volmar told Stephen about the Satan incident. He was very upset, as you know. And the bishop said she shouldn't treat people like that; that he was hardly the first, wouldn't be the last and that perhaps a scare might do her good.'

'And when better than the autumn equinox to help her see the light?' says the bishop.

'How do you mean?' says Volmar.

'A scare, like cancer, can make us look at life differently; it helps us adjust our understanding. She is over-reaching herself, Volmar. A scare will be a gift.'

'I suppose it's only a part in a musical.' He's not sure. Self-doubt overtakes him and he's looking for an exit.

'No, she does much worse things than making Satan of you, Volmar. In fact, she can do a pretty good impersonation of the old rascal herself! Come to the summer house tomorrow at 1.00pm.'

~

'So, it was the bishop's idea?' says Bancroft. 'I didn't see that coming.'

'No, it wasn't the bishop's idea.' Bancroft is enjoying his ploughman's. Meals had been sporadic recently and the tuna sandwich hadn't been enough. He could eat another of these very easily. 'Who else was in the summer house?'

'Louisa?' he says, choking a little on a mouth full of bread and cheese.

'Are you all right?'

'I'm always too hasty with cheese.'

'It was Louisa who made the bishop bold. He was her useful idiot. I think we know what passed between them.'

'I just wonder about the future of the convent, bishop.'

'Its future?'

'I mean, its future in Hildegard's hands.'

'Oh, I see.' He didn't see; or perhaps he didn't dare to see.

'And its reputation in the diocese, obviously – in the Lewes area. The place may become a rather large stain on your legacy.'

'Well, I hardly think ... '

'A wonderful woman, of course.'

'Definitely.'

'Quite outstanding – but that doesn't mean we wish to live with her! I joke, I know.' The bishop is glad she jokes. 'But between you and me, I wonder if she may be more suited to Wales than the home counties. Somewhere more *rugged*.'

'Somewhere more – far away?'

'Well, the "wonderful" do look better from a distance, in my experience – a great distance. And I'm sure that is true of many of the saints: better from a distance. She just needs to move – or to *be* moved on.'

There is silence. The bishop has no idea what is being suggested. He feels uncomfortable. 'But I have no power to do that, Louisa. You are aware of that. I'm the Bishop of Lewes but I have no power here.'

'Oh, I hate pathetic men, Bishop! No power? No wonder she out-shines you.'

'Out-shines me?'

'Everyone thinks so. But I don't. And neither do I imagine you're the sort to take things lying down. Not for a moment do I imagine that. Good Yorkshire stock, aren't you, Stephen?' The bishop nods with coy pride, as if someone has just discovered he's World Long Jump champion. 'Let's meet in the summer house tomorrow at 1.00pm. I may have a little joke we can play on her.'

~

'It was always the Green Chapel as far as Louisa was concerned,' says the abbot. 'It was taking the convent in quite the wrong direction. Louisa wanted the place famous for its orthodoxy.'

'What's that?'

'Well, literally, it means "right worship", so, perhaps I should say, "traditionalist".

'What's that?' Explaining the church to an outsider is a bad idea in the abbot's book. It takes a while, makes no sense to the sane and achieves a large portion of nothing.

'It's about taking the credal formulations seriously.'

'What are they?' The abbot feels ready to die.

'The point is, this approach has no place for things like environmental concerns. None at all.'

'How's that then? It's the only thing that matters, isn't it?'

'Maybe – but they are not in the creeds. And if they're not in the creeds they don't count. They believe in the Father and the Son and the Holy Spirit. They don't believe in green energy. A priest not far from here once said to me, "Jesus never mentioned the ozone layer, so why should I?"

'I don't suppose he spoke about hospitals much either, but they seem to have caught on.'

'The thing is, the Green Chapel would have made the convent famous for all the wrong reasons, a bonfire of unwanted publicity. So, a different bonfire was planned, one to give her a bit of a shock, a warning.'

'And Louisa felt she had this right? I mean, she's not even a bloody nun! 'Scusing my language, Abbot.'

'Oh, Louisa always feels she has the right. Being entitled means never having to say you're sorry; and always having the power. And she understands power; how it must draw others into simpering complicity. It is called "negative intelligence" and it's there in all despots. The intelligence to see people's flaws and how they can be used. She could see the bishop's jealousy; Volmar's rage – and Richardis' infatuation, her need for a mother-figure.'

'And it was Louisa, Volmar and the bishop in the summer house.'

'Those three inside, looking out. And Michael outside, looking in. He was considered harmless as they made their plans – at one point they waved to him, apparently. And referred to the whole thing as their "little game".'

'Didn't quite end that way.'

'Why's he looking at us?' says the bishop. Michael stands there at his surly best, staring straight at the summer house.

'Because he's a moron, frankly, and of no great concern to anyone. Why Hildegard employed him ... '

'Something of a mystery,' says Volmar, glad to be in the club.

'A polite but sharp smack on her over-bearing bottom,' says Louisa. 'That is all we now provide.' The September sun in her eyes; the summer house is an absolute sun trap.

'Quite!' says the bishop, greatly amused by the image; and perhaps a little aroused. Louisa was an attractive woman, though on second thoughts, perhaps 'handsome' was preferable – better for public consumption. A male bishop cannot find a woman attractive unless she is his wife. But she can be handsome.

'And she will not be harmed,' says Volmar sternly, already weak.

'Only her ego, Volmar, only her ego! Call it purgation, an inner cleansing. The fire will hardly have started, the chapel will only begin to warm, before you open the door, pretend surprise and happily apologise for the mistake.'

'So, who will lock it?' asks Volmar. He wants to be sure of the details. 'Who will lock her in?'

'None of your business is best. Need to know, I think. What is important is that none of us is nearby. We will all be conspicuous around the fire.'

'And Hildegard alone.'

'We won't get sentimental, Volmar. The bishop invites her to a meeting in the chapel. And with the point made, you let her out. It's all very simple. The worst she'll suffer is a bit of a fright, which might be the saving of her. And a little note of warning delivered to her office. We don't hurt her, Volmar – we help her. It's a kindness.'

~

'Unfortunately for them, the moron is a fine lip reader.'

'He's also mad,' says Bancroft. 'You didn't see him round the fire with the whipping thing.'

'He realised early in life that it gave him power. His disability took power from him; but lip-reading gave it back.'

'But through glass?'

'He did need to be sure he'd heard aright. So later, he pretended to Volmar that he was in on "the little game" – and had it confirmed that Volmar was the one to release Hildegard.'

'Only he didn't make it.'

'Because Michael spiked his drink as the fireworks exploded in the sky, with everyone's eyes busy elsewhere. He then puts it about that Volmar can't handle his alcohol. "Not a drinker, that one – went to his head!" And so, while he played Mr Life and Soul of the party, singing ABBA songs around the fire, Hildegard burned in the chapel.'

'And he was the only one who knew. He must have hated her.'

'He would say he was putting things right – "Putting things right, Abbot, putting things right!" – after what she did to Daisy. With Hildegard gone, Daisy could become a nun which was all she ever wanted. He did it for her, a twisted mess of revenge and hope.' Bancroft is now reaching for his thermos and a chocolate bar. Whatever he's doing, and however busy, he's never too busy to eat. Some people say they 'forget to eat' sometimes ... not Bancroft. 'Michael can't put things down,' continues the abbot. 'He can't let go; he has to win. And when he heard the conversation in the summer house, a solution presented itself.'

There is a face at the car window; it is Sister Rowena. Peter winds it down.

'Is this a private meeting?' she asks.

'Not at all, Sister. I'm merely the lunchtime entertainment for Bancroft.' Bancroft nods in her direction, spilling his coffee. It's never been easy drinking coffee in a car. 'And is it true that you are the only candidate for the post of abbess here?'

'It seems so, yes.'

'Then my "Good Luck" is a little unnecessary.'

'As well as blasphemous.'

'Oh?'

'Well, was Paul's conversion on the road to Damascus lucky? I am *called*, Abbot, not *lucky*.' Peter extracts himself from the car. Bancroft will be happier free from this debate.

'Quite.'

'Though I suppose you *were* our white knight in a way.' He smiles with the memory of their recent exchange. It seems a long time ago.

'In a speckled way, perhaps. And still on your side.'

'Which, as previously noted, may be a mixed blessing.'

'Unmixed for those who don't murder or maim.'

'But not the same as friendship.' She is testing the water. She likes him.

'Maybe it already is, Abbess.'

And they both know this to be true, however these things happen; so, Rowena moves briskly on.

'And *becoming* abbess of the community is not the challenge, believe me.'

'I do believe you.'

'Looking after the rabble, "Hic labour, hoc opus est!"' Peter nods.

'It is good to hear some Latin again.' And with his coffee finished, Bancroft is now alongside them. 'Wouldn't you say so, Bancroft? Good to hear some Latin again. And don't say "It's all Greek to me."'

'Never crossed my mind,' lies Bancroft.

Sister Rowena looks around, as if to check who is listening. 'But forget about *my* future, Abbot. It is *your* future which is the bigger story surely?'

'My future, Sister? I'm sure I don't know what you mean.'

# And six months later

Peter and the new abbess meet again. The occasion is the laying of the foundation stone of the new Green Chapel. It is not the size originally intended; but a place of private prayer to replace the old prayer chapel, now filled in – and Hildegard's tomb.

'Let me introduce you to the new abbess, Tamsin. She was recently appointed to huge acclaim.'

'Congratulations,' says Tamsin. 'If that's what you're meant to say.'

'It'll do.'

'I mean, promotion is generally celebrated in the world, though whether that's true here ... ' She does suddenly wonder. 'I'm not religious, I'm afraid.'

'I don't think I am either,' says Rowena.

'The abbess was previously a choreographer,' adds Peter. 'But she won't do a plié, I've already asked.'

And then suddenly abbess is moving, spinning and whirling like a Dervish, with such ease and control, such grace and speed, like a greyhound released, stretching one moment, crouching the next, her habit and body at one in seamless union. And then at rest, still again, the choreographer gone; the abbess returns.

'Well!' says Peter in amazement.

'The convent dance nights should improve,' says Jason, who is hastily introduced to Rowena by Tamsin.

'He's a cartoonist, I'm afraid; and couldn't be more embarrassed to be here if he tried.'

'Then it must be love,' says the abbess.

'Oh, I doubt that,' replies Tamsin, rattled.

'How do you do,' says Jason, shaking Rowena's hand before she is called away. Everyone wants the abbess on a day like this.

'She does move well,' says Jason, watching her leave them. 'And when did I last say that about a nun?'

'So, what do we do now?' asks Tamsin. She feels awkward. She doesn't wish to be here. 'This is hardly a networking event.'

'Unless you're thinking of the sisterhood, Tamsin. Stranger things ... '

'I'm not.'

'We're just milling,' says the abbot.

'I hate milling.'

'I'm not a huge fan myself,' admits Peter.

'No, but I actively hate it.'

'Jason, where are you in the milling debate?' asks Peter.

Jason sighs but affirms. 'I can mill.'

'And glad to hear it. Milling definitely has a place.'

'It has no place.' Tamsin is looking around at the nuns close by.

'If I *was* going to mill, though,' adds Jason, clarifying his position, 'I probably wouldn't choose a convent. It was Damson's idea not mine.' Tamsin snarls.

'So, noble of you to come,' says Peter.

'He's just looking for cartoon ideas,' says Damson.

'*Myth*,' says Jason. 'Why do people think cartoonists are always looking for cartoon ideas?'

'Because they are?'

Jason got this all the time. People would say 'I don't want to turn up in one of your cartoons!' – when it was clear as day that they would like nothing more. Politicians paid him good money for originals of cartoons in which they featured, however rude

– it was about *them*, and that's all that mattered. Something about the sunlight of attention; any attention ... even abusive attention. And in truth, he probably would have to include a nun or two in a cartoon soon; maybe a dancing nun ... but with affection. The Green Chapel was clearly a great idea. He felt these were good people.

'And so, Sister Patience really did fall on her sword?' asks Tamsin, alone with the abbot for a moment. She is out of touch with convent matters; her world has moved on, other cases to attend to. 'I mean, with her promotion plans. Didn't she want to be abbess?' Whatever she may forget, Tamsin always remembers promotion plans.

'She fell on her conscience, yes,' says Peter and Tamsin is dismayed. 'She feels she colluded with events in some manner; allowed something to be, which should not have been. She confessed publicly to the community. It was very moving, by all accounts.'

'Imagine a world where leaders apologise and step down,' says Jason, who has joined them again. 'No, sorry – can't do it. It's too far-fetched.'

'She's looking after the hens now; much more challenging than nuns.'

The laying of the Green Chapel's foundation stone by Jenny, the new Bishop of Lewes, had gone well. The resignation of her predecessor, Stephen, was muddy water under an ecclesiastical bridge familiar with mud passing by. He had separated from his wife Margaret. She had suggested it. And there was to be no pretence of a 'trial' element to the process. It was definitely goodbye, 'and then we can both move on with our lives, Stephen'. Although she would move on quicker than him. The public shaming – of which his lost marriage was part – left him more desolate than he could have imagined; and in a very dark pit of self-recrimination. But helped by a counsellor friend, he stopped dreaming of suicide and was now training at Plumpton Agricultural College to become a farmer, so he could join his brother on his land in Cumbria. He was looking forward to getting away from the south of England, which he had never taken to. 'Too much of a plain-speaker, me.' His received English, so carefully cultivated over the years, was turning more northern by the day. Re-invention of the self takes time and lies – but he would get there.

And so would the chapel, 'which we see as the *beginning* of our green adventure, rather than the end,' as Abbess Rowena declared during the ceremony. 'Our planet, as well as its people, must be at the centre of our calling. You cannot serve one without the other. Think people, think planet – that shall be our dance!'

The westerly wind blew hard across the sea, throwing paper plates and sausage roles all over the place. So, it was difficult for everyone to hear her precise words, with someone asking why she was talking about Thanet at such an important moment in the convent's history.

No one had heard from Louisa since she moved out of the cottage. A large van appeared one night for her furniture; and she followed behind it in a taxi. No 'goodbyes'. Just an empty home, as dawn broke across the shingle. She had returned, it was said, to daddy's estate in Scotland, avoiding Westminster and TV studios as much as possible. She was quoted as saying she 'wished to spend more time with her family' – the same family she despised and had travelled to the other end of the UK to avoid.

~

'I did try and tell you, Peter.'

'Tell me what?'

The abbess has pulled him away from the crowd, saying there is someone he must see.

'You asked me about the murderer, remember? While I was mending the fence in the dark.'

'Yes, I remember. You said you were unqualified to comment. And then started showing off with big words like "proprioception".'

'And then I told you about the cock.'

'How could I forget?'

'About the cock protecting newcomers; about the cock being powerful – and therefore needing to be good.'

'Louisa?' It struck him suddenly. How slow had he been? 'Louisa protecting Richardis?'

'There was something about her; and it wasn't good. But what did I know? She was popular; she raised money, huge sums. What's not to like?'

'But you didn't like. And I'm afraid I missed the message of your parable.'

'You made up for it. And I believe you have met Sister Magnhild,' says the abbess, moving on.

'The name doesn't ring a bell.'

'She wanted to see you.'

'Not words I often hear.'

'Magnhild was a Danish saint.'

'Really?'

'An obvious choice, of course.'

'I'll take your word for it. I'm hoping she speaks English. My Danish is unforgivably rusty.'

'I think you'll manage.'

A nun is standing in the doorway of the chapel. 'Daisy?'

'I'll leave you to talk,' says the abbess. 'I have an open day to attend to.'

'Beats chasing the bloody chickens, eh?' says Daisy, loud enough for the abbess to hear without her having to reply. Though she's aware Sr Magnhild will need to watch her language if her novitiate is to proceed in a satisfactory manner. This may be difficult.

And Daisy looks different in her habit; so utterly different. And different beyond it as well; thinner in a face which speaks of stress and worry. Peter can imagine the cause.

'It's good to see you.'

'Good to see *you*, Abbot. Or maybe not? I mean, are you an abbot or aren't you?' He stands before her in civvies; in the same gardening trousers and thick blue jumper he wore after events became heated in the prayer chapel; when both of them had said goodbye to life. He had not worn a habit since that night. On seeing the ashes the following morning, he knew it was over; all confusion gone. The abbot had died that night and there was no going back; just a decent burial to arrange.

'But why get rid of it all?' says Sister Magnhild. 'It's who you are!'

'I'm taking a chance.'

'On what?'

'On the idea that you can let go of a role – and still exist.'

'You're mad.'

'I'm not sure I'll take that from *you* in your insane new clothes.' Manghild mock curtsies. 'And how's the scream?'

'The scream? It won't ever go, will it?'

'Probably not. She's your friend, in a way.'

'I don't cower these days, though. I talk with her. Every scream has its reasons.' Peter nods. 'And your abbot days are really done?'

'That's right, no longer an abbot. There, I've said it! You find a habit, just as I lose one. And Michael?'

The novice is serious again. 'He's on remand. No bail granted. He's in Lewes prison fortunately, so I can still visit. It's appalling in there.' The abbot nods.

'Is he OK?'

'He's sanguine.'

'Sanguine?'

'It's a word I learned from the chaplain. She told me Michael was sanguine and I didn't know whether to look pleased or angry. So, I went and checked my school dictionary, which I've kept, God knows why. And now I use it all the time.'

'The dictionary?'

'No, the word. Sanguine. It's pretty decent, as it goes.'

'He's not denying it? Denying events, I mean.'

'No, he knows what he did. His lawyer thinks he should go down the "unsound mind" route. But he doesn't want to. I don't know. What do you think?'

'I don't think anyone's mind is sound.'

'And the chaplain is talking crap anyway.'

'How?'

'He's not sanguine – he's bloody suicidal when I see him. He wishes he'd thrown himself on the fire, which he would have done, if P.C. Bancroft hadn't interrupted and Sister Patience hadn't grabbed him. He won't recover from what he did – to us.'

'To you.'

'To me, yes. He just cries "Sorry" and I say, "It's all right, I understand," though I don't understand – I don't understand how anyone can bloody do that.'

'Self-preservation trumps everything. We'll sacrifice anyone on the altar of our frightened ego. And the force of Michael's shame ... '

'But he didn't murder her,' says Sister Magnhild.

'He caused her death; a close relation.'

'Lots of people caused it. The worm, the snake, the ego ... '

'We'll not imagine law is concerned with justice, Daisy.' Arched eyebrows call him to order. '*Sister*, sorry.'

'Forgiven.'

'The law is a rough attempt at order and no more. Justice will always have to whistle for its supper.'

'So, he's in the slammer on suicide watch and Louisa, who's knee deep in shittery, is sitting on a large throne in Scotland ordering fresh coffee and haddock and eggs for breakfast.'

But she isn't in Scotland. Louisa is standing behind the altar, beaming.

'Louisa?' says the abbot, almost feeling the chill.

~

'What are *you* doing here, Bancroft?' The Chief Inspector is happy to find someone not in robes. 'Fancy a day by the sea or something?' Bancroft is in smart casuals, his clothes of choice. And Wonder almost doesn't recognise him; the boy brushes up surprisingly well. 'Not on the pull, are you?'

'I was pretty involved in the case, sir.'

'Of course, you were. How could I forget?'

'I don't know, sir.'

'Heroic stuff, Bancroft! And, er, CID now, of course.' He remembers just in time.

'Yes, sir.'

'Sounds like one hell of an evening for you.'

'It was quite a night.'

'You filling in for the D.I., who was having a smooch in Lewes, from what I hear. Lucky man, eh?'

'Sir?'

'Lucky man, whoever he was! Between you and me, of course.'

'Well, I think the lucky man is here, sir.'

'Oh? Well, I mean ... '

'He's definitely here should you wish to meet him. I could find him for you.' He'll be glad to be free of Wonder, who makes him nervous. Authority does this with Bancroft; it makes him uncomfortable. And it's impossible to socialise with your boss. 'He's a cartoonist.'

'A cartoonist?' Wonder is flabbergasted. *'Really?* Bloody hell. ' Bancroft nods. 'You'd think she'd want someone doing something, well, valuable.'

'Takes all sorts, I suppose.' Bancroft's tone suggests Jason is a loan shark or sex worker.

'I mean, I'm all for a laugh, Bancroft, don't get me wrong – but cartooning? It isn't a *job*, is it? Not a *proper* job.'

Though Bancroft sometimes wonders whether policing is a proper job – or an exercise in box ticking, form filling, arse-covering and, oh – putting the wrong bloody people in prison. How is Louisa not behind bars today? The thin blue line may be holding back the chaos – but what if the thin blue line is part of the chaos? In fact, what if there isn't a line? Bancroft has become a cynic and quite outspoken on the matter of late, especially in the canteen. 'I mean, which of these politicians has a right to be roaming the streets, with the number of lies they've told?' It didn't go down well with the Tory boys – which, as he discovered, was most of them. But then his mother had lied as well. She'd lied about his father; she'd lied about everything – lied and then lied about the lies. So, he knew how lies corrode.

'Are you a policeman?' asks the young woman. She's shorter, and more elf-like – but still reminds Bancroft of Princess Diana; the same avoidant eyes.

'I am, yes.'

'I thought I'd seen you here. During the troubles.'

Bancroft is surprised at the approach; and Wonder frankly cannot believe the young man's luck. He has only gone and pulled in a convent, which was a bit of a thing; and she's a pretty one as well. So, well done to the lad!

'Is the abbot here?' she asks.

'The abbot?'

'I need to speak with him. Urgently.'

'We don't call him that anymore.'

'Oh?'

'Well, I do, and probably always will; old habits and all that. But yes, he *is* here. Shall we go and find him?'

The chance to get away from Wonder is keenly seized. Right now, Bancroft would take a skunk back to its slightly disappointing family, if it meant escape from his boss.

'The Naked Abbot,' says Louisa, holding court in the chapel. 'Or whatever you call yourself now. Is that too rude?'

'Why are you here?'

'And fat Daisy also changing her name. Going Danish, I hear – to save her bacon. Very commendable weight loss, by the way. It's never too late.'

'But you remain "The Snake",' says Sister Magnhild. 'Hildegard wasn't wrong there.' Louisa shakes her head, a weary smile.

Simon Parke

'Poor, poor Hildegard, a wonderful woman; and a strong woman, wholly admirable. We need more strong women; it's a crusade of mine. But sadly, not strong enough to withstand Michael's horrible hatred.'

'Shut it.'

'And to have such a man as a brother. You must feel terrible. I can only imagine your loss of appetite.'

'I'd prefer him as a brother, to you as a sister, you cow.'

'So, you'll get used to the old prison visit. "Look, but don't touch."'

The abbot really can't stand this; so much anger coursing through him. 'The bishop told us you thought Hildegard would be better off in Wales.'

She laughs. 'Well, Wales, whatever people say, is better than a coffin. Some lovely views apparently. But this is all speculation, obviously.'

'So, why are you here, Louisa?' asks Peter.

'Why am I here? That's a rather existential question, which I will neatly side-step. But why am I here today, *by the sea,* which I actually hate? I just had to visit to remind myself what a pathetic and misguided little place it is. I shan't be back.'

'They wouldn't have you.'

'I wouldn't have them. I regret every penny raised. It's a fake after all – every flag stone and arch of it.'

'I think you were the fake, Louisa – a little lost girl in search of an identity. But if you can't rule, you can't stay, that's how it is, isn't it? So, what happened to your soul? Do you ever wonder?'

'Not really, no. I'll leave that to the poets who have time for their endless omphaloskepsis. Oh, it means *navel-gazing,* Daisy, you'll have to keep up, such a Tide Mills girl! But me? I have an everlasting agenda of things to do, which is a quite brilliant system for avoiding all useless introspection, Abbot. Keep busy, I say, keep busy. Busy-ness dispenses wonderfully with the need for abstract contemplation about the meaning of existence – or the purpose I might have on this planet. Who knows the answer?'

248

'Well, we're certainly struggling,' says the Tide Mills girl.

'Keep the mind busy, Abbot, that's my advice.'

'And the *Dead Angel Society* at Oxford?' The abbess had spoken of it and Louisa's shock is apparent.

'Oh, you have been doing your research. Or did naughty Rowena tell you? It was a bit of a shock meeting her here, I can tell you. And even more of a shock for her! Oh, the stories I could tell about Rowena!'

'But you don't talk about it, do you? The silence is deafening. As with your friends in the press. No column inches there. Yet you were *president* of the nightmare.'

'It was just a piece of fun.'

'Not for your targets.'

'No one was hurt, not really. And if they were, well, don't blub – just get on with it, as Daddy would say. That's what I had to do.'

'"If nothing means anything, then truly anything goes." Wasn't that the society's motto?'

'We were students, Abbot! Or whatever you are. Though despair is strangely liberating; you should try it. It might help with your pomposity. We were just girls having a laugh – girls to whom nothing mattered.'

'And is that still the case, Louisa?' She walks towards him.

'Best not to ask, Abbot, best not to ask.'

'I am asking.'

'But what if you find that nothing does? What if – contrary to everything this chapel stands for – there really is nothing? What if the hokey cokey *is* what it's all about?' She smiles at her joke. 'Best not to look under that stone.'

'And you wrote the note, didn't you? The note to Michael asking him to move the fire from its usual spot this year – and to build it on the stone.'

She smiles. 'I couldn't possibly comment. Conjecture, your honour.'

'There's a court case coming and it won't be a joke. Michael will testify.'

Simon Parke

'Michael the pervert? Michael the murderer?'

'And others too. Others will testify, Louisa.'

'Oh, blow the court case, Abbot. Blow it all down! I'll apologise, sound humble. I can do *contrite*. And then the news cycle will move on.'

'Truth won't.'

'Truth? If you still imagine people care about that ... '

'And the bishop ... '

'*Ex*-bishop, post nervous breakdown, post marital calamity ... so sad.'

'And Richardis ... '

'My little elf. I'd be surprised if she ever made it to court.'

'She will. And I will. I will testify.'

'Ex-abbot joins ex-bishop. Disgraced in some way? People can't help but put two and two together. And my friends in the press, they'll support me, I'm good for them – I get things done.'

'Until you don't, Louisa; until you aren't good for them. Then friends like yours disappear.'

'Waffle, Abbot – piffle and waffle.' She is disturbed but pushes the dark clouds away. 'No, really, we mustn't be defeatist. That's not the way at all. No dark cumulus of despair! We shall beat it away with broomsticks! I'm very happy just blasting on; and that's what I'll do. As Bismarck says – daddy's favourite man – "He goes farthest, who knows not where he is going." And on that note, with appointments calling, I need to go.' And she does go, slipping out through the vestry, leaving by the back door, she's gone ... and now only the silence remains. Peter finds himself gripping a chair for support, as if the survivor of an assault. Daisy is pale.

'It'll be all right, Daisy.'

'It's Sister Magnhild now.'

'Of course.'

'And she's stronger than Daisy.'

'I have no doubt. You put on a new self. And it will be all right.'

'Not for Michael.'

Silence.

'She is a terrible emptiness, is she not?' He sits down with a sigh of recovery. 'To meet Louisa is to meet an abyss; but an emptiness of such force.' He wonders if he's ever experienced such darkness.

'Michael will be crucified in court.'

'It won't be beautiful, Sister. Though sometimes the crucified rise.' The empty cross sits quietly on the altar before them. 'And *we* did, if you remember. We came back from the dead.'

'That bloody crossword clue.' The hint of a smile; though it could be a sneer.

'Ah yes, the crossword. You were better than me at the crossword. Though in the end ... '

A shared look and the two of them are back there. They are back in the prayer chapel on the night of the second bonfire, dumped there by Michael, sealed in and desperate. They know again the fear, they feel it, the body doesn't forget – the stones warming, sweat dripping and the abbot obsessed with the cook, or with her secret, 'forty-five seconds to the prayer chapel and back'. And the conversation which followed on the night neither wished to remember ...

'How did she get here in that time?' asks the abbot. 'Forty-five seconds? Impossible. There must be another way, Daisy. There *must.*'

'She might be telling porkies.'

'Let's bet on the truth, because the lie can't help us.'

And together, using the abbot's habit, warming even now, they had shuffled across to the south-facing wall, the one nearest the kitchen – and found nothing there, just stone. The walls were heating faster than the floor, but the floor would catch up; the floor would soon be red hot coals and then the habit would count for nothing, and their feet would be on fire.

'We're looking for a gap.'

'What do you mean?'

'My spiritual director in the desert, Brother Andrew, before becoming a monk, he travelled the world as an escape artist.'

'Do you have his number?'

'He said that every escape was a puzzle in which you had to find the gap. "Every puzzle has a gap, Peter; wherever there's a crisis, there's always a gap – you just need to find it."'

'There's no gap here, Abbot. How can there be a fucking gap?' She is overwhelmed by the sense that life disappoints endlessly, always had, always will – and so bloody unfair. 'That's life, girl, get used to it,' as her pitiful father always said. And she had got used to it. Only *The Scream* made sense. Only the scream is true. So, of course, there's no gap and no escape.

'What's in that?' He points to a small stone cupboard.

'It's just a cupboard.'

'What's in the cupboard?' He hadn't noticed it until now. It wasn't there to be noticed; it was there to blend in. For Daisy, it had just been another alcove to clean. 'Communion stuff – wafers, wine.'

'Open it.'

'The last supper, very appropriate.'

She pulls at the vermiculite door; and inside, on two small shelves, neatly stored, all things necessary for the Eucharist – a chalice, a silver plate, wafers and wine, service booklets – and Peter reaches forward and with an angry sweep of his arm, clears the shelves, everything falling.

'Have you lost it, Abbot?'

'No, I've found it, Daisy.' He points to a keypad now revealed, numerals and letters, previously hidden behind the stuff of religion. And beneath the keypad, what was it? A clue of sorts. *'It's the gospel truth, 4109'*

'I hate crosswords,' says the abbot.

'Which is bad news for us both.'

'Loved mainly by men in need of control.'

'Michael loves them.'

'You don't say.' He focuses. 'Let's see. It could be easy. Maybe the gospel truth is the number.' The abbot keys in 4109. Nothing.

'It's not just the number, is it, Abbot? It's the gospel truth.' This is a reprimand. *Think, abbot! For God's sake, think!* 'It's

Matthew, Mark, Luke or John, isn't it? So what if the '4' indicates the fourth gospel?' she asks.

'Which is John. So, John 109.' He tries it in the key pad – again, nothing.

'Try again – you may have slipped. Try again.' He tries again; and nothing again. 'The gospel of John doesn't have a hundred and nine chapters.'

'Every day's a school day.' Her head drops. 'Michael would know the answer.'

'Are you giving up?'

'I'm seeing sense.'

'You're giving up.'

'Michael ... '

'Maybe Michael *is* the answer,' says the abbot. Suddenly he is hearing their conversation again, as he blocked the abbot's exit from the kitchen. *"I'm afraid I am the door, Abbot; and I'm not opening."* 'That's it!' he says.

'What's it?'

'"I am the door!" It's Jesus.'

'I don't see him.'

'John 10.9 – "I am the door."' His fingers are hurting with the heat, the blistering begins, they are starting to shake, all slippy and slidy, and his feet burn as he types in *John 10.9*. It has to work, because he types in an oven, the wall is scalding, Daisy screams in pain, there's no protection for their feet now, and this is it, this is the end, unless ... and then the give – the wall easing back, some mechanism released, and Daisy's singed arms flailing and falling forward into the darkness. And for a moment – a moment later remembered – she's somewhere else ... this darkness is the cavern of her soul, as if she falls into herself, and finds the place filled with light, a many-coloured luminosity of startling brilliance, as if she herself is the brilliance; as if this radiance and glow is Daisy.

'Oh, wow!' The excitement must speak. 'Oh wow!' she shouts. All pain is gone; the scream dissolved. And then the abbot lands on top of her, before rolling away.

'Is this Narnia?' she asks.

'I could do with the snow.' His scalded feet beg for cool. 'But we've got to get out; we've got to get out, Daisy! Like the cook used to – in forty-five seconds.'

~

'What I'm asking, Abbot, is *"Why?"'*
 'Be careful, Richardis.'
 'Careful?'
 'Don't ask a question unless you're ready for an answer.'
 'I am ready.' Peter's laugh is dismissive; and he regrets this. But who is ever ready for the truth?
 He is sitting with Richardis in the snug. He is catching up on her life. He discovers she has been living in London since the terrible night; though, in a way, it had been the making of her. 'The worst of times can do this, eh?' She remembers the moment, and it took place in this very room. She remembers Louisa dragging her along to speak out against Michael, to declare him a sex pest. She remembers how Louisa called her into the room, with the D.I. and Peter waiting, and so in control of everything, just like she always was.
 'Tell them about Michael,' she'd said. And Richardis had just stood there, looking at the ground. So, Louisa tried to remind her, cajole her into action. She was good at this. 'About him being a sex pest, Richardis. Like you told me earlier, when you were crying. You know it's for the best.'
 'He isn't a sex pest.' It's out before she knows it and Louisa's face contorts in shock. 'You're making it up, Louisa, because Michael scares you.' And Richardis fully expects the sky to fall in; she feels the heave of terror inside her. Who is she to use her voice in this way – and against one so strong? But the sky doesn't fall in, it remains intact; and she gathers herself, and catching the abbot's eye, feels strengthened. Her breathing deepens a little. 'You're asking me to make it up, Louisa. I'm not going to. I'm not going to.' There, as simple as that – Richardis had spoken; and then she had walked out.

'Not a compelling testimony,' says Tamsin to Louisa. 'Yours, I mean.'

'The girl's frightened. He's threatened her.'

'Well, you'd know all about that,' says the abbot. 'You're a charming but purposeful bully.'

'Still upset about not getting the job, Abbot? You really must let go.'

A moment of silence between them.

'We're done here,' says Tamsin, exhausted.

'One final question, Louisa.'

'Make it interesting, Abbot.'

'Do you feel an apology is in order?'

She looks incredulous, like an aggrieved teenager. 'An apology for *what*?'

'Yes.' The abbot nods to himself in bleak realisation. 'And, in my eyes, Louisa, that's the question, and those are the words, that most damn you.'

~

And since then, Richardis had stayed in London with friends, determined to be happy, grateful for the sky and the tennis club she'd joined – she'd always liked tennis. 'I'm a happy person,' she'd say. 'And don't tell me otherwise!'

She worked in an art gallery run by a previous boyfriend, who could be a bit of a bore. But she always knew she must be here today, because she couldn't keep the happiness up, something was eating away at it, like a mouse at midnight, consuming it slowly. And maybe, in part, it was the fact that she had locked the chapel door, wedging it shut, the door that Volmar was meant to open – so no harm done; or no harm done until he *didn't* open it and Hildegard couldn't get out. Then harm *was* done. She hadn't asked why Louisa wanted it closed – something about a joke, something about cleaning, she couldn't quite get her head around it. But she'd just followed instructions 'like a puppet on a string', which was a song she'd always liked, though not so much now.

'Why do I end up in the thrall of strong women?' she asks.

'That's not really the question.'

'Well, it *is* the question.'

'But the true question is this: why do you stop existing in their presence?'

'I don't know what you mean.' She did know. But she didn't want to know, which would make it difficult. Don't ask a question unless ...

'You need to look at your mother.'

'My *mother?* How come? My mother is my hero.' She is suddenly angry, defensive, dismissive. 'She taught me to be independent. I have total respect for her. *Total.*'

'Like I said, Richardis, don't ask a question unless you are ready for an answer.' There is a pause. Peter feels only weariness; denial brings this on. Richardis' eyes water a little.

'I do exist.'

'It's not me who needs persuading.'

'You're saying I don't.'

'I'm telling you your life story, which, in a way, you asked me to do. A story of a little girl with no voice, with her voice removed, whose only existence was found in looking after Mother, in meeting Mother's needs, Mother's little helper. *Then,* she existed, but only then. And God help her if she didn't meet Mother's needs; punishment of some sort. Perhaps the silent treatment? Recognise anything there?' No response. 'So, you were very easy for Louisa. She asks you to jump and you jump as high as you can, because you want, *so much*, that she likes you. You *need* her to like you. Just like all those years ago.'

Richardis looks like she has been shot. Her large eyes are glazed, the eyes of a deer, the moment before death; as if something has hit home, lodged deep inside and it is the end. 'The truth is sometimes a bullet. It may set us free; but first it destroys.'

They sit in silence.

'So, what now?'

'That's up to you, Richardis. But you could try freedom. You could try existence. And I witnessed both in this very room, remember?'

'When?'

'The day you chose to exist, Richardis. A great day. Louisa hauled you in to play her patsy, to spout her story, to be a good little girl, to please her – and you said "no".'

'I did.' She looks sneakily pleased.

'You chose to exist, Richardis, which is the beginning of your story, not the end.'

$\sim$

'I'm on my way to the hens,' says Patience. She is the former sub-abbess, now with other responsibilities.

'They're a labour, I'm told,' says Peter, on a mission of his own.

'Rather.'

'Foxes and rats, they never give up.'

'And neither do the seagulls, Abbot.' How could he forget the seagulls? 'They come for the food as well and Sister Rowena was a little soft on them, perhaps.' Peter can see sterner times ahead for the seagulls; but they'll survive because it's what they do. 'Some new netting should stop them.'

'In my experience, nothing stops foxes and nothing stops seagulls.'

'We'll see, shall we? We'll just see,' says Patience, tightening her jaw. Let battle commence.

'And you don't now wish you were back in your office overlooking the Thames and wearing jeans at the weekend?'

'Why do you ask?' She is suddenly tense. Does he know? But what does it matter if he does?

'No reason. Is there a problem?'

'No, well, maybe there has been.'

'But it's sorted?'

'I think so. We're walking in the same direction, actually. Before the hen house, I have something to do.' And so, they travel on together, out of the convent and towards the sea.

'And while you're keeping the chickens safe, Sister, keep yourself safe.'

'I'm sure I shall.' What is he saying? She's a bit on edge. 'But I don't always feel safe.'

'Well, there's no predator worse than self-judgement. Like the fox, it breaks through all defences. But then you know that.' They walk on in silence for a while.

'I have joined the Stormhaven Mermaids,' she says.

'Is that good?'

'They are all-year swimmers, every day, no matter what. 7.00am. Be here.'

'I won't be. But brave of you.' He could have added 'insane'.

'This is where they meet.'

'Is that penance?'

'No, no, *no*, Abbot. It's a mercy. I will bathe in the sea of mercy every day. They say you just make a friend of your fear,' she adds, more to herself than him. The abbot nods and together, they stand gazing across the restless drift of the waves towards Newhaven harbour.

'What's in the bag?' she asks, because the abbot appears secretive about it; and Patience believes secrets should always be exposed to the light, where they do less damage. She really has no time for people keeping secrets. What is gained by that?

'Oh, nothing really,' says the abbot, which isn't an answer.

'So, what's in the bag?' And will he tell her? Is it any of her business? He needs to decide. This was meant to be a private affair.

'Ashes,' he says.

'Ashes? Ashes to be scattered into the sea?'

'Into the sea, yes. A final letting go.'

And then an admission. 'I do know, actually.'

'You know what?'

'I know what's in the bag.'

'How do you know?'

'The abbess just told me. I'm sorry, I never meant to interfere.'

'You haven't.'

'No, I have.'

'Well, yes, you have.'

'I know I have,'

'But it's OK.'

'It's your ... '

'It is, yes – my habit, the remains of it at least, collected from the chapel floor. And it's appropriate you're here, in a way.'

'Oh?'

'Your voice was important in the decision, in the letting go.' He still remembered her dismay on hearing he belonged to no community. 'So, you can come along, if you like ... as a witness.'

'I may be a participant. If that's OK?'

'How do you mean?' She's not saying something. She's awkward, hesitant.

'I have a bag of my own, Peter.' She draws out a plastic shopping bag from her deep nun's pockets with something inside. 'It's my jeans.'

'Your jeans?'

'The remains of my jeans. I haven't been quite truthful about letting them go.'

'Being quite truthful is hard.'

'And I've not quite managed it. I said I had, but I hadn't. Not quite. But the bonfire that nearly killed you – its embers consumed my jeans.'

'Ah.'

'And I have the late-night visit of Bancroft to thank for that. He came to my bedroom.'

'The mind boggles.'

'It needn't. But now – well, maybe I am to do what you are here to do. Scatter the ashes.'

Their feet crunching on the stones, they arrive together at the sea edge, all white foam and bubbles. It is calm today, a gentle southerly in their faces. The abbot is taking off his shoes and socks and rolling up his trousers.

'I will walk on a little further,' says Patience.

'You're letting go too?'

'I am, yes. My jeans and your habit – our former lives set free.'

'Well, we better hurry before it becomes a festival.'

He wades into the water feeling the stones biting his feet and sharp cold on his shins. He looks back. She is now twenty metres further along and wading in herself. He lets her be – and the water is now over his knees, his trousers are soaked. The sea doesn't allow for half-measures. You come in swim wear or take the consequences. He finds his spot, now waste deep. And as he leans forward, the cold quite forgotten, everything quite forgotten, the ashes of his habit, the clothes of another life, are gently committed to the water.

'Thank you,' he says.

And here is no easy goodbye; no ease at all. On reflection, this habit had saved him twice. It saved him in his twenties, giving life order and hope, when neither had been there before. And then saved again, in a different manner, in the chapel with Daisy, as the stones warmed, giving them time. It had saved him twice; but could not save him now. Life is change. And what helps you in the morning might hurt you in the afternoon. Jung said something along those lines and they possessed the ring of truth. Dust to dust, ashes to ashes – and they remain afloat for a while, riding the surface, bobbing on the briny, and then in a blink, they soak, expand, become heavy and sink. The habit is gone in a moment, joined to eternity as, on the sky line, the Newhaven ferry makes its way towards France.

'It is finished.'

And then the abbot sinks, as if in pursuit of his habit. He disappears under, as along the coast, but no great distance, Patience lets go of her jeans; lets go of a colder, harder self who fought her way up from Peckham – and with the wrong coloured skin – to something like the top. 'Well done girl!' she says. It's good to celebrate success and it was always the jeans at the weekend, clean crisp jeans for chilling out, though chilling was never her thing – what did it even mean? She always had too much to do, 'a life most organised' as a friend said. But now the jeans are gone, this secret apostasy burned to cinders and joining the sea, as one wave becomes another: 'Grant me a humble spirit, O Lord.'

She looks across for the abbot. She doesn't wish to intrude but he must be finished by now. And there's no one there. She looks around, concerned. Has he waded back to the shore? But she would see him and the shingle is deserted. There's only silence.

And now she's wading towards where the abbot had been, sudden fear inside her, it shouldn't be like this – but had her words found some weakness in the man? Was she to blame? Too many thoughts snipe at her; she's in the water, up to her breasts now, but without a clue what to do, because it shouldn't be like this. Where is he? And then sudden movement, making her stumble and fall in the water, as Peter emerges like a monster from the deep, gasping for air. He finds his footing, still breathless. And then looking up to the sky: 'For all that has been, thank you! For all that shall be, yes!' The words are a cry.

'I was worried,' says Patience, so relieved to see him but irritated at the drama.

'Re-birth,' says Peter.

'You could have told me.'

'I didn't know. Spontaneous. I rise again!'

Patience had never been spontaneous. Perhaps one day. And they return to the shore, the wash dragging against the stones, making them unsteady. Peter stumbles out of the water, and Patience follows him, still holding the plastic bag.

'All done?' he asks.

'All done.' The relief is evident.

'So, what's left?'

'How do you mean?'

'What's left of you?'

'A kinder more submissive spirit?'

'Be careful who you submit to. Power is generally abusive. Cold, isn't it?'

The wind is blowing sharp against their skin. They start to walk.

'So, what now for you?' asks the Jackal, shivering.

Good question.

'Am I allowed to hug you?' he asks.

'One mustn't get emotional.'

'No, of course ... '

'But, I mean, well – yes.'

So, they stop, face each other and hug in damp union, a mysterious silhouette on the shingle and Peter speaks.

'May my strength be yours, Patience, and may your strength be mine.'

They hold each other by the sea, exchange strength – and then part and stand awkwardly.

'Thank you,' she says, and there could be a tear in her eyes because they do not always obey the rules.

'Though I may have done better in that exchange than you,' says Peter. 'As one who gives a penny and receives a pound.' Patience smiles.

'And to repeat my question: what now?'

'I don't know, Sister. I have no idea.' He turns to walk on and then stops. 'Possibly a visit to a clothes shop, God help them. But really, I have no idea.'

'We both return to nothing – *Peter.*'

'And out of nothing, something.' He's finding it difficult to speak; too much is arising inside him, his voice struggling for sound. 'That's how it is, isn't it? Out of nothing, something.'

Patience nods, she feels it could be true; and together, Peter and the hen keeper, free of habits, free of jeans, they walk slowly back to the convent, the sea wind behind them, the future in front.

And although it's hard – as hard as hard can be – neither of the walkers looks back.

# Author notes

Those familiar with the 11<sup>th</sup> century figure, Hildegard of Bingen, will note many similarities to her story. This is a work of fiction; but draws on her very real life which I researched, feeling it could be a fascinating novel of its own; and, of course, it could. But for now, she appears in the final Abbot Peter mystery. And here are some of the truths smuggled into the manuscript.

1) Hildegard, with her concept of Viriditas, was a powerful and poetic forerunner of the Green movement today.

2) She was eight years old when handed over by her parents for the religious life, a thank offering, and initially, taken under the wing of Jutta of Sponheim.

3) She became a prolific writer of letters to the powerful around Europe; and of works of theology and medicine.

4) She only took upper class women in her convent, believing the mixing of social classes to be unhelpful.

5) Volmar was a mentor to her in her youth; and a most loyal companion as she rose to power as abbess.

6) Hildegard had a will of her own; and took on any men who opposed her. (It was usually men.) She was savage about clergy who she felt were not up to their calling.

7) She did become gravely ill when she refused to write down the visions given to her. She recovered when she expressed them. And did not hold back thereafter.

8) She wrote possibly the first example of musical theatre, music and words, a show performed by her nuns, in extravagant costumes.

9) The young nun Richardis was particularly cherished by Hildegard. She was deeply upset when Richardis decided to leave for another convent.

The convent's architectural history was inspired by a stay at the Bailiffscourt Hotel near Littlehampton, West Sussex. You too may be fooled.

And, as ever, Stormhaven is a thinly disguised version of Seaford, now my home. We do have small religious communities here and abound in good works. But there is nothing quite like the Community of the Holy Fire, which is invention-by-the-sea.

It's been a pleasure.

Lightning Source UK Ltd.
Milton Keynes UK
UKHW040809251022
411061UK00004B/550